MORAINE'S EDGE
BOOKS

In the Ramsdell Family Series

Rosette: A Novel of Pioneer Michigan (1856–1913)

"Blizzard" (1888)

Solomon Ramsdell: A Novel of the Civil War Era
(1857–1867)

Forthcoming: A transcription of Rosette's
journal (1856–1858)

Solomon Ramsdell

A Novel of the Civil War Era

CINDY RINAMAN MARSCH

This is a work of fiction based on historical facts, including public records of birth, marriage, property ownership, military service, and burial. Some details and names have been conflated to unify the story, some family members omitted, and some characters invented. In *Rosette* the Watson farm was located in Grattan, but research shows the property slightly west, in Cannon Township. Solomon did buy his own farm in Grattan.

Select details in this book have been confirmed or supplied by the work of William Robert Brittenham (deceased), *The Garter Family of New York and Michigan* (Poughkeepsie, NY: 2006), used by permission of his family.

Sources that inspired details of historical record in the novel include the following:

"Gettysburg Cemetery Dedication," in *The Lansing State Republican* (Lansing, Michigan: November 25, 1863), from Chronicling America—The Library of Congress

J. H. Kidd, *Personal Recollections of a Cavalryman with Custer's Michigan Cavalry Brigade in the Civil War* (Ionia, Michigan: Sentinel Printing Company, 2006)

John L. Ransom, *Andersonville Diary, Escape, and List of Dead, With Name, Company, Regiment, Date of Death and Number of Grave in Cemetery* (Philadelphia: Douglass Brothers, 1883)

The notion of husband-and-wife trees comes from Katherine Grossman, in a remembrance of her beloved husband Rick.

The article "Pioneer Profile" by Susie Fair in the Afterword is transcribed and slightly edited from an image provided by Nancy Brown from family records and used by permission of *The Rockford Squire*.

First released in the United States of America 2021
Print ISBN: 978-0-9971127-3-3
E-Book ISBN: 978-0-9971127-4-0

Moraine's Edge Books
154 Dight Road
Slippery Rock, PA 16057
www.MorainesEdgeBooks.com
www.RosetteBook.com

Join the Readers List at RosetteBook.com to receive news and special offers on additional publications

Dedicated to the honor and memory
of my family members who have
served in the military,
especially
Colonel James Curtis Rinaman, M.D.,
United States Army Reserve,
physician and prisoner of war
in the Philippines and Japan
during World War II

CONTENTS

TESTIMONY FROM THE PENSION RECORD OF SOLOMON RAMSDELL

Transcribed from an image of the handwritten document

Oct the 29 1890

I was aquainted with Solmon Ramsdel all through the war after our enlistment he was in the same company with me and we were both taken prisoner the 12 of June 1864 at Trevillian Station to the best of my knolage I should say he was a sound man up to that time While in andersonvill prison he sufferd with chronic Diarhea and rheumatism he was peroled Some time in the Winter I don't remember just the time but while he was there he suffered every thing but death No one but God knows what us boys Suffered in those Rebble Prisons he is worthy of all the help you can give him. He was a good Soldier and a good [Sivilian?] a man that lived through those prisons is good for nothing to earn a lively hood

Yours truly John Van Wagner

PROLOGUE
JUNE 1864

"Welcome to Belle Isle, gentlemen!"

The red-haired Rebel guard tipped his pristine Union cap. "The James River resort offers only the finest for our Yankee friends." The boy waved along the hundreds of prisoners passing him on the footbridge. "Y'all have been starving out Richmond, so we'll return the courtesy."

Private Solomon Ramsdell, bugler with the Sixth Michigan Cavalry, was not as lame as most after the sixty-mile march from Trevilian Station; he was a farmer, accustomed to many miles of walking in the course of a day's work. The officers, who'd spent the war mounted, had suffered greatly on the march, and they'd been diverted to a riverside warehouse called Libby Prison. Only the enlisted men were in the file now—sergeants were the commanding officers.

As the taunts of the freckle-faced young guard faded behind him, Solomon shrugged his slim leather pack more securely against his back. It was under his shirt, its straps looped over his shoulders. He'd worn it this way into each battle, knowing capture was possible. In it were a few things he could trade, including a woven towel, a tiny bottle of laudanum, two pencils, three buttons and a needle and thread, and two precious nuggets of maple candy wrapped in waxed paper.

From here, he could make out little of Belle Isle. But the stream of men being poured along the path into the depression in the island's center accounted for his still having his bag—the less conspicuous possessions must have escaped the Confederates' notice.

Plenty of time to confiscate it later, Solomon thought. He could see tents poking up here and there above the mass of men, like frontier Indian tepees he'd seen in drawings. Surely there weren't enough for all of them. Behind him, hundreds more prisoners still pressed toward the island, and no doubt the battles up the river weren't even finished yet.

The current below the footbridge stirred up a little breeze, but one like the gusts of steam from a washday kettle back home . . . How his wife would glow on laundry day, brown eyes bright as she pushed damp strands of hair behind her ears, her ambition stirred by the order and cleanliness she established in her world.

But here there was only stink, and heat, and an inescapable soddenness that increased their misery. That redheaded guard—or the rat-faced one ahead who was officiously poking at the prisoners to hurry them along— they'd as soon increase the Yankees' misery as escape it themselves.

He'd read in the papers about these prisons not a year before—how the guards would steal the supplies sent in by the Union, then sell them back to the prisoners for whatever cash they hadn't managed to confiscate when the prisoners first arrived. These guards hadn't taken anything from the Union men yet . . . *Maybe waiting for the best of the lot.*

Finally herded past the ditches that served for prison walls and let into the central pit, Solomon, like the men around him, collapsed onto a clear spot of ground. Just to be off his feet, lying still, was exquisite pleasure, and only his growing thirst and distant hunger threatened the glory of that simple rest.

The approaching midsummer evening brought little relief from the heat and promised the arrival of swarms of mosquitoes. After a half hour supine, Solomon found his way back to his feet and into a line for river-water-and-rice soup. He tasted little difference between the broth and plain river water, but the soup eased his pangs, nonetheless. There would be no place for him in a tent, but perhaps the night would be cooler outside, with hope of a breeze. He found a slight rise in the land and prepared to make camp, which meant just finding a smooth spot to lay himself out.

A week before, the brash Custer had led the cavalry through days of hard riding and marching from Cold Harbor to Trevilian Station; their assignment was to take out the railroad while Sheridan brought his own cavalry forces down from the north to join them. What a magnificent tale Solomon could tell his father about the horses and mounted men in all their glory, pressing strong into their attack. They managed to overtake a supply train and destroy a piece of track while Custer flashed through the ranks on his horse, stirring up excitement and energy.

But that was where the glory ended.

Like the footbridge, Custer's path had led the Michigan cavalry units to a place where they found themselves surrounded by Confederates. And all of a sudden, Custer's riding to and fro looked more like desperation. He managed to send a message by swift horse to Sheridan, but despite Sheridan's troops coming to their aid, the Union cavalry was hemmed in and cut off. No measure of brashness could keep the Rebels from picking off many Union men and gathering prisoners as if they were herding pigs and sheep.

"Stuffed it right inside his jacket!" one of Solomon's fellow prisoners had marveled on the long march after they were captured. "I saw it myself. Custer wouldn't suffer the battle flag to be captured—"

"Though maybe he didn't mind so much about *us*!" another man had snapped.

A forced march is a dulling, shaming thing. *Why could we not manage to preserve ourselves to fight on with our brethren?* Solomon lamented. But he was merely one in the long column of the day's casualties. When they were captured, it was a simple relaxing of the arms to release the gun, to slide off the horse, to surrender his bugle.

Solomon was a signal man, conveying the commanders' orders to the men with notes bright and round and thrilling. Sometimes—if the men had lain quiet until that moment—he startled flocks of birds from the trees with his blast.

Now he'd be signified by a tally mark in the papers when the reports of the battle came out. *How many killed, how many wounded, how many captured . . .* And what would become of Hector? Solomon had brought his fine animal— judged worthy of battle—when he'd mustered into the army, and from that time on had been able to see him only from afar. Officers rode Hector, while Solomon, a lowly private, took whatever stock horse was available—when he was allowed to ride.

In a stupor from fatigue and heat, Solomon had no interest in making the acquaintance of the men who shared the little rise that caught what wisps of air stirred around them. He wanted to be alone with his thoughts as his body restored its soundness, easing his fatigue and stirring his heart and mind to face whatever came next.

The summer haze veiled the stars, but he lay on his back contemplating the heavens in any case. From somewhere far across Belle Isle came the plaintive wail of a harmonica. Solomon chuckled bitterly to himself.

Yes, Father, I've seen that prison we read about by your stove that November night, he thought, picturing the sterling Jacob

Ramsdell, a citizen always ready to uphold the highest ideals, or to recruit his children to carry out those ideals. *Now I've come on your behalf, not to liberate the camp as we plotted with saucers and apples upon the kitchen table, but as one of the horde needing rescue.*

Prisoner exchanges had broken down, and as the young bridge guard had pointed out, Richmond was starving. There were far too many men on this island already, and surely more to come.

Solomon watched the dim stars wheel through the sky above Virginia as they had above Michigan, and he found comfort in that, even as fear and doubt grew within him. *What will become of us?*

BEGINNINGS
JUNE 1857

Wagon

MID-JUNE BREEZES TOSSED apple-green leaves on their branches, the early afternoon light dappling the dirt road that curved over the river bluffs and wound out of sight. Solomon Ramsdell brushed some dandelion fluff from one knee and curled the knot of leather reins more firmly in his fist. The tight-sprung wagon bounced a little as it sped along the road. *Well, we're almost there.*

Jennette Watson sat beside him, hands folded in her lap except when the wagon jolted enough that she had to brace against the bench they sat upon, one small boot planted against the buckboard. Since they'd crossed the Flat River, only a half hour from her home, she had grown quiet and prim.

* * *

Their journey to Cannon Township had started friendly and easy that morning at his parents' home, where Jennette had stayed the night so they could get an early start. It was the custom for schoolteachers to board around in the community, but the young ladies who had stayed with the Ramsdells over the years usually held themselves back, unsure how to join in the family's activities. Jennette was different—she'd entered into Sally Ramsdell's breakfast preparations without hesitation, lending a hand just where it was needed, and reciting a few lines with his young sister Ellen from a poem she'd taught her that week in school. All had been warm and lighthearted.

"Here, take this to your mother, Jennette," his mother had said, holding out a paper-wrapped two-pound lump of the maple sugar they produced each year from their sugar-bush, and then tucking it into a willow basket that Ellen had lined with a blue-checked cloth.

Solomon's father had likewise handed him a copy of *Hunt's Merchants' Magazine,* but had addressed himself to Jennette. "Your father might like to see this issue . . . pieces on prospects for the railroad."

"Yes, thank you," she'd said, with no need for ceremony.

Solomon knew that as far as the Ramsdells were concerned, Jennette was already part of the family—her own family just needed to be brought into the agreement. His little brothers had scampered around Jennette this morning, asking her to remember them to her older brother Daniel, who'd spent happy weeks with them in the fall learning Jacob Ramsdell's farming techniques. When Andrew Watson had come to fetch his son in December, he'd stayed two nights, poring over diagrams and machinery with Jacob by firelight and striding over the fields on the frosty days.

When the Watson men had left, Jacob had nodded his verdict to Solomon. "Son, Watson has a daughter—two, in fact—and you would do well to see if one of them pleases you. Children favor their parents, as Daniel evidences, and I've found a kindred spirit in their father."

* * *

Solomon looked over at the young woman beside him. She fairly glowed with vitality and wit. *And have I found my match in you, Jennette?* Besides the Kings, his own family was the most accomplished in the area—but he'd always known he could find some cousins back in New York if necessary. He'd struck up a spark of courtship with the fall schoolteacher, but nothing had come of it. And his trips to Kalamazoo when his elder sister Rosette was teaching there hadn't turned up anything more than flounces and giggles.

And then last month, when the planting was done, Jennette Watson had arrived to take the school—and took Solomon by surprise as well. She was fair-haired but dark-eyed, and slim like Rosette. But Jennette was a different sort of schoolteacher. Rosette drilled her students in multiplication tables and busied them with spellers, poring over education journals to learn the latest theories, but Jennette read to them and encouraged them to tell stories. And she'd created a chapbook of their poems to display in the schoolhouse. One day when Solomon had happened by as school was dismissed, she'd showed him the little handmade volume bound with a red ribbon. "I made it pretty so they know it's worthy of their best penmanship," she'd said.

"But what of their spelling lessons?" he asked.

"You'll find all the words spelled correctly. They were eager to do their best for their book."

Of course they were, he thought. If the end could be met by other means, why not pursue them? *She's not bound by custom, but called by wisdom . . .*

And so he had found himself longing to learn more of her and had put himself in her path whenever possible. In fact, he was finding himself increasingly unable to do without her. But he hadn't yet said so, even with events unfolding that required him to declare his intentions.

Jennette seemed willing to keep company with him, and had even begun to look expectant when he came into a room. But she didn't sidle close to him as Rosette had to her Otis Churchill. Those two had tumbled into marriage without even a shanty of their own; Solomon wanted more dignity and preparation for himself and his own bride.

So when they'd started out that morning, the basket of gifts stowed in the bed of the wagon, they'd been a little stiff, both knowing what this trip to her parents meant for them, though it was as yet unspoken.

Once his home was out of sight behind them, Solomon had cut his eyes toward Jennette and caught her cutting her eyes at him. They had both burst into laughter.

"So, here we are," she said.

"Indeed. On the road to your home," he replied, "so you might see your family."

"So I might see my family . . ." And leaning forward and twisting around to look up into his face as he drove, she held an imaginary lens to her eye and squinted. "And my family see *you*!" She sat back with a satisfied laugh, and he laughed too, relaxing.

She caught me there.

"So I know your father from his visits here," he said, "and Daniel became like a brother in his season of working with us. But tell me more of your mother. She's a Sally like mine . . ."

"And I might have been a Sally too, since my middle name is Sarah, after my mother. She's much like your mother in other ways, too, though softer, I should think," Jennette said. "Sally *Ramsdell* goes about her kitchen like a lieutenant, carrying out the will of the general—your father. But my mother accomplishes much the same count of pies and crocks of butter—though proportional to our smaller household, of course—in more mysterious ways.

Mother is a bustling little bird, flitting here and there with bright eyes and tiny hands, singing a little as she goes."

"No, my mother does not sing." Solomon leaned back a little as the horse drew the small wagon down the bluff to the river road. "And neither do you, come to think of it."

"You wouldn't want me to sing," she said with a laugh. "I can follow the music to play our piano—I follow the notes up and down the staff and the rhythm across the measures. But it's calculations only. Calista says plainly that I cannot sing a note."

"No wonder you're so quiet with the hymns in meeting!" he said. Jennette's earnest voice was beautifully modulated for speech, but perhaps not for song.

"I do love hearing your violin, though, and I can dance enough to take part."

"But you say your sister has an ear?"

"Oh yes! Calista sings gloriously and plays even better. I'm glad you're bringing it. You'll enjoy playing with her and I'll enjoy watching."

"I had thought to play with your brother," he said. On his first night with the Ramsdells, Daniel Watson had brought out his own violin when Solomon began tuning his after supper. Without a word—Daniel was quiet by nature—he'd picked up Sol's opening phrase and echoed it with a turn, inviting Solomon to add his own improvisation, and thus began almost nightly sessions of music. Word got out and folks called for dances just to hear the two of them play.

"Well, all three of you should play together!" she said.

"But I don't want to appear to be showing off . . ." It was trial enough that he must win the family's—no, the *father's*—approval before he expressed his intentions. "Has Daniel told the family that I play?"

She looked thoughtful and gazed down at the slow-flowing river beside the road. "No, I don't believe he said anything about it, because I was surprised when I first saw you play . . . It was like being back at home, and it eased my way coming to keep a school in a strange place. Though I do remember asking Daniel all about you Ramsdells."

Solomon enjoyed the image of her launching a barrage of questions at her stoic brother. "But Daniel doesn't say much."

"Calista and I leave him little room to do so!" She laughed. "Ah, Calista . . . I've missed her."

"Tell me of her," he said. "Does she have a middle name? My sister Rosette's middle name is from Shakespeare—Cordelia."

"Calista Diantha," Jennette said with a sigh. "It is ever so much more enchanting than *Sarah*."

"Is she like you?" *Fair and shining,* Solomon thought, *supple as a willow switch.*

"She speaks her mind, as I do," Jennette said, "but with perhaps more pepper than honey. She's four years my junior, you know, just sixteen but well grown. Sometimes she seems older than I . . . especially when she broods over the piano. Too serious for her years, perhaps."

"And her appearance? Is she fair like you?" he said, glad for a safe opportunity to offer a compliment.

Jennette bowed her head a little, then lifted her eyes to hold his gaze. "I have often thought that if we were flowers, I'd be a daisy and she a tulip, perhaps a purple one—she's deeper and darker. I envy her curls and . . ." She glanced at down her slim figure and said no more.

"*Ahem!* Golden curls then," he announced, straightening up to arrange reins that didn't need it.

"Oh, no. Calista is more bronze, or tending to pewter, if we're naming metals. And I do hope"—she paused—"I hope she likes you."

"Well, so do I! What should I do to impress her?"

"Your music should do that," Jennette said. "But I don't want it to seem that we are showing you off . . ."

"Ah, I know," he said. "Shall we just be forthright with each other? I'm not taking you home for a visit because I'm the family member free to do so. In fact, my father would have liked another opportunity for confabulation with yours. He was loath to let me go in his stead."

"And my father will be disappointed not to see him, I'm sure." She gazed at Solomon expectantly.

"We've spent many hours together in the weeks you've been teaching our school, and I find myself missing you when you board elsewhere. You bring the sunshine back with you when you return." At last he could say these things aloud.

"I'm not at liberty to return your sentiments without my father's leave," she said. "But I *can* say that I'm glad to be here with you on this journey, and that I look forward to introducing you to my family. How's that?" she asked with a grin.

"That's just fine," he said, returning her smile. "So what should be done to make the best impression on your severe sister?"

"Well, she's not so bad as all that. But she *does* pride herself on her judgment—and judges quickly." She knotted her fist a moment. "She seems always to have the advantage of me."

"Could we, perhaps, trip up her judgment a little?" Solomon tugged on the brim of his bowler—better than his working hat, but still modest.

Her fist opened in her lap and she cocked her head at him, waiting for more.

A golden bird, he thought. *Something of her mother there?*

"You said Daniel hasn't told the family I play . . ."

"No, not that I can recall. As I said, I was surprised to see you with your violin."

"Well, we won't be able to fool *him*, obviously, but I was not around much when your father visited, so I know *he* hasn't heard me play. And Calista likely hasn't heard of my playing. What if I were to make a poor impression on her to begin with?"

"Oh, but you mustn't make a poor impression!"

Solomon laughed. "No, I'll be much the gentleman for your family. But if your sister is passionate for music, perhaps there . . ."

"Ah, now I see!" she said. "You could lead her astray—"

"—by playing terribly and being terribly proud of doing so!"

"Mother will be dismayed too," she added, "so you'll want to take special care to please her elsewise."

"Sally Ramsdell has taught me my manners, so I hope they will suffice for Sally Watson. And your father?" With the question, Solomon pointed out the dark shapes in a far cleared field—tom turkeys fanning their tails for the females gathered around them.

She nodded without commenting on the sight. "Father appreciates music, but it's not his passion as it is for Mother, and especially for Calista."

As the wagon drew near the turkeys, the females scattered and, with a ruffle of feathers that tucked sleek against their bodies, the toms adjourned their display.

"Do you think a word to Daniel would help our scheme?" Solomon asked. "I can be sure to take him aside for that."

"He likes a good joke, and suffers quite as much from Calista's quickness as I do. Daniel will be glad to play along."

While they rode on, Solomon contemplated how he might carry off the deception.

Then about midday, in a place where the road was flanked by the river on one side and woods on the other, Jennette asked, "Could we stop here a moment, for a rest for the horse and a drink?"

Though they had encountered only a few other travelers that day, and could probably have stopped in the middle of the road, Solomon waited for a place to pull off where they could find privacy in the woods and where he could easily descend the riverbank for a bucket of water.

After he'd climbed back up the bank and poured some water into a flat basin for the horse, Solomon found that Jennette had already returned to the wagon, loosened the horse to crop grass beside the path, and unwrapped the ham and bread that his mother had sent. They ate standing up, leaning against the wagon, the bucket on the ground between them.

It was all very practical and pleasant, with mingled scents, spicy and sweet, wafting over to them from the wooded riverbank. But then, when they'd finished, she filled the dipper with water from the bucket and held it out to him, silently bidding him to drink first. Though they didn't touch, it felt as if they had. He took the dipper and drank, and then she carefully took it back, looking at him as she drank, the ripple of the water reflected in her brown eyes.

In that shared cup their hearts began to knit together.

If only I could hold this moment, just here, he thought.

But the moment passed, and Jennette busied herself pouring out the last of the water for the horse and packing away the leftover bread. She babbled nervously as they climbed back up into the wagon and got on their way. ". . . I believe it's only an hour from here, and this was the way they took when they brought Mother the piano—what it took Father to get that through canal, lake, river, and road for her!"

Solomon, recalling the moment with the dipper, hardly heard her.

Watsons'

THEIR ARRIVAL AT THE Watson home near Bostwick Lake was just as Solomon might have expected. A big brown dog ran down the lane and barked as he circled the wagon.

"That's Puck," Jennette said, and shushed him until he settled down—though he still thrashed his hindquarters excitedly with his feathered tail. Andrew Watson and Daniel stepped out of the barn with tools in their hands, and two ladies—presumably Sally Watson and Calista—came out onto the porch and the younger hurried down the steps.

Before Solomon could climb down to help Jennette to the ground, Calista had already run up to her sister's side of the wagon and urged Jennette down into her arms. Jennette, though petite herself, was half a head taller than Calista, who still seemed somehow the elder sister, despite her childish exuberance.

After nodding a greeting, Daniel unhitched the horse and led him to the barn, and Solomon climbed down and took the hand Jennette's father extended to him, each matching the other's strong clasp.

"Well, Mr. Ramsdell, I was expecting your father," Mr. Watson said. "But I'll be pleased to better make your acquaintance in any case. Thank you for bringing our daughter home."

"I was pleased to do it." Solomon replied, hesitating to add more without a prompt.

Mr. Watson gestured toward the porch and they both walked over to Mrs. Watson. Jeannette was standing alongside the path with Calista's arm about her waist, both watching.

"Sally, dear, this is Solomon Ramsdell, Jacob's son. He's a farmer himself, clearing a place near his father's in Ionia County. Mr. Ramsdell, may I introduce my wife?"

"Pleased to meet you, Mr. Ramsdell." Mrs. Watson extended her hand as if to give him the choice of taking it or kissing it. He clasped her fingers and bowed his head a little, his bowler already in his other hand.

"My mother sends her compliments and a bit of something from Orange Township," Solomon said, gesturing toward the wagon. "She hopes to make your acquaintance soon. Perhaps you can visit us in Ionia to see how Miss Watson's school progresses."

"That would be lovely," Mrs. Watson replied. Jennette and Calista had by this time walked up the steps, and Solomon stepped aside so the sisters could join them on the porch. Jennette embraced her mother and then clasped Calista's hand, looking to her father to make the introduction.

He obliged. "Mr. Ramsdell, this is my daughter Calista." She extended her hand as her mother had, but regarded him with keen attention.

"Miss Calista," Solomon said, briefly taking her hand.

"Well then, I'll have Daniel help you with the horse and wagon, *Solomon*," Mr. Watson said, establishing their relationship with the emphasis on the name.

"And we'll see to supper," announced Mrs. Watson, holding open the door. "Girls, come with me."

After Daniel and Solomon fetched a few items from the wagon and had a brief tour of the barn and the kitchen garden, they had a few quiet words between them and then made their way to the house to wash up. While the men sat on the front porch, waiting for supper, Solomon could hear through the open window that Calista was whispering insistently and Jennette mildly replying as they set things on the table in the large kitchen beyond the front room. But he could not make out the words.

"Mother!" Calista called, "we're finished with the table! I want to take Jennette upstairs to tidy up before supper."

"Very well," answered Mrs. Watson from the kitchen beyond. "We can wait a few minutes to begin."

Solomon could hear the sisters more clearly when he turned to watch them climb the stairs. "I expect you knew who it was bringing me as soon as we drove up," Jennette said with a laugh, reaching up a hand to squeeze Calista's arm. Then they were upstairs and he heard no more.

Solomon turned his attention back to the Watson men, who had fallen into a discussion about the farm. He heard the word *seed* and picked up the thread of their talk of crop yields and speculation until the sisters' feet clattered down the stairs again a little later. Daniel rose at the sound, then Mr. Watson, who held the front door for Solomon.

Jennette was standing at the bottom of the stairs, her hair arranged into smooth wings on either side and twisted up into a knot at the back, and Calista was behind her, fixing the knot with a ribbon. Solomon hadn't seen this style before—he supposed it was Calista's doing—but it was lovely, highlighting the blond sheen of Jennette's hair.

Calista herself had a spray of lavender meadow rue tucked into the dark curls behind her ear.

"Ladies," he said, bowing his head. They returned the gesture.

At the table Solomon made pleasant conversation, adding to Andrew Watson's knowledge of how Jacob Ramsdell managed some problem on his farm. While deferential to his father's ways, Solomon also made it clear he had ideas of his own. And he made sure to direct questions and observations to each of the others in turn: he declared that Sally Watson's dried-apple pie rivaled his own mother's, and he told Daniel of the progress they'd made clearing the land and improving the road to town.

"And Miss Calista," he added as they began to stir from the table, Jennette's gaze upon him, "your sister tells me that you make music."

Calista reddened and glanced at Jennette. "Well, yes, I do love music."

"Mr. Watson, Mrs. Watson, could I beg the favor?" he asked. "Miss Watson has been telling me of her sister's talents. Would you be so kind as to let her play for us? Perhaps even give us a little song?"

"W-well, I don't know," Calista said, clearly uncomfortable at being the focus of conversation. "It's growing late . . ."

"But you won't be alone," Jennette said. "I persuaded Mr. Ramsdell to bring along his violin."

Solomon shrugged and smiled warmly at Calista. "So you see, we are both put on the spot. And there is no help for it."

"No help at all," Jennette declared.

While Mrs. Watson cleared the table, Mr. Watson opened the piano bench in the next room and began selecting a few pieces of music. Solomon went out to the barn for his violin. As he was returning, he heard Calista's voice carry out into the yard. "But Jennette, you're tone deaf—how do you *know* he can play?"

Solomon made sure to bang about a bit as he came up the steps with the violin. *She's probably in a panic, wondering if I'll screech and saw—and if Jennette will know how to keep from encouraging me!* Would Calista bear it with good will, knowing good will was everywhere around her? He was amused at the dilemma they had set up for Jennette's sister. But he knew—and Calista would know—the music must be right.

All the Watsons were waiting in the front room when he entered. Solomon swung the instrument out of its case and tucked the bow under his arm and the violin under his chin. Then he put one foot up on a handy stool. He made a fierce face of concentration and plucked a string as Calista played an A. He got two strings in tune, but oh, the third! He nodded in satisfaction as Calista's eyes widened in horror, and then he tuned the final string from the ruined third one, pulled the bow out from under his arm, and nodded. "Your pleasure, Miss Calista. What shall we play?"

"Oh, I . . . I don't know." She shuffled through the music, then looked over her shoulder to where her parents sat on parlor chairs and Daniel lounged against the mantel. "Maybe Daniel could come play his own violin . . .?"

"I know!" Solomon said. "How about 'Nobody's Jig?'" He tapped his bow on her stack of music and glanced at Jennette, who was standing quietly by the piano, holding her face very still.

"Well, yes," Calista answered, "but that starts with you, properly, and then I come in a bit later."

"And it's danceable." Solomon nodded to Jennette. "Well, let's have at it, then." He took a big breath, laid his bow on the strings of his instrument, and made a preliminary sawing motion that squealed the long, swooping opening phrase, then jumped into the quick dancing rhythm. Calista winced around her smile.

It's as bad as she feared, he thought as he galloped wildly around the rhythm until he finished his verse and it was time for her to come in. He nodded encouragingly with his whole body as he scratched away at his violin, and Calista answered with her soft and bouncing chords.

But then, after she'd gotten a line or two into her part, Solomon smoothed out his playing, his runs lilting and carrying them both up and over the lines of the music, badly tuned strings and all. And on the next verse, when the piano was the solo instrument, Solomon quickly adjusted the tuning pegs on his violin and joined in to echo Calista's dancing melody with harmonies that played with the lines every which way—revealing his mastery a line at a time.

Calista shook her head as she played. *She knows she's been had,* Solomon thought. Jennette laughed delightedly and drummed out a rhythm with her fingers on the top of the piano until Daniel claimed her for a dance. Her parents nodded and tapped their feet at the show before them.

They'd finished three or four more verses of call-and-answer improvisation before Daniel got out his violin to join them. Solomon knew he had won over Calista with his playing—she was so swept up in it she couldn't bear to quit. She started shuffling through the music and held up a favorite concerto that she said Daniel had never been able to manage but that she longed to play.

And so the evening passed, the music expressing what their words couldn't say.

THE NEXT MORNING, Solomon, who had slept in Daniel's room, got up early with him to help with the chores. As they emerged from the barn, each carrying a pail of milk, Andrew Watson came down the kitchen steps. Solomon handed Daniel his pail of milk and turned to shake hands and fall into step with the older man as he headed to the barn. Jennette walked lightly, with a little swing like her father's, Solomon noticed. Watson was slender like his daughter, though he had just the beginnings of a pot belly above his waistband.

Solomon was wearing a clean shirt, still creased from careful folding, and he was freshly shaven and had combed back his hair. Watson looked him up and down in silence.

"Mr. Watson," Solomon said, "I understand from Daniel that you've been successful with fruit here. The apples we had in the pie last night were excellent—even dried they were firm and sweet, with few blemishes."

"Mrs. Watson saw to that." Watson chuckled, softening a bit. "No doubt we'll have the brown and noduled ones after you've gone."

"Just as my mother would have done. Nevertheless, I understand you have a good yield."

"They serve us well, though I am looking to more cultivation of the berries that grow wild throughout the woods here. The soil by the river is good for them." He paused a moment at the barn, as if to deliberate, and then bypassed it and led Solomon to the field and fence line behind it.

"We have more floodplain in Orange," Solomon said, "good once we get the trees and stumps out, but—"

"And so it was once here as well. We spent years burning out those stumps after sending the trees to mill."

"The land goes through seasons, it seems." Solomon put his hand upon the rail of the fence they had reached. "First we find an Indian path to travel, and then we broaden it into road. And then perhaps we cultivate a sugar-bush. One season we chop and mill and burn. And another season we plant for our own food, or for seed to sell."

"And one man comes in ..." Watson paused for a leisurely inspection of a slat that had fallen from its leaning post. "As I was saying, one man comes in to build a mill, another man a forge, and before we know it, we're a village or a town." Solomon pulled the post straight as Watson refitted the slat, each knowing what to do without a word to the other.

"I have land just west of my father's, and my brother-in-law a half section just west of mine, but there's one small quarter section in between. South of us runs a branch and a fine sugar-bush, as you saw when you visited. In one place we've not yet used are the remains of a sugar-bush clearing that someone made before we ever settled there. Though it was just twenty years ago, it seems almost before time to me."

"Were you born in Michigan, Solomon?"

"Yes, sir, but in Wayne County. My parents hadn't made it this far west when they had to stop for my arrival. From there we went to Kalamazoo County, where my sister Diana—now gone—was born, the first white child in the county."

"I am sorry for your family's loss—we are fortunate not to have known the loss of a child ourselves." Watson looked up, as if to judge the time to move on from the topic.

"Jennette was nearly the first white child born here," he said. "Stout over there"—he gestured in the direction of a neighbor's place—"he and I had the first farms here—known as Plainfield then. His wife managed her Mary's birth just two hours before Jennette's, that they might have the claim." He chuckled. "No matter. So, Kalamazoo . . . your father told me he helped found that town."

"Yes, he was a judge there, and drew up the plans for the streets. Have you heard of his giant rocking chair?"

"No, I haven't. What would be the use of that?"

"It was just for the fun of it. Father and some others constructed a giant rocking chair that takes climbing to get into. And though he's a rather dignified man these days, it tells a bit of his character to mention it."

"He's not the only one in the business of making outsized articles," Watson said. "Perhaps Daniel—and the girls—can take you to see our local Gargantua today."

"That certainly sounds intriguing! But I'm here to be of help if you'll have my services today, and to attend worship with your family tomorrow before taking Miss Watson back in the afternoon."

"Well, we've finished planting, and not much is ready to pick this early. Wild strawberries, maybe . . ." He reached down to inspect some strawberry plants at the base of the fence, then straightened with an involuntary groan.

"Daniel mentioned some good fishing in Bostwick Lake near here," Solomon said, stretching out his own back in sympathy.

"Yes! And with the help of the Gargantua, you might provide for our supper."

"Now you have me perplexed, Mr. Watson. I suppose I shall have to let Daniel show me."

"And the girls, too. Jennette and Calista never pass up fishing expeditions."

Solomon took a deep breath. *I might not get a better chance.* "Speaking of your daughters, I had hoped . . ." He stuffed his hands in his pockets to still their trembling.

Watson stopped at a broken slat and propped it up a bit for show, though it wouldn't hold against a determined cow. "I need to get this one repaired," he said, then turned to face Solomon. "I expect you have a *particular* hope?"

"Yes, sir," Solomon answered. "I had hoped to secure your permission to court your daughter."

"Jennette, correct? Though it's possible she's said enough about Calista that you've admired *her* from afar."

"Oh . . . y-yes, Jennette!" he stammered. "Though Calista is a fine young lady, too."

Watson smiled and gave a courtly nod. "No fear, young man. I know what you mean. With four years between them, and you older than Jennette . . ."

"Yes, sir. I'm twenty-four. Just turned."

"Well, Jennette is more your age. But I'd like to know what you admire in her. I want to make sure she's properly appreciated."

"Oh, well, she's just so easy with her pupils in the school, and so learned. No doubt your doing, sir—and Mrs. Watson's."

"Jennette has always been one for the books, Calista for the music—and Daniel, he does a little bit of everything." They passed a promising patch of raspberries along a length of the fence, though it would be weeks before they were ready. Watson bent to reveal a deep-red wild strawberry beneath its leaf and picked the tiny fruit. He held it out to Solomon, who took it with a nod and murmured with pleasure as its sweetness filled his mouth.

"So, why are you twenty-four and not yet married, to get straight to the point?"

"Well, sir, I've been working with my father and clearing my own land, as well as working on the roads that I mentioned. And I've managed to save enough to build my house and furnish it modestly. I've also been learning what my father does with the local government and school administration; I want to learn as much as possible from him while I can, before setting out so fully on my own that I no longer have his guidance."

"That sounds like a sensible approach," Watson said. "Daniel is doing much the same here." They turned at a fence corner and walked along the newly sprouting wheat and through the pasture, knee-deep in wildflowers that grew up to the fence.

"Actually," Solomon continued. "I've been watchful for a young lady who would be a suitable wife"—*Oh no! Not watchful, as for a robber!* "Th-that is, keeping an eye out for a young lady. I've known for some time that a schoolteacher is just the sort I'd be most interested in. We're a family of schoolteachers—my father one himself in days gone by, and my sister Rosette a teacher until her marriage this year."

"What makes a good teacher, do you think?" Watson said, turning at another fence corner at the base of a hill. They began to walk up toward a wooded area that had not yet known the axe. The swooping birds of the fields gave way to rustling birds and chipmunks on the forest floor. The light-speckled gloom brought their voices lower.

"Beyond the usual things that made my sister a good teacher?" Solomon asked. "Rosette kept an orderly class and cared for details like spelling and penmanship . . . but Miss

Watson—Jennette—went beyond those things and made a book with her class. What I would have given to have made such a thing when I was in school! She thought of it herself and did it with them, simultaneously answering to children's desires and helping them learn in spite of themselves."

"A child's heart can be foolish, desiring what's not good for him." Watson tipped his head back to study the tree canopy. "No child wants to learn his figures, though he must."

"You echo my father!" Solomon said, his voice garbled by his own head tipping back to watch the light filter through the new leaves. "He made sure we all knew our mathematics. It was his specialty." He picked up a long twig and snapped it in the middle to have something to do with his hands. "But the beauty *behind* the numbers is what feeds his passion for them. My father is a rare man in that, and I see that same quality in your daughter."

"Go on," Watson said.

"You already know my father, and the family I would be drawing her into. I've made a good start on a farm and home worthy of a wife like Jennette, and her care for her students shows me she would make a fine mother."

"You praise her prettily." Watson stopped at the next turning of the fence to raise his foot onto a boulder. "But do you care for her? And how has she responded to you?"

"I wanted to speak to you first, sir, before declaring myself, as is proper. But I think my intentions have become plain over the last few weeks. Yesterday I hinted at them and she seemed pleased, though she stopped me from saying more until I'd spoken to you."

Watson waited, and Solomon felt he must add more— *less business, more heart.*

"As I've come to know Jennette these weeks, my heart has been called toward hers. Although it would be foolish for me to declare myself more fully without her reciprocation"—he twisted his hands together—"I am prepared to say that—indeed—I do love her."

"Well, to be frank, Solomon, it's not all your doing that you've been drawn to her. Your father and I spoke of this possibility last year, measuring out between us how we might encourage a match between our children. We came up with the idea of Jennette working as the Orange Township schoolteacher for a season, but we didn't want to declare it openly. Jacob and I think so well of each other, it seemed natural to join our families thus."

It was not all my doing? Solomon felt confused. And then indignant. "Why wasn't I told?" he said, cracking his twig into splinters and dropping them on the ground. "Father told me I ought to consider your daughters, but I thought—"

"Your father and I wanted only to see you happily settled—both of you—and now it seems you will be! So yes, you may court Jennette. And when you're sure, you may write to ask my permission to propose, and I will grant it—provided you continue to cherish her and do right by her. But she'll know well enough whether that's the case." Watson turned back toward the house and waved an arm for Solomon to follow.

Like a child, or a dog, Solomon thought. *So sure of me.* All that had seemed to be working itself out in his hands was suddenly not in his hands at all, but in his father's—and her father's!

He stumbled along behind Watson until they came in sight of the house, where Jennette appeared at the kitchen door, her hand shielding her eyes from the morning sun as she looked in their direction. *Is she, too, in on the scheme?*

* * *

Solomon endured breakfast somehow, with strained politeness and silence. Jennette and Calista carried the conversation for all of them.

"Are you weary from your journey, Mr. Ramsdell?" Mrs. Watson finally asked him. "You're quiet this morning." She offered the jam pot. "More jam?"

He held up his hand. "No thank you. And yes, I am a bit fatigued."

Jennette knit her brows at him and then cut her eyes toward Calista.

Is she worried she's been found out, then?

"So," Watson said, "I told Solomon here about our neighborhood Gargantua. I'm thinking perhaps you young people could go to see it this morning—and perhaps fish for our supper?"

"Oh yes!" said Jennette. She wiped her mouth with her napkin and turned to her brother. "Daniel, you must take us." Daniel nodded but Solomon remained stone-faced. While his uppermost thought was that he must defend against being a mark and a buffoon, below this his mind raced to and fro with warring ideas. *Could she seem so straight and clear, and yet be working womanly wiles against me?*

"I haven't told him what the Gargantua is, however," Watson continued, "so you can decide whether to surprise him or tell him before you get there."

Why begin telling me things now?

All of them rose from the table. The women began to clear up, and Daniel invited Solomon to help him get the fishing poles ready, grabbing a small, chipped cup and a dishcloth as he left the kitchen. They walked to the barn in silence—Solomon's filled with pounding in his ears—while the big fluffy dog worked to herd them until Daniel gave a little calming whistle and ruffled his head.

And what's Daniel's part in this?

Solomon waited as Daniel climbed a short ladder built onto a sturdy barn post, then took the poles Daniel retrieved from their resting place across the rafters. Daniel then handed Solomon a box with a leather strap before hopping down from the ladder and leading him outside to a bench where they could work.

The poles, simple flexible branches cleared of their twigs, were smooth where many hands had held them. They inspected the knots on the attached lines and replaced the ones that had snapped, securing a hook from the box on each line and preparing a cloth pouch with additional hooks, a spool of line, and a claw-like tool for drawing in the catch.

Daniel tucked his knife into the sheath at his waist and tied the pouch there, then went back into the barn, returning with a hand spade and picking up the cup and cloth. Solomon stood to follow Daniel to the nearby compost heap, where Daniel handed him the spade, and Solomon thrust and twisted it, turning up rich black soil squirming with pink and gray worms that Daniel plucked out and dropped into the cup.

"Now we're ready," Daniel said as he tied the dishcloth over the cup of worms. "C'mon, Puck—you can go, too," he said to the dog. He nodded toward the house where Jennette and Calista stood on the porch in their bonnets, Calista holding a basket. Solomon shouldered the poles while Daniel secured the cup of worms with the cloth and nestled the cup into the box he slung on its strap over his shoulder. The sisters joined them as they came near the porch, and Solomon followed the three Watson siblings around the house. They took a path into the dark of the wood, then Jennette looked over her shoulder at him.

"It's just a mile or so more," she said, then returned to her conversation with Calista. The gloom in the woods matched Solomon's mood as he trudged beside Daniel. *No need to chat with me, then, now that I'm secured?*

Lake

Before long, the lake was visible through the trees, a mirror reflecting the late-morning sun, and Puck ran ahead of them. When it was fully in view, Solomon estimated it at a couple of hundred acres. Trees grew right up to the edge in most places, but there was a bit of clear shore here and there, and the dog had run right in to swim, spreading arcs across the still water.

"And now"—Calista spread her arms—"we will show you a wonder of Michigan!" Daniel dropped his box, and Jennette the basket she'd been carrying the last part of the walk, and the three siblings hurried a little up the shore and crowded one another in an excited push into the woods. Solomon stood where he was, holding the poles.

"Solomon! Give a man some help!" Daniel called from inside the forest. Solomon propped the fishing poles against a tree and followed the sounds of the sisters' voices, picking his way through the brush where there was no path. As he approached, he saw a massive fallen tree, larger than any in the vicinity—and then he saw it was clean, stripped of its bark. But no, not a log . . . a canoe! It was an enormous version of the small dugouts he'd seen Indians use on the Grand, and massively heavy. It slanted down toward the shore and rested on a ramp of logs that just barely held it out of the water.

Jennette beamed up at him from behind the canoe and smacked her hands on the wood. "Have you ever seen one this big? Thirty feet!"

"Never," Solomon said, forgetting his dark mood in his effort to work out the puzzle of the thing. How had it gotten here? Who would use it? "How many does it take to get it in the water?"

"Well, I'm hoping just the two—or four—of us," Daniel said. He and Calista were clearing branches and old leaves out of the canoe.

Calista dumped an armload of branches on the ground. "I don't think it's been used since last fall, by the looks of it."

"Years ago this whitewood tree was felled south of Cannonsburg," Jennette said. "A Chippewa was entreated by the agent—Bostwick—to make it into a dugout canoe, but to the scale of the tree."

"No one gave thought to what it would take to launch it when it was done," Daniel added, "and there was no body of water larger than a creek within miles."

"So how did the Bostwick fellow get it *here?*" Solomon asked, thinking of all the logs his family had dragged to the mill over the years, difficult even over proper roads.

"It took all manner of oxen," Calista said.

Daniel nodded. "Four yoke, five miles."

"And now we use it for fishing and lake parties," Jennette said, "when we have the ambition and numbers to launch it. Will you help?"

Not just assuming I will, then? What was in her mind?

"Of course," he replied.

For Daniel's sake, in any case.

Solomon studied Jennette for a moment as she cleared brush out from underneath the vessel, then he walked to the front of the canoe, stepping off the length for himself. Fully thirty feet, and long poles inside for directing it.

Daniel saw him drawing out the poles and said, "No paddles, as it would take too many to gain any speed. We just pole out a ways and then pole back." He returned to his work at the bow, adjusting the smooth logs that had been arranged for launch.

"How will we—?" Solomon began, but Puck had just raced back from his explorations in the water and on the shore and shook vigorously, spraying Solomon with lake water.

"Get it back up onshore?" Jennette laughed at Solomon wiping his face. "We can't! We'll launch for the summer and push—and pull—the bow up on the bank when we return. Since it's the same on both ends, whichever end points toward the lake is the bow. The last to use it in the fall— probably us again—will bring a larger crew to drag it out of the water."

"Won't last too long that way," Daniel said, "but it was a silly thing to begin with."

Calista waved a hand to dismiss his comment. "But we can get more than a dozen in it for the Independence Day party! And the lake will echo when they shoot off the cannon."

"From Cannonsburg, of course," Jennette explained, then brightly told of how a Mr. Cannon back East had provided plots for the unlanded to make a town when she was just a little child, and how he thought a gift of a cannon would help them to remember him. "And his agent, Mr. Bostwick, gave his name to this lake. The cannon has been a trial, though, because whenever they fire it at New Year's or Independence Day, someone who doesn't know the business always manages to rush in and get himself hurt. So a few years ago they buried the cannon to put a stop to that—"

"But *somebody* dug it back up," Daniel said, eyes sparkling.

"And *you* wouldn't know anything about that, would you?" Calista said.

Daniel smirked. "No, nor Father."

Solomon appreciated the good-natured teasing of siblings. "As I recall, Daniel, you really know your guns. Jerome and Frank told me of the small game you shot at our place."

"He once got a bear," Calista said proudly, "right between the eyes!"

"Yes, well, let's get this boat on the lake," Daniel said, then cleared his throat and turned away, tugging at his collar.

With a careful arrangement of levers and logs, and some mighty shoving from them all, the giant canoe began its slide into the lake. Puck leapt right in and sat in the bow, awaiting his ride. When all but the stern was launched, Solomon and Daniel held it in place while Calista and Jennette hurried to grab their lunch basket and fishing gear. The girls climbed into the middle of the canoe, where they knelt, waiting for the launch, and the young men heaved and pried, and when they finally released the last bit of the vessel from the land, they flung themselves into the canoe as it glided out into the lake.

"Good thing you didn't have to wade in," Calista called back as Solomon and Daniel stood to wield their poles. "It's ice-cold."

* * *

After a couple of hours, the fishing party came away with six panfish and a lake trout, having thrown back the catfish Daniel caught with some bacon from his pocket. They'd enjoyed a floating picnic, the girls leaning far over the bulk of the canoe to trail their fingers in the water. Jennette seemed at ease so long as Solomon kept up a natural rapport, but she looked closely at him when he kept too long a silence

As they landed the canoe, Puck delicately disembarked, leaving off his swimming for the day. They left the stern— now the bow—partially extended into the lake. The wood, though close-grained and tight, was showing some breakdown from years of such treatment.

As they walked the path back to the Watsons', Solomon let himself fall into place beside Jennette and noticed that Daniel glanced over his shoulder, then said something to Calista, and they stepped up their pace, Puck alongside them. The poles bounced on Daniel's shoulder, and Calista swung the lunch basket.

I'll just have to venture the thing, Solomon thought.

"So now that we're on our own ..." He pulled down a dried vine from an overhead limb, then folded the vine over on itself and wound it around his wrist, one way and then the other. "And I can ask you what I've been wondering since this morning ..."

She looked up at him to hear more, and the turn of her head sent her sweet, sharp scent his way.

He took a breath to steady his nerves. "Your father seemed pretty pleased with himself when he told me that he and my father arranged our courtship, as if I had no part in it at all. He gave me permission to court you—without a thought."

"Well," she replied with a single note of laughter, "it does seem to have been neatly done."

"But what I want to know is this—did you come to Orange at your father's direction, intending to snare me?" Solomon twisted the vine savagely around his wrist, then flung it into the woods.

"No, it was not that at all!" she cried. "Father spoke well of your father and said a little here and there about your family—that you were at the head of a suitable community for my teaching. And he didn't hesitate to send me there, though he wouldn't let me go to other places."

Solomon kept silent, looking down at the ground as they walked.

After a minute or so she added in a low voice, "I am only what I seem to be," and then she stopped in the path and looked down, the brim of her bonnet hiding her countenance from him.

I've distressed her! His heart grew heavy and sank within him, and without thinking he snatched her hand and held it between his. "Jennette, I cannot bear that I doubted you! But more than what I imagined you might have said or done, I felt betrayed, felt made a fool, by the whole *idea* I've had."

"What idea?" she asked, gently pulling her hand away. She lifted her head and began walking again.

"I set a purpose for myself to find a partner for my life, and then you came to us and appeared to be all the things . . . you seemed to be the answer to my purpose."

"So it distresses you that our fathers might have arranged for us to discover one another. And now I hear that you wanted to have it all in hand yourself . . . that you might *boast* of it?" She was walking quickly now, down one knoll and up another, rapidly catching up to Daniel and Calista.

"No," Solomon said as he kept pace with her, "but I see now that they didn't draw you into their conspiracy, and that's all that matters."

"Because you can retain the boast, then?"

"No!" He slapped his hands on his thighs in exasperation. "I don't know *what* I mean to say! It's only that"—he stopped and faced her, taking both her hands in his. "Jennette, the last several weeks my whole life has come to a realization I couldn't have expected—all my hope for a helpmeet is met, and overmet, in you."

"Are you overwrought?" she asked softly, teasing, "like one of the heroes in Rosette's novels?"

His face flamed. It was so.

"Never mind," she said, squeezing his fingers and releasing them before she turned to walk again. "If Father has given permission, then I'm all anticipation for how you might court me ... Wagon rides, maybe? We've already had one of those!"

He fell into her play, abashed but giddily relieved. "Flowers, perhaps ..."

"How about nosegays?"

"Surely ... but what on earth is a nosegay?"

Her laugh rang through the trees as an answer, and she left the path to snatch up a little blossom of trillium and some bright greenery to surround it. She demonstrated holding it to her nose and then held it out for him to try.

He took the tiny bouquet, and her hands as well, and drew her to himself.

SEPARATION
1861–1863

Idyll

THE TOWHEADED CHILD stumbled over a furrow and steadied himself, calling and pointing before him. "Grappa o' dere! O' dere!"

Solomon lifted his head where he was squatting further along the furrow, setting out seedlings in the newly turned soil in his upper field. Two fields away his father was doing the same on his own land. "You're right, Sy! That's Grandpa over there!" He stood and brushed his hand off on his thigh, put two fingers in his mouth, and whistled a curling note that raised his father's head across the way. Then he knelt next to Seymour and they both waved until Jacob Ramsdell lifted his hat and waved back.

"Grappa see me!" Seymour shouted and galloped about.

Solomon sat back on his heels and looked around at his property—all was fresh and damp in late spring, just a trace of the winter's snow mounds still melting into the ground at the northwest corner of the house. Soon the summer sun would reach Jennette's flower bed there for much of the day, and the tulips of weeks ago would be followed by midsummer blooms. The first spring that her lilacs had bloomed, when Seymour was an infant, Solomon had brought Jennette a cluster in a glass dish.

"Not that I need cheering," she'd said before pressing her lips to their son's brow. "But it's a fitting celebration of spring giving way to summer." She'd closed her eyes and inhaled deeply, as if adding the lilac scent to her memory, then nodded for Solomon to do the same.

His sturdy son was approaching the box of seedlings, so Solomon rose to intervene. "What have you got there, Sy? Let's see about putting the rest of those in the ground."

Jennette came out to the clothesline with a rug to beat. *So it's just late this year,* he thought. *The annual airing out.* Each spring she would throw open all the windows—never mind the temperature—and haul out all the goods that softened the edges of winter. From upstairs and down, out the door he had painted soft blue just for her, came first the rugs to be beaten, then the quilts and curtains to be piled up and washed over the next few days. She'd sweep out the cobwebs from top to bottom, and the ashes that had settled on dressers and shelves, and nothing would go back into the house until all was clean. If she didn't finish in one day, and if the night was cold, they'd shiver in the midst of all the emptiness.

* * *

"To remember the martyrs, perhaps," she'd said two springs before when they'd been huddled in their four-poster bed with the one old green-and-brown diamond quilt she'd washed early for just this occasion. "On this one night, we can, in our privation, look about this bare room . . ." She dramatically turned her head to both frosty windows, which were free of their curtains, black panes revealing the cold night sky.

"And wish for a burning-at-the-stake at which to warm ourselves?"

"No!" she cried, pretending to swat at him. "No," she continued soberly, "we can think of what others have suffered in the past. And with just a small taste of their pain, our appetites will be sharpened to better enjoy our pleasures when we have them."

"You've provided just enough comfort"—he held up the corner of the quilt that was wrapped around them as they sat cross-legged together against the headboard—"that we can still our shivering long enough to contemplate such things." He pursed his lips and nodded as if in a brown study, then sneaked his arm around her back and pulled her to him quickly for a kiss, resting his hand on top of her belly, which was full with their child.

She smiled a firm little smile at the kiss and pressed his hand to a spot where the babe was drawing a heel or elbow across her belly. "So have you seen to the cradle and cupboard this little one will need very soon?"

"Well, yes . . ." Solomon hesitated; he'd wanted to surprise her with the finished cradle. "But surely there's still time. The mite won't have call for it for weeks yet. Your spring cleaning is the earliest I've ever known."

"That's as may be, but readiness is all. I've done my part, but sometimes I fear you might not have everything in hand." She held up her hand and touched each finger to thumb in turn to enumerate: "There's the spring washing, which will be done within a day, and stores of wheat, corn, salt pork, beans . . ." She made a fist.

"Have I ever failed you as a provider?" he asked indulgently, pulling open her hand.

"Well, we did have to go without light bread that week you forgot the saleratus from town."

"As I said then, I don't know why you couldn't have used some of Rosette's, or even Mother's or the Kings'—"

"Because, as I already told you"—she planted her palms on either side of her body and stretched out her legs to ease them, breaking their embrace—"it does not do for my mother-in-law to have cause to doubt my housekeeping. And Rosette needn't be bothered by one more thing in her day . . ." She left the rest unsaid.

"But surely Lucinda or one of the King girls could have provided it."

"Perhaps, but then your mother and sister would have known in due time!" Jennette exhaled a big lungful of a sigh that became a frosty cloud before them—and relaxed into a chuckle.

She drew back a moment and mirrored his pursed lips and furrowed brow, pulling at an imaginary beard, perhaps to acknowledge that she'd been the cause of his dour expression. Then she kissed him again, pulled back laughing, then planted another kiss. He put his hands on her shoulders and faced her, adjusting the quilt around them. *Right here, right now, is all I have ever wanted.*

Her eyes reflected the lamplight from their bedside table.

"You would have us contemplate the martyrs, and matters of housekeeping, but I would rather contemplate you," he said quietly.

"And so you shall, all our life long. I mean to keep you wondering sometimes, though." She traced a finger across his brow and down to his jawline, curled her hand into the thick beard he'd grown the first year of their marriage, and drew him in for another kiss. "Wondering and warm," she said as she leaned back and scooted down the bed, somehow arranging the quilt to cover them both.

* * *

"Well, son," Solomon said, brushing the dirt from his hands after planting the last of the currant seedlings, "we'd best stay out from underfoot, lest we hinder the cleaning and find ourselves freezing and hungry tonight." He swooped the toddler onto his shoulders and marched into the barn, where he set him loose in the hayloft so he could make some repairs to the horse stall while Hector was out to pasture. When Seymour tired of romping in the remains of the winter hay, he whimpered to come down, so Solomon popped him into a feed box and gave him a stick of wood. While the father hammered nails, the child banged the slats of the feed box, and thus they passed a happy hour until they both grew hungry and Seymour tried climbing out of the box.

"Yes, let's make our escape." Solomon helped Seymour haul himself up and over the rail. "Run on up to Mama, now. See where she is by the house?" Seymour waddled along the muddy path, falling and picking himself up several times, while Solomon kept an eye on him. Jennette was billowing some linens over Seymour's outgrown cradle, which she had pulled into the sunshine to air, and Solomon noted when she spied her son toddling toward her.

"There's my big boy!" she called, holding out her hands. When Seymour at last reached her, he fell against her and buried his head in her skirt, scrubbing his face into the gingham in his sleepiness. Her words to Seymour carried across the field to Solomon on an easterly breeze: "We'll get you some dinner and then a little rest." She spread her hand on top of the child's head.

Solomon turned toward the southeast horizon, as if by facing that direction he could make sense of what had, of late, been running through his mind as he'd read the news, talked of current events in town, and whittled on his father's porch while his younger brothers took up their own favorite strands of speculation and judgment.

Their father was born not long after the nation itself had come into being—to New England patriots who congratulated themselves on the settled new order and a promising future. He had only ever had the concerns of a frontiersman. What was that thing John Adams had said? The patriots fought that their children might plant and keep shop, that *their* children might paint and sing . . . *and play violin, no doubt.* Solomon and his brothers were in that comfortable generation, with no need to wander as their father had wandered across the Michigan landscape from the New York of his birth, and the Massachusetts of *his* father's birth. Solomon was born here in Michigan and had settled within view of his father's farm and his sister's husband's place, and in a few years his younger sister and brothers would no doubt have farms nearby themselves. The cousins would grow up together, not needing to rely on stories and letters to weave together the threads of family lore as their elders had been forced to do over the years.

His father had taught him well the principles of government and of law, drawing from the ancient sources and later the best ideas of the previous centuries. But these lessons would have crumbled to ash if Jacob Ramsdell hadn't also been a wise leader as teacher and magistrate, and a successful farmer and businessman. He lived out his ideals and thereby commanded respect.

The ideals of Abolition that had drawn both Solomon and his father to support Fremont back in 1856, arose from high-minded principles, it was true. But backing Fremont also served their private interests: pursuing trade and prosperity in a market unhindered by the unfair advantages of slavery. They campaigned for Lincoln, too, as the ideals of Abolition became more complex. As long as the South sought only to secede, Michigan was in no danger of invasion, but what if the pressures of war stung the Confederates into retaliation? After all, Fort Sumter was property of the United States Government, and the Rebels had invaded the island. Some Michiganders suggested there could be a threat from the South—were they just fearmongers?

But Rebel troops marching through his sugar-bush and across his creek, firing his fields and barn and threatening his wife and child—this was not the only thing that could ruin them . . . Solomon was willing to put his life on the line to defend and promulgate the principles of the Union, but not if it meant leaving his land and family unprotected from poverty. A man must bend every effort to provide for his family, and Solomon knew leaving his farm would expose Jennette and Seymour to all kinds of dangers—even if a Confederate soldier never came within a hundred miles of them.

Principles were one thing, but recent events had exposed practicalities of a different sort. Fort Sumter was the flashpoint, and Solomon could almost hear the hoofbeats and the squeak of leather and the clank of artillery pieces drawing him into the midst of the melee.

"Sol!" Jennette called, breaking his reverie. "Solomon!"

He blinked and shook himself back to the present. *Dinner. Yes.* He raised a hand to acknowledge her call and trudged alongside the newly plowed furrows, smiling to himself.

Like a painting, so lovely. His wife, their son, a house so well cared for in the midst of land that supported them all— and more children to come, he hoped. Fort Sumter suddenly seemed ages rather than weeks ago, and the possibility of being drawn into the war seemed remote.

Grand Rapids

SOLOMON PULLED HIS going-to-town bowler down on his head and walked out to the porch with Seymour as Jacob Ramsdell rode up, flourishing his top hat. The three-year-old climbed down the porch steps still slick from a morning shower as his grandfather swung down from his saddle and looped his reins over a branch of the five-year-old shagbark hickory.

When Solomon had built this house, he'd planted the tree behind the enormous boulder that marked the boundary of his front yard. Pale gold leaves fluttered down through rain-blackened branches onto his father's shoulders.

"Fine display there, Sol," Jacob said, brushing a leaf from his coat. "Even better in a decade."

"It's hard to imagine that this smooth trunk will earn its name in later years," Solomon said, nodding his thanks for the compliment. "Even harder to imagine it will outlive us by eight to ten generations."

"A man plants a shagbark when he intends to stay put. Seymour's children will be the first to enjoy a good nut harvest."

"When I planted it, I thought of how you weren't settled until you came here. Rosette and I were almost grown by then—and Diana gone." Solomon paused. "It seemed the right thing, to plant a good tree and watch it grow up with my family."

Seymour came back to Solomon and tugged on his hand, straining toward the horses. Solomon led him over and handed him a loop of Priam's dangling reins, and Seymour murmured to his grandfather's horse while Hector snorted companionably.

"Are you ready, then, Sol?" Jacob asked.

"Yes, sir. Just waiting a moment for Jennette." Solomon cinched the girth on Hector's saddle.

Jacob turned to Seymour and handed him a piece of sugar from his pocket. "You may give it to him, Sy." He bent down to demonstrate holding the sugar on a flattened palm, and after the horse whisked it away, asked softly, "Want up?" Seymour brightened and nodded, and his grandfather lifted him to put a foot on the edge of the saddle, as if in a stirrup. The child tried to swing his leg over in a proper mount, then bent forward—though he could hardly reach—and stroked Priam's shoulder.

The blue front door swung open. Jennette stood on the threshold, nestling newborn Callie on her shoulder. "Grandpa Ramsdell! Look what we have here!" she called. She crossed the porch and went down the two steps, bearing a little bundle in her free hand.

"Well, what *do* we have here?" Solomon's father said, walking to meet her. He bent over the child Jennette presented for his inspection, then unwrapped the fabric from the bundle she handed him, revealing a sweet bun.

"It's currant," Jennette said, "a little something for your ride. Father Ramsdell, you know I want you to bring my husband back to me from Grand Rapids. Don't let him sign with a regiment."

He nodded graciously and took up the formality he used in affectionate jest with her. "Young Mrs. Ramsdell, you must know I have only limited influence with your husband." He then added in a stage whisper, "But *your* influence is such that you may be assured he will return to you in two days' time."

"Shall we, young sir?" Jacob asked Seymour, holding out his hands to help him down from the saddle before mounting the horse himself.

Solomon kissed his wife and children, swung into his saddle, and guided Hector toward Jacob, who waited by the rock on Priam, who was stepping restlessly. Then they picked their way down the slight rise to the road and trotted north along the edge of a neighboring farm, then west toward Otis and Rosette's. As they approached the house, Solomon heard the small percussion of six-year-old DeWitt chopping at kindling with his own little wooden axe. When the boy saw them, he ran up to the road.

Jacob leaned down over Priam and said, "Where's your mother, DeWitt?"

The boy shrugged. "Pa's went to town."

"Is she inside, then, your mama?" Solomon said.

"S'pose so," DeWitt said, swinging his axe first in front of him, then behind.

"Well, here . . ." Jacob took out the bundle Jennette had given him. "I have a sweet that you may have." DeWitt stepped up to take it, opened the corners of the cloth for a peek, and then closed them up again.

Solomon turned Hector back toward the road and said over his shoulder, "DeWitt, tell your mother we stopped, and that Jennette will be around to see her after dinner." The boy just stood there, mute, holding the bun until they left.

A few rods away, Solomon broke the quiet. "Grief has brought that whole house low."

"I fear Rosette does not bear up well," his father replied. "It's a sore thing to lose a child—for a woman, especially."

"And two lost to fever the same week!" Solomon shook his head and sighed. "It's been months, but Rosette cannot see the Heavenly Father's care that would help reconcile her to the loss."

"We're not meant to reconcile these types of things, son. In our minds, perhaps, but in our hearts it won't ever sit right. Your mother still mourns Diana, and the grief rises up unbidden sometimes, as if her heart had only just remembered."

"Is it harder for Rosette, do you think? She's always measuring herself by one thing or another. Three children born minus two lost equals judgment?"

"I expect Churchill could ease her grief," his father said. "But he's not sympathetic enough to think of it."

"I try to send Jennette—or she sends herself."

"If anyone could comfort Rosette, your wife is the one. Perhaps the infant will help things a bit—though she's just as likely to increase the sting, I recognize."

They made their way northwest to Ionia, took care of some brief business at the bank, then rode on west, stopping at a boarding house for the night. The next morning they traveled along the river to Grand Rapids. The fence marking the fairgrounds bore tatters of bunting from the summer's activities—Solomon knew many had answered the recruiters' calls to the cavalry, infantry, and artillery.

Solomon had hoped the new president could lead the hearts of *all* the people. But it had come to this—to war. The attack on Fort Sumter had led to skirmishes and a simmering unease that bubbled like a soap pot, releasing vile heat. But if that unease could be contained, there could come a good product, like soap coming of ashes and lard. That was how Solomon thought of it, anyway.

Winter had settled it all down for a while, but it had also brought the diphtheria that claimed Rosette's babies. A pall had settled on the Ramsdell family, which had not known such a close death since Diana's a decade earlier. Solomon had nearly turned his back on the Churchills in order to shield himself from the prospect of losing his own child. *What brought this calamity?* he'd wondered. *What dangers might I forestall?* No, now was not a time to go to some far-off battlefield and leave Jennette and the children vulnerable.

"Look there!" his father called as they approached the town. A park had been fenced off and trees planted to form a public square. The fine fall Saturday had brought peddlers with wagons and sawhorses to line the boulevard, where horse racing had recently been outlawed in the interest of respectability. Hardly an Indian could be seen in town anymore, nor a single wigwam along the roads leading into town. They had even abandoned the island in the river where they'd kept a summer village in years gone by.

"You'd almost think it was in New York," Jacob said. "A fine river town, commerce . . ."

"Even an opera house!" Solomon reminded him as they came near to Squier's.

"With the railroad meeting the river here, and the ability to float lumber in, they're well set up to manufacture furniture, and supplies for the war. I've been thinking about getting in on that," his father said. "Myron King is, too. He's working on a deal to trade farms with a man out this way. I'm thinking of Lowell."

What? Our whole family has settled in Orange Township . . . It's our home.

But Solomon just said, "I don't favor the bustle myself," then turned his horse to avoid a wagon. He patted Hector's neck to settle him in the unfamiliar tumult.

They rode up to a saloon they knew and without a word dismounted and gave their horses into the care of a stableman in a side alley. As they had agreed when Solomon offered to accompany his father on the trip to town, Jacob visited the railroad offices to discuss prospects and make acquaintance with those whose knowledge and influence would be of use in the future, and Solomon wandered through town. He peered into the storefronts and carefully read the playbills posted at Squier's. *Would Jennette enjoy hearing an opera? Maybe a play.*

After an hour the men met back at the saloon and went in and had a meal. Jacob was full of ideas and Solomon half-listened while longing to be back home. When they emerged onto the boardwalk and clattered down to cross to the new park, they found themselves in front of a sawhorse-and-plank table covered with a striped cloth and draped with bunting—all in red, white, and blue.

"Honor for our country, protection for our land!" called a man from behind the table. He was dressed in a soldier's jacket and cap. "Join the muster of the Sixth Michigan Cavalry!" The man held out a leaflet, which Solomon took and idly pocketed. He and his father went on to the next display, where a peddler thrust out a deep canvas bag suspended from one shoulder by a strap, with a dozen-or-so walking sticks flaunting their decorative handles at the opening. Solomon drew out a silver-handled one and tried leaning upon it. *Too short . . .* though the knob felt right in his hand. He tried a simpler stick with a brass handle perpendicular to the shaft. It had a thumb rest that balanced the grip. *Yes, this is the one.* He lifted and twirled it up under his arm.

His father raised his eyebrows comically. "Are you a drum major, then?"

"A good walking stick gives the right impression," Solomon answered, a little abashed. He brought the cane down for quieter effect and tested it out for a few paces.

"No need until there's need, though," his father said. "Now *I* could make use of such a thing, in light of my years—but I won't give in to a stick until I must."

Solomon laughed. "So it seems we both nurture a bit of pride . . . I'll take this one," he said to the peddler, counting out the money. "And Father, you may borrow it once you feel the need. How about that?"

They continued along the displays, a brisk fall wind setting tablecloths and leaflets aflutter as they walked by. Town dwellers in light outerwear and folks from out of town in traveling coats and hats mingled in the street. In their midst, a familiar gait and the glint of a gun drew Solomon's attention.

"Daniel! Daniel Watson!" he called. His brother-in-law turned and scanned the crowd, his face clearing when he spotted Solomon, then closed the distance between them and extended a hand first to Jacob—who took it in his right and wrapped his left arm around the younger man's shoulders—and then to Solomon.

"What brings you to Grand Rapids?" Jacob asked.

"I've just taken the bounty for a wolf!" Daniel said, pointing to the muzzle of the gun slung on his back. "There were several menacing the town, and they put out a call—"

"And you couldn't resist." Solomon grinned.

"I had to have my try, and just the second morning out I spied him and got him. I'll set the money aside for when I get back—and set up my own farm."

"Back from where?" Jacob said. "Have you enlisted?"

"Yes, sir. I signed with the Western Sharpshooters in Kalamazoo—Company D, boys from a bunch of states. I'll join up with them in a few weeks' time."

"What settled you?" Jacob asked. Solomon tried a few poses with his new walking stick while he listened intently to their exchange.

"With Calista's help, and Mother's, Father can manage the farm well enough for a time. It seemed the right time to go, with the Rebels gaining strength this summer and the president's call for men in July . . . even before Antietam."

"But we farmers can just as well support the Union with our work here, can we not?" Solomon said, tipping his cane from one hand to the other, its point stuck into the dirt at his feet.

"No doubt the Union needs that, too, Sol. But the plea for sharpshooters was more than I could resist, to tell the truth. I have an important contribution to make—and no family yet to care for."

Solomon bent to study his hands atop his cane, and then looked up with a little smile. Daniel looked concerned. "I . . . I didn't—"

Solomon held up a hand. "No need, brother. I'm at ease with my choice . . . And perhaps my choice will change."

"Yes, perhaps!" Daniel said, relief in his voice.

"Actually, Mrs. Ramsdell and I are contemplating a change, ourselves," Jacob said. "The boom that has come to Grand Rapids has spread to just south of your father's place. I have been conferring with men here today about the possibilities, and I have my eye on a parcel in Lowell. It's enough for a family home, but my real business would be in town. I'm thinking of opening a saddlery . . ."

Solomon followed Daniel and his father as they chatted about the prospects in Lowell while inspecting the offerings on different tables, buying something here and there, including some sweets to take back to the children. He felt ill at ease and was glad of his father keeping up talk with Daniel, who usually didn't say much in any case. *Is Daniel the better man, enlisting?*

When they came to the end of the new picket fence that surrounded the city park, Jacob turned to Daniel and shook his hand. "We honor your service to the Union. When did you say your regiment departs?"

* * *

After Jacob conferred with a saddler near the stable, the Ramsdells collected their horses and began the journey back to the boarding house.

"The Union *does* need our crops," Jacob said into the silence of the gathering dusk as afternoon gave way to night. The lamp of the boarding house gleamed ahead.

"I am only now bringing my farm to its maturity," Solomon replied. "With you selling up for Lowell—"

"Not certain yet, son."

"But what would become of Jennette and the children without you there—or without the Kings—if I were away? And what of Rosette?"

"Others would take over our farms."

"They wouldn't be family," Solomon said as they reached the house. "And Otis has little enough care for family."

"Then it's just as well you're remaining in Orange."

A boy with a lantern came out and took their horses, and Jacob began to wash up for supper at a bowl on the porch. "I struck out on my own for New York at your age."

Solomon, too, washed his face and hands, then pulled out a handkerchief to dry them. As he did so, the recruiter's leaflet fell to the boards of the porch; he picked it up and tried to read it but was unable to make out the words with the light coming from the window. They stepped inside— just in time to join the other lodgers for supper—and after he sat down, Solomon spread out the leaflet on the table, revealing a drawing of the battle flag of the Sixth Regiment, a swallowtail flag with a seal in the middle. Words curved over the top and under the bottom of the seal: "Fear Not Death. Fear Dishonor."

Newspaper

ANOTHER YEAR PASSED with Solomon enjoying success with every crop he put his hand to, his wife and children blooming with health, and the rumblings of the distant war bothering them mostly as they read about and discussed them as they rested of an evening. He missed having his father to talk to about the battles and policies—for months now the elder Ramsdells' house had lain empty across the fields.

When Solomon came downstairs after putting the children to bed one evening, Jennette was at the kitchen table with a lamp, bent over a bowl of cracked hickory nuts. She was picking out the nutmeats and saving them in a smaller bowl. She looked up and patted the bench beside her. "Come sit here and read the papers to me while I finish. I just need to fill this up for my Christmas cake."

She nodded at the slim book in his hand. "So you read Sy some Aesop, then?"

"Yes," he replied as he slid onto the bench beside her. "The one about how the strength of the sun makes a man shed his coat, while the wind only makes him draw it closer."

"And did Callie make you sing?"

"Indeed—holds her mouth open to show me how." He laughed. "It's the only way to make her sit still for the reading. She's a little lark herself—or will be," he said, sorting through the newspapers from Lansing.

"How was Otis today? Rosette seemed cheerful enough when she brought DeWitt to play with Sy. We had the boys crack these nuts on your boulder."

"He was either quiet, as usual, or grumbling, as usual." Solomon folded back the page with news of the war, then looked up. "He isn't taking to the new neighbors—seems Riker isn't as willing as Myron King to loan out his tools and is more liable to ask to borrow some."

"Well, with both the Kings and your folks gone," Jennette said, "we all must take stock and decide what we can share of what we have, and what we need to hold back to invest in our own families."

"And not so many neighbors to share with these days, with no new men coming in." He paused to read, then said, "I know what became of some of those men—it says here they dedicated the Gettysburg Cemetery last week— reburied fifteen hundred and left two thousand where they were. I wonder how many were from Michigan ..."

Jennette shook her head slowly. "So many."

"There were forty or fifty thousand at the ceremonies ..." He tapped his finger on that place in the paper. "The main address—by Edward Everett—was *two hours.*"

"I hope it wasn't cold!" she said with a shiver.

"It doesn't say, but look here—they printed an address by the president. I wish I'd seen him. When Father saw him in Kalamazoo in '56, he said Lincoln was ridiculous to look at—like Irving's Ichabod Crane—and he couldn't believe he'd be eloquent. But his words are like those of the orators of old." Solomon began reading aloud and finished with the line, "'. . . all mankind are created equal by a good God.'"

"Sometimes we have to remind ourselves of that, don't we?" Jennette said. "The slaves . . . the Confederates—He made them all, and us, too."

"We'd do well to remember it. Let me continue—it's just this much." He measured the passage in the paper with a finger and thumb.

"That must have been a mercy after Mr. Everett's two hours!" Jennette offered a nut half to Solomon on the end of the pick. He took it between finger and thumb and held it as he continued reading.

"'. . . for those who here gave their lives that the nation might live,'" he read and then stopped.

"'Greater love hath no man than this . . .'" she quoted.

Both Solomon and Jennette gazed quietly into the lamplight, until Jennette looked away to the light flickering in the stove. Solomon continued to read. "'The brave men, living and dead, who struggled here have consecrated it far above our poor power—'"

"When I think of those men," Jennette said, "and the boys we know—Daniel! Is he safe?" She knuckled away a tear. "But I'm thinking of Thucydides, too. Isn't that funeral oration like this? You know the one . . ."

"Pericles."

"Yes, the recalling of the ancestors, the honor of the sacrifice—"

"And the call to the living," Solomon said, putting the forgotten nut on the table and laying a hand on hers. *I feel the flicker of a call rising in me now,* he thought, *but I will not leave her while she hesitates.*

"Solomon, I've pondered what it means for us. When I first came here to Orange and your family's farms, I saw what I would be a part of—a family much like my own, all so familiar and so lovely, especially with you." She smoothed her hands along the tabletop Solomon had so lovingly fashioned for their home the winter he'd waited for her before their marriage. He'd made it sturdy and practical, but with a rounded edge that spoke to his care. Jennette gripped that edge.

He waited for her to continue. *"And yet," she'll say. That's how she usually ventures a new idea.*

"And yet . . . it seems selfish to care only for ourselves. We have so much and are so happy, with plans for the future. The war merely *threatens* to overrun our happiness . . . but for those in the places of battle, their homes are *in fact* overrun."

"The war could come here," he said. Some spoke of that possibility, though it would take more powerful allies for the Rebels, or more attrition in the Union ranks, for the war to threaten Michigan.

"I know. It's not just to aid our distant neighbors that you might go, but to protect our own home. It makes me ashamed to think that I may be willing for you to go only now that I realize that."

"It's my duty to keep you from that dilemma by making the decision myself," he said. "But I wouldn't make it without your consent."

"Go on," Jennette said in a low voice, glancing toward the newspaper. "What's the rest?"

"'The brave men, living and dead, who struggled here have consecrated it far above our poor power,'" he read again. "'The work we little heed.' Their work on the battlefield, do you think?"

"Surely."

"'Let us long remember what we say here, but not forget what they did here . . .'" He read on, pausing at the heavy phrases. "'Dedicated here to the unfinished work that they have thus far nobly carried forward . . . the great task remaining before us; for us to renew devotion to that cause for which they gave the full measure of their devotion.'"

Does my work go beyond growing this family, this farm? Can death and destruction, if it's for a noble purpose, be a calling, too?

"Sol," Jennette said. "We can go to my father's, the children and I."

"But *I* must care for you—I must be with you!" He crumpled the newspaper and cast it aside, clasping both her hands so that she dropped the nut pick.

"Must you? This farm will keep, and we can leave it for a season. Otis can check on it from time to time."

"This isn't what I wanted for us! Since I was twelve and my family came here, my mind has been set on this farm and this life with you, before I even knew you. I used to walk these fields when they were woods, fields only in my mind. We cut the trees, burned the stumps, carried the wood to the mill to build this house not six years ago."

And until I had you, I could only cry these things in my heart. Now I can say them aloud. How can I leave this?

"But what of those young men in the ground at Gettysburg? And Bull Run, and all those other places? Didn't they have dreams, too? What of the ones Pericles praised so long ago?"

"They were born to the sword. I was born to the axe and plow."

"Our grandfathers and great-grandfathers fought in their own time," she said.

"Why should I leave what I've worked so hard for? I've given my voice to the Abolition movement since I cast my first vote for Fremont!" Solomon slid off the bench and began pacing—two or three steps and a turn—in the little kitchen. *Wasn't that enough? I got men to vote for Fremont and then for Lincoln! Why couldn't Lincoln turn men's hearts?*

If Solomon left, who would preserve his holdings, or feed his family? And what if he *didn't* return? What would become of Jennette and the children? Who would teach his son as Jacob had taught him?

"Dearest," Jennette said, "you want to be happy, and to be happy you must be free—"

"And to be free, I must be brave—I know how it goes," he said, irritated to be instructed.

"I *know* you're brave, Solomon. But if other men are to be happy, they, too, must be free. That's why they're fighting."

"Perhaps some of them. Some are conscripted, too. Others fight for glory, or for the right to decide for themselves how to live. I understand that. I can see how a man in South Carolina, having found his plot of land and been persuaded to plant it with cotton, say—to clothe the North. How that man, now prospering and with a view to the future, could rise up indignant when the North decided to remove from him the means to produce it."

"Perhaps that is the bravery needed now," Jennette said, "to be willing to cast aside what has long been worked for in the interest of freedom for another . . . or in support of a nation that can teach others what freedom is." She swept the stray hickory shells into the larger bowl and got up from the bench. Solomon stood with his hand to his head, and she stepped close to him and laid her head against his shoulder so he couldn't help but embrace her with that arm.

To be willing to lay down my life . . . Not just go into battle and risk the breath in his lungs, but walk away from this home he'd made—to lay down *this* life.

"We'll be fine with my parents," Jennette continued. "Mother has been unwell for a long while, and Calista bears most of the housework herself. She would enjoy having a sister with her again and would be such a dear aunt to the children. She might even be freed up to teach—I know she's longed for the opportunity to do so. If you can see fit to spare us, we can cheer that household." She squeezed him around the waist and then emptied her bowl of shells into the kindling basket against the wall. "One day our own hickory shells from the tree you planted can go into our stove, and our own nuts into my Christmas cake."

"I can better be sure of that if I'm here to tend to it."

"But you can't keep it better than the Almighty, can you? In olden days, Pericles called men to bravery who worshiped virtues as their gods. But *our* God is not far from us, and He can keep what concerns us. Speaking of that . . ." She untied her apron and pulled a page from her folder of scrap paper, then moistened a pencil tip. "Let's consider what must be done to make this move to Cannon Township . . ."

So it begins. All philosophy and sentiment tucked away for the time being, Jennette's bright practicality took over the room—and his evening—and he picked up the nut from the table and popped it into his mouth, then settled himself on the bench for an hour of murmuring assent as his wife laid out her plans for their future.

INTO WAR
1863–1864

Leave-taking

THE WATSON HOME WAS FULL of Christmas cheer overlaid with brave high spirits in anticipation of the separation. The adults escaped their private tension by focusing on the children, and Seymour and Callie happily partook of every treat and amusement their parents and aunt and grandparents offered. Neighbors came, too, with gingerbread or nuts "for the children," but in those gestures really seeking to shore up Jennette and Solomon.

The Watsons took instruction from Dickens for how to celebrate the holiday, as Jennette had urged them to when she'd become entranced by "A Christmas Carol" as a child. The Ramsdells, being of New England Puritan stock, had never made much of the holiday—they'd even held school that day when Solomon was growing up, since his father was the superintendent. But who could resist when Jennette made paper crowns for each of them and steamed a pudding?

The day after Christmas, Jennette packed up sweetmeats to take to two poor households she knew of in Cannonsburg, and Calista held Callie in her arms and kept a firm hand on Seymour's shoulder so he wouldn't run out to join his parents in the sleigh. Solomon and Jennette would be alone for a few hours of the precious time they had left together.

I might as well say something, Solomon thought as they glided out of the yard behind the rhythmic jingle of the bells on Watson's mare, though nothing came to mind. *So few words for so many thoughts.*

Jennette, too, sat quietly, her hands in her mother's fox muff. "For special," Sally had said when she'd handed it to Jennette. The bright fur had been Daniel's gift when he'd left for the sharpshooters the year before.

"What do you think, Solomon . . ." Jennette held up the fur sleeve warming her hands. "Is this Daniel's revenge on the fox for all the chickens he stole? Is this fur all the softer and all the glossier because of the chickens the fox ate before he met his end?"

"I doubt there's any great meaning in it," Solomon said, not ready to banter. "But I suppose it's just as well to have something useful to come of the killing." He winced at his words. *That was not the thing to say.*

Jennette was silent a few moments and then took a big breath and said, "Did you see how Sy loved those pencils Calista gave him for Christmas?" Her voice had a forced brightness. "Already he's made a picture for you to take with you. It's his own self-portrait, with his initials I helped him write. I didn't want to wait until you opened it to explain, when all will be in such a rush . . ."

"I hope he'll learn to read and write before I return, so he can write me a letter, and I write him."

"Oh yes! He'll be eager."

Less than an hour later they came to the main road through town. The snow was already packed down by the horses and sleighs that had passed through since the previous night's fresh fall. "Here, make a turn on the road behind the church—Mother Barlett is just back there. See the house?"

A tiny wisp of smoke was rising from a crumbling chimney on the crooked roof of the shack, and their horse and sleigh made the first marks in the fresh blanket of snow that surrounded the place. A little path had been beaten out from the door to the woodpile, where a decent store of wood lay stacked for the widow's use.

Solomon helped Jennette down from the sleigh, and the two of them made footprints up to the door, their feet punching deep holes that they had to lift out of with each step. Jennette held up her skirts to keep them from dragging through the snow, her muff pushed up one arm, and Solomon carried the little basket she had tied up with a red ribbon. At the door Jennette knocked and called, "Mother Barlett! It's Jennette!"

After a few moments they heard things being shoved around, and the door opened a crack, a beady eye peering out at a child's height.

"Mother Barlett, do you remember me? It's Jennette Watson come to see you!" The door opened a little further and two bright eyes in a wrinkled old face peered up at them. "This is Solomon, Mother Barlett. My husband. May we come in?"

The door closed an inch or two, paused while the sound of murmuring came through the crack, then opened again to reveal the little old woman shuffling back to her chair at a slanting kitchen table, one of its leg far askew.

"Oh dear, what's happened to your table?" Jennette asked.

"Fell into it when I brought in a load of wood last week," the old woman grumbled.

Solomon set the basket down on the table and squatted to inspect the damage. "Mrs. Barlett, I believe I could fix this for you right away if you have a little hatchet."

"That I do." She nodded toward the woodpile by her hearth, where a hatchet lay in the litter of wood and splinters, then raised a crooked finger to point at Jennette. "It's been a long time since you been here, girlie."

"I'm sorry, Mother Barlett, but I live a long way up the river now. Our home is there—our farm and children. But we'll be close by for a time now, living with Mother and Father again."

The old woman wrinkled her forehead. "So then this young fella has given up farming to let your papa keep him?"

Solomon raised his head sharply.

"No, no!" Jennette said. "Our farm is still there. But Solomon here is enlisting with the army—"

"Going to war, then?"

"Yes, ma'am," Solomon answered from where he crouched, testing the tightness of the table leg with the splinter he'd driven into the hole. "And hope to return soon."

"Well, bless you for that, son. You go to keep us safe."

"I certainly hope to do so."

"My papa fought the British before I was born," Mother Barlett said, "and my mama had to keep some o' them Redcoats in our house in Massachusetts. I weren't born until the year the U.S. Constitution came about—a change o' life baby for my mama—but I heard all about it."

"Yes, ma'am," Solomon said. "My folks are from back East, too, and a line of us Ramsdells is there still."

"Do you 'spect we'll be keeping them Rebels in our houses here? 'Cause I got precious little to board 'em with."

"No, Mrs. Barlett, I intend to keep the war far from Michigan, if I have anything to say about it."

"That's why he's going," Jennette said.

"And because I believe in the principle," Solomon added. "I voted for Abolition the first chance I got."

"Well, I don't know about that Abolition," Mother Barlett said, "but mebbe those Rebels ought to be let alone, like we wanted to be in my papa's time." She shook her head over her gnarled hands clasped in her lap. "Don't seem much different to me."

Solomon looked up at Jennette from where he was finishing with the table leg. She shook her head a little.

"Well, Mrs. Barlett, I thank you for your father's service to our country," he said as he stood up and patted the table. "This should stand strong for you for a good while now."

"I thank-ee kindly," she said with a formal nod, then unclasped her hands to reach for Jennette's basket and set it on the table. "And what's in here?"

Jennette bounced a little where she stood, flushing with pleasure. "A little something for you for Christmas—from all of us. Mother and Calista and I made these." She reached in and took out a cookie with a dot of jam nestled in a thumbprint on top. "We hope you like them."

Mother Barlett held out her hand for the cookie and giggled as it crumbled at her first toothless bite, her eyes sparkling with pleasure.

"There are some other things in there, too—a good slice of ham and a bit of apple cake."

Solomon moved nearer to the door to signal it was time to go. "We wish you all the best for the New Year," he said, brushing wood chips from the bowler in his hand.

Jennette bent to adjust the woman's shawl around her shoulders and kissed her cheek. Then she raised her own hood and said, "Father will be in town the next day or two and will check in on you again."

"Young sir!" Mother Barlett called to Solomon, "keep your musket clean and your eyes clear, as my papa would say."

"Much obliged," Solomon replied as he held the door open for Jennette.

They picked their way back to the sleigh, then delivered a basket to another poor family in the town. It was well below freezing, but clear and still, when Solomon drove the sleigh to the top of a smooth rise where the afternoon sun shone brightly on their faces. Jennette drew a blanket around their shoulders, then leaned her head against him.

"Jennette," Solomon said formally, "it's my foremost duty in this life to care for you and the children. I go only because it's an extension of that duty to keep our country whole and safe as well, else our home cannot be secure. Our son must see that a true man is willing to do these things."

She nodded into his shoulder.

"And I mean to prove as good a soldier as I have tried to be a farmer and a husband. I want to be the best of what a soldier can be—loyal to my commanding officer, a friend to my fellows, and fierce as needed against the enemy."

"That's the part that concerns me," she said, lifting her head. "I cannot see you shooting another man—or running him through with a sword—when he's standing before you. We haven't known a man yet that's been evil enough for that. You've never had to do violence before . . . not even a thief in our chicken house—"

"Other than foxes," he said with a squeeze around her shoulders.

"You know what I mean," she chided. "There are sharp dealers and lazy men in Orange and Ionia, but no one set on doing us harm directly."

"But yet we know such men prowl about. And in a war they're massed together, with real power in arms and in leadership. That must be met with opposing force, and I'm ready to take part."

"Are you, indeed? You've always been my champion, pursuing good in the world, bringing order to our land and riches to our table. You've had to kill beasts and spend yourself in exhausting work with land and lumber. But you haven't had to rise up against an enemy matched with you in strength and purpose."

"I'm confident in the machines of our army," Solomon said. "Alongside my brother soldiers, I'll do my duty."

"And you'll come home to me whole and well? Oh, I am of many minds, Solomon! You make pretty speeches—and I know your heart is noble, so that's fitting—but I'm not eager to be a war widow. I would that you'd come home after all that—you and Daniel both."

"That's my intent as well." He turned her face to his and kissed her tenderly.

Solomon could feel Jennette shiver a little as the sun sank closer to the horizon, bathing the white expanse in a rosy glow; she buried herself a bit further under his arm, her knees tucked beneath his on the seat of the sleigh, while the horse stamped and jingled the bells on her bridle.

Engagements

IT WAS LATE MAY, and Private Solomon Ramsdell, Sixth Michigan Cavalry, polished his bugle while looking this way and that to find something else to do . . . maybe split some more wood. Once they'd joined up with the cavalry, there'd been weeks of drills and forming up in parades, but after that they had idled many days—or marched hard and set up camp, only to idle again until it was time to decamp. So military life was a lot of idling, he'd learned, but for the hard work of keeping everyone fed and warm and equipped before battles and doctored after. In early March, only three hundred of their number had been chosen for the first attempt on Spotsylvania, Solomon not among them. But that had failed because of some missed connection or other.

Sherman's cavalry had later found renewed purpose at Wilderness, Yellow Tavern, and the second attempt at Spotsylvania—but since then they'd been idle again. Solomon was well drilled, his rifle cleaned, his buttons tight—and the few rents in his uniform mended with the needle and thread Rosette had spared him from her sewing box. He'd written cheerful letters to Jennette and the children, but not too frequently, lest he betray his uselessness here.

Solomon put down his bugle and stood, smacking his cap on his thigh in frustration, then made his way to the woodpile. As he split logs, he thought of their last day together back in Michigan.

* * *

Jennette's cheeks were bright from the fire and her brown eyes haunted with the ghosts of brave tears she'd banished. Sometimes she stopped to look deep into his eyes, holding his gaze, pouring into it all the things she hadn't yet said, though she'd tried to say so many things. She was of a firm purpose in his leaving, and cheerful and bustling about her parents' house, getting everything ready for his journey.

"Take these few things to Rosette as you pass by," she said, handing him a small bundle to tuck into the leather pack his father had fashioned for him. It was made flat, like an envelope, to lie against his back under his coat. After closing the flap, Solomon ran his finger over the letters his father had tooled there: "S. R. 6th Mich. Cav."

Jennette said something that Solomon missed, but he heard her next words: "I know she must be lonesome this Christmas with Mother and Father Ramsdell gone to Lowell." Strangers had moved into the farm where Rosette and Solomon had grown up together with Diana and Ellen, Jerome and Frank. *What must it be like for Rosette to walk out to the road and look down to their place,* Sol wondered, *knowing they're not there?* She could no longer send Otis over to borrow some spice from Mother, and now she wouldn't be able to count on things from Jennette, either. But Jennette said she and Rosette were planning to write one another, to ease their loneliness.

Solomon knew Jennette felt the sinking regret of a duty not done. She'd had to loosen her grip on her care for her sister-in-law, letting it slip between her fingers for the sake of Solomon's going to war.

* * *

So much for her sacrifice. Solomon thought. He sighed and split another log into quarters and kindling. *Naught for me to do here, really.*

But oh, how bravely he'd set out that January morning with the muster. Like some others, Solomon had offered Hector in service to the Union, and the officer had agreed he was one of the rare farm horses that, with training, would be fit for cavalry service. Solomon had even been allowed to ride Hector for part of the journey. They'd picked their way over frozen fields, their horses walking an endless, narrow row, never turning to double back and furrow the land as they would have at home. Their way lay before them in an eastward and southerly direction, through fields pocked with boulders and icy puddles. The horses plodded forward at their masters' bidding.

Once they joined the rest of the regiment, Solomon kept falling in beside John Van Wagoner, a cheerful, energetic young Montcalm man who'd joined up in '62. The two compared notes on places they'd been and business they'd done in Ionia County over the years. For Solomon, John bridged the great divide between life before and life after war, and his spirits lifted every time he spied the Montcalm man among the rest.

Solomon carried a bundle of kindling with him when he went to visit Hector. The horses were tethered at the end of the camp, cropping the lush spring grass in what had once been the fenced field of a prosperous Virginia farmer, the fence boards and posts long since torn down for Union army fires. Hector raised his head and came over to Solomon, who rubbed his nose and told him the news from Jennette's latest letter.

The beasts needed this idleness after the bloody raids that had taken so many of their kind—and Solomon's. Even before the brutal carnage of the campaign had begun, the poor horses had seemed bewildered, perhaps a result of the constant state of readiness. Each night the troopers had prepared themselves to light out for a raid at a moment's notice. The horses were saddled—though cinched only loosely—their reins looped through the riders' hands as they slept in tents at the horses' feet.

* * *

The first days of May weeks earlier, ten thousand mounted soldiers had paraded at Culpeper for General Sheridan—who had just taken command of the cavalry—and their purpose coalesced. That was the finest moment of Solomon's career as a soldier thus far, but it was eclipsed soon after, when the grueling chaos of the Wilderness had overtaken him. Most of Sheridan's cavalry had massed on the field, but the Second and Sixth Michigan gathered under General Custer in the woods. Then the daring young cavalry officer rode out into a clearing before his brigade, and the men fixed their eyes on him. Custer called for the band to play, and Solomon raised his bugle to take his part in "Yankee Doodle." While Confederate shells rained on them, Custer's Wolverines advanced into the ravine, their Spencer carbines loosing their deadly array and repulsing the enemy.

Custer then called the troops back, and Solomon bugled "Rally" with the others; most of the glorious saber-wielding riders who had paraded so proudly just hours before—moments, it seemed—dismounted, strode out of the woods, and "engaged the enemy," as they called it. The horses they'd left behind reared and whinnied in terror, even in the shelter of the trees, as if horrified by what men were capable of.

Solomon wondered then if Hector was one of the horses still in the battle. He pictured Hector's eyes turning back in their sockets, blaring white in his terror as he shied from blades and leapt over corpses strewn before him on the battlefield . . . Even as a saber thrust found its mark in a man's body, sliding between ribs and catching on a spine as easily as it sliced a leather belt, and with the same impunity . . . Even as the soldiers wreaked havoc from afar and thundered with their guns, their mighty cannons, rifle after rifle reporting in a volley . . .

* * *

Why do we center all our pity on dumb animals in the midst of a battle? Solomon wondered, absently stroking Hector's shoulder. Even while attempting to destroy all the gray world facing their blue, the soldiers had bent over their mounts while awaiting their turn on the battlefield, embracing their horses' necks and fondling their manes. They'd breathed soothing lullaby words to the animals, lovers' words, fathers' words.

Lullaby words for dumb beasts that had not chosen to be there, as Solomon had. Lullaby words while a boy as young as his brother Frank had lain at Solomon's feet, the last few beats of his heart bubbling blood from his mouth.

How could we? Solomon thought, shaking his head. *And that was only the beginning.*

* * *

Immediately following the Battles of the Wilderness, as the Philadelphia paper called the engagement, Custer led them in other battles, other marches, destroying and building bridges—mostly hunting Confederate General Jeb Stuart. One harrowing night they followed the Fifth Michigan across a destroyed bridge, hopping from one railroad tie to the next while under fire. Once they were all across, they blew up what was left of the bridge and then limped with empty bellies to the Union lines and a few days' rest.

There were better times, too. Unaccountably, one evening the field musicians formed up and began to play rousing band tunes while bodies still soaked the battlefield in blood. How were they able to play so jauntily, so proudly—as if they'd gone from parade to music without the hell in between? John Van Wagoner appeared in the firelit crowd that evening, his familiar face rooting Solomon in the firm ground of home—reminding him of what was enduring, of what they fought for. They fought so that all men would have leave to gather by a fire, to sing, to laugh, and then go home to their families.

Even more inexplicable, the Confederate band answered them from across the river. For hours they played call-and-answer, the music echoing beautifully across the water, buoying their hearts together in their shared purpose—even if that purpose *was* to kill one another.

One day Major Kidd, commander of the Sixth Michigan, brought General Sheridan among them. Solomon was able to get a good look at the leader of all the cavalry and thought him uncommonly handsome and dignified, every bit a noble soldier—though because of his short legs he seemed taller when he was in the saddle. Just the sort of man made for a horse . . . or made *by* a horse.

And at Yellow Tavern, despite the mix-up of the lines of the Fifth and Sixth, the cavalry made the ridge at last. Some Michigan gun or other—every man hoped it had been his—had taken down Stuart himself. That was the only kind of battle Solomon had been able stomach: at a distance, the enemy anonymous, no faces to go with the bodies being cut down. But he'd seen enough of it up close that he was beginning to go numb.

Not long after the battle at Yellow Tavern, they had come to a quiet success at Hanover—including the liberation of a group of prisoners and the seizing of a supply train, which had meant good eating for days. But now, weeks later, it was just idleness and waiting for the next raid along the way to Trevilian Station.

Solomon said goodbye to Hector and, after crossing through the camp and arranging his kindling at his tent, looked around for something else to do. He made a deep, shuddering sigh. *If only I had my violin.*

THE CRUX
SUMMER 1864

Andersonville

THE RUMBLING TRAIN carried the weary, stinking prisoners from summer-sweltering Virginia into the depths of the South. It carried them away from the rich farmlands and dark woods they'd known in their Northern homes, from hills and cool streams into flatlands. Deep shade of hardwoods gave way to hard red clay and scraggly stands of pine. The intense late-June heat was relieved only by the slight breezes of the train's movement across the landscape. The sun leaned closer down upon them, and though the land seemed dry and brittle with all its pine straw and pale earth where clay became sand, nevertheless an oppressive washday steam clogged the men's airways. They gulped and threw open their collars for air they nearly had to drink to get down.

Solomon closed his eyes against the yellow fireball hanging just outside the hole that served as the boxcar's "window," and the flickering shadows of pines crossed his eyelids. The opening let in ashes and soot with the fine orange dust that crept up his nose and settled gritty on the backs of his hands. Sodden air hung close, sealing in the sweat that gathered on his skin but couldn't dissipate.

When the train finally stopped, Solomon, like all the men, was soaked and sluggish, and he could barely move. He had only distant thoughts of hunger that were shouted down by his longing for the tinny warm water passed around in a bucket.

The train had ceased roaring now, and screaming cicadas shrilled their pulsing beat. The platform was new-sawn planks, the landing place for prisoners, with no bustle of ordinary commerce—there was no hurry. Prisoners could wait while Confederate officers and soldiers took their slow time with arrangements. Ears ringing with the sounds of the insects, Solomon waved away the mosquitoes and gnats that poured through the ventilation holes, and squabbles broke out about whether to cover the holes or keep them open—all was misery.

Just to get out, to walk a bit, would be heaven, Solomon thought. But his mind would not rouse itself to consider the prospects.

After an hour or two the doors were opened and the men filed out with their poor packs of this and that—whatever memento or tool a man thought might come in handy in faraway enemy confinement, clutched compulsively as he was taken into custody on the battlefield, now reduced to remnants after Belle Isle. Solomon pulled on his cap, felt for his cup and slit-handled spoon on his belt loop, and adjusted his rolled blanket tied with short ropes. His precious leather pack against his back, concealed beneath his shirt, held most of his little treasures he hoped would be of use in the days and weeks—surely not months—to come. The medicine and towel had gone first, at Belle Isle. Only one of his candies remained, but he still had the paper from the other, the pencils, and Rosette's needle.

The man before him in the press had to grip the side of the doorway to pull himself forward, and Solomon realized he had not cared to know the men on this journey beyond a hooded-lid nod to the fellows from his own regiment. Each had his own nightmare to endure. The regiment would form up again in the camp, as they'd been trained.

The struggling man hesitated at the steps, and Solomon squatted to help support him on the way down, grasping him under the arms. The man's legs bent beneath him as he reached the platform, and the soldier supervising their movements eyed him until another prisoner reached out to take the man's arm that was blindly reaching out for help.

Most were stirred to a little liveliness by the change, and they stood in ranks as bidden, then made a small effort to march along a curving dirt road that became a dust cloud with their shuffling feet. Modest hills gave way to farms tucked into the woods and then a town—Andersonville, Georgia, someone said. The final small summit revealed Camp Sumter, a vast clearing surrounded by two rows of wooden fencing—log palisades—with pigeon roosts along the walls, guards using rickety ladders to climb up to keep watch over their charges. A glimpse of the prison ground itself showed throngs of men milling about, some in a line, with a few cooking fires sending tendrils of smoke into the air. The summer sun was sinking red, retreating from the enclosure where gloom was already gathering around the captives.

Their queue was processed into registry books full of columns and details, but the Confederate soldier clerks seated at the tables were shabby and washed-out compared to the lively soldiers from the battlefield who had led the Union prisoners to Belle Isle and transferred them to the care of low, filthy guards. Some of these prison soldiers had scruffy beards, others wore their uniform jackets open for a breath of air, and a couple seemed to have no uniform at all, or just a cap set at a casual angle. The grizzled old man who took Solomon's papers grunted out his questions around a twig he was chewing, never looking up, and kept scratching at the fleas that hopped off his head onto the book before him.

Once they were all recorded, a gate in the palisade was opened and a small group of new prisoners was let inside to the area between the wooden fences. Once they were all in the space, the outer gate was closed and the inner one opened.

"All the way past the deadline," ordered a boy guard with a squeaky voice. As they filed through the gate, he indicated a single fence rail that ran around the camp a rod-and-some within the palisade. "Keep to that side of the deadline," he added.

The stench from the enclosure fully engulfed them, and Solomon shuddered as he realized the heap of refuse just inside the deadline was a pile of corpses, barefoot and naked or with the merest tatters left on their bodies.

The few dozen men stood still, and Solomon was unsure of what they were to do next. No rations had been given them, and the other prisoners seemed hardly to notice their arrival. *Where is the military order?* Solomon wondered.

A Sergeant Harris from the Fifth Michigan, now the senior officer, stepped forward to speak to three of the prisoners who were walking up to greet the newcomers. Harris approached the three with authority, standing straight. As they spoke, the tallest of the three gestured both to the corpses and to the camp at large while shaking his head. The shorter of his companions—his stance suggesting a once-powerful build now reduced to flabby withering—added a word here and there and chewed on a scrap of leather, then spat occasionally, as if it were tobacco.

The third man stood silent, hunched over a stick the height of a rifle.

Sergeant Harris's weariness visibly overtook him during the conversation, and he began to shrink into the lax posture the two other men held. Only the tall one stood straight.

That's a man to watch, Solomon thought.

As Harris returned to the clutch of new prisoners awaiting instructions, he drew a deep breath, his head turned away from the corpses, as if steeling himself for what came next. The three prisoners he'd spoken to separated and faced the new men, waiting.

"Men," Harris said, "there is not here the order we would expect in a Union prison. They're much reduced, and we must shift for ourselves. But these men are here to take us in groups to their areas of influence, that we might take our places among them. Divide yourselves and go with them where they lead."

Solomon knew he wanted to be with the tall man, and he reached out to his Montcalm friend, who stood next to him, and gestured where he thought they should go. "John," he said, "I have a hunch about this one."

John whistled for their other Sixth Michigan fellow, William Davis, and nodded him over. The three found their way to the space before the tall man, who waited silently for whoever would gather with him. But Sergeant Harris had drawn a few men of the Fifth to stand before the once-muscular man.

With an apologetic wave to Solomon, John followed William over to Harris and the man who would guide them into their new life in the prison. Solomon was alone.

No solidarity for the Sixth, then?

The tall man spoke: "I'm Robert Kinley, Pennsylvania—don't matter much my regiment and such anymore. But I speak for the high ground here, and with me and mine you'll have a better chance than these poor souls." He nodded toward the corpses. "These are just the ones that died since morning in here. Every morning they take a line for the infirmary—if they don't need to be carried, they're not ready—and not much of anybody comes back. Others die in the night, and their fellows drag them down here, too."

He paused. "Whatever you have on your back or in your pockets is your currency for livin' in Camp Sumter. You can barter it, sell it, or eat it yourself—leather and paper look pretty good before long. But don't set it down or you'll lose it. Any soundness of limb or constitution you have right now is the best you'll know in this place—my condolences for those already ill. That's the way of things here, as you'll soon learn."

He turned and started walking along the perimeter of the camp, lightly pantomiming a touch of the single rail, but two feet short of it. "This is the deadline, and they mean it. Any man ventures a limb across this line"—he tipped his cap to the musket-bearing guard in the pigeon roost—"will soon know the consequence."

As they approached the noxious swamp that divided the prison grounds, Solomon saw men squatting at the edges, relieving themselves of thin squirts of the flux, others a little upstream rinsing out their cookpots.

"Are there no latrines?" Solomon asked, breaking the silence of the stunned new prisoners.

"No, private," Kinley said. "The ground is too swampy for it, and the general hygiene allows for this arrangement to help—water supply from the first half and latrine for the second half of the course. But that's just for the men strong enough to get here . . . The stream there feeding the swamp? That's the Sweetwater, doncha know." He smiled crookedly while that sank in, then asked, "Where you from, prisoner?"

"Sixth Michigan Ca—"

"Ah—just Michigan will do."

The group of a dozen or so continued along the deadline, watched by hollow-eyed men squatting at little fires or simply lying down, some on ground cloths, some not. The few barracks seemed a token attempt to house the tens of thousands that must be here. All seemed drained of what might have once made them soldiers, or even men.

The ground rose slightly at this end of the prison grounds and Solomon considered the advantages of being away from the swamp, away from the gate with the corpses. This was a higher circle of hell.

When they came to the far end of the enclosure, Kinley stopped in a cleared place before a respectable-looking tent where several men were engaged in businesslike conversation, but cross-legged on the ground as there were no stools. They looked up and wearily stood at Kinley's approach and looked the newcomers over. One stepped close to Solomon and reached out and felt the contour of his pack under his shirt. Solomon pulled away protectively and a couple of the men chuckled.

"We'll be keeping this one here," said the man who had touched the pack, smirking at his companions.

"Enough of that, Miller," Kinley said. "But he's a likely one—asked about the latrine arrangements—so he might do for us. And he's Michigan like you."

He turned to the group of newcomers. "These are the heads of our lots up here, and I'm the head of all the lots. This is our lot in life, you see." He laughed grimly. "Some stick to their old regiments here in Camp Sumter, but we don't bother with that. We do find it friendly-like to stick with our states for our domestic arrangements in our lots. I'm Pennsylvania, and that head there's New York, and there's others . . . so go and sort yourselves out."

Ransom

SOLOMON REGRETTED WITHIN DAYS that Miller was the leader for the Michigan lot, but Kinley seemed a force of personality and strength that few others retained in this place, and perhaps he could keep Miller in line. Still, Kinley carried a hint of the brutality, too, and it was likely no virtue that enabled Kinley and those under him to produce bits of food and other necessaries, like the occasional sliver of soap. But what choice did he have?

In a bid to show himself valuable, and preferring to offer before being robbed, Solomon brought out his remaining piece of maple candy for Kinley's inspection the first morning in his new place. Kinley nodded toward Miller, who snatched it up. Kinley later traded it for a store of yams and beans—and half of a pigeon someone had miraculously snatched from midair as it flew over the camp.

As soon as Kinley learned of his education and skill in business, Solomon began to hear "Ramsdell!" called out whenever Kinley needed an emissary to other points of strength in the camp. Kinley had heard of a small group of Michiganders who had adopted rules to stay as healthy as might be. On one of Solomon's visits to that group, housed in two makeshift but priceless tents they'd attached together, a barber named John Ransom explained that they had pledged never to eat meat with worms, no matter how hungry they were, and never to put a cup to their lips unless the water inside had been boiled. For all their precautions, Solomon saw their position on low ground was a problem for Ransom's men, while Kinsley's stake on the higher ground kept his lot out of the miasma of the swampier areas.

Ransom kept a diary where he recorded his time in the camp in tiny script, and the sight of him bending over it reminded Solomon of Rosette laboring away at her own journals. She'd carefully kept each volume, lining them up on a shelf from year to year, and she'd lovingly cared for her pens and ink. From their parents' home, where she had few domestic cares and wrote in a schoolmarmish way, she'd gone to her first home as Otis Churchill's wife, where she had to bend over a baby in her lap to get in that day's entry by the light of the cookstove. But she had doggedly pursued her task just as Ransom did here. As Solomon watched Ransom sitting on the bare earth, licking a stub of a pencil to record the horrors around them, he realized the pity he'd felt for Rosette in her rough newlywed shanty was naive.

"Are you telling the worst of it, John?" Solomon asked him one day.

"My purpose here," Ransom said, "is to keep accounts, but I ease the language some. The men who survive this place will know what lies beneath the words."

"Well, then," Solomon said, "you bear witness to it for us all. But if . . ." Would Ransom's writings ever leave the prison? Would the pages be torn out for burning by a prisoner suffering in the cold? He'd heard that frost did eventually come to these parts. Or would the book just end up in a pile of refuse when the man who treasured it slipped away, like many of his fellows, into delirium and death?

"I know your question, Sol—will I be able to spirit it out of here? I have a man devoted to the idea of it, so he'll be a help, but if we both succumb, will you take charge of it?"

Solomon didn't answer that day. But as the weeks went by and his own health declined, and he carried many men to the gate in exchange for an extra spoonful of beans or meal from a guard, Solomon began to understand what his new friend had asked of him.

One evening, after he'd been in the prison for almost two months, in the brief respite between the intense heat and the onslaught of the mosquitoes, Solomon visited the chronicler of their imprisonment and found him shockingly reduced. He offered Ransom his last precious pencil as a gift. "John, I'll carry your writing away with me— if you cannot—for I mean to get home."

"We all did," Ransom answered. He was lying on his side on the ground, propped up on a broken box so he could write. He struggled to speak. "P'rhaps this book . . . these books . . . are proof I *still* mean to get home. I have mem'ry of life before . . . before *this* . . . for hope."

"But your men here are the finest I've seen, even with your illness! You'll rally again, I know it."

"No," Ransom said, his voice a dry croak. "Likely my last week. I've seen how it goes . . . Can hardly sit up a quarter hour—the weakness drags me down . . . and the mouth sores . . . growing . . ." He held out a bony forearm. "Flesh falling away."

"But they're even now saying that they'll move some of us—you can hold on until then."

"That old rumor . . . just a jest." Ransom laughed weakly, then took many moments to catch his breath. "Nearly dragged m'self to the infirmary line yesterday . . .

but having the strength to get there reminded me I wasn't ready. When I can't get there myself—they'll take me."

* * *

When Solomon got back to his lot, Miller crawled out of their ragged tent and scrambled away, returning a few minutes later with Kinley.

Their commander, for so he was, squatted down by where Solomon lay on a blanket, resting after the difficult climb up the muddy hill. Kinley pressed a finger into Solomon's shoulder and said, "I know you've been to Ransom's group. What'd you find?"

Solomon lifted his head in surprise. *Why does he care?* He pushed himself up on his elbows and then to sitting, and he said John Ransom was ailing.

"Only three of them left, then, and only one still strong enough to resist," Kinley said, "as I understand it." Then he looked at Solomon with an intense gaze.

Solomon grew cold within. He'd seen that lowered brow before as Kinley pressed a man into some dubious service "for the lot," Kinley would say. *My turn has come.*

"You and I both know they have barber tools," Kinley said. "Best we get them before they're free for anyone to claim." He looked down and traced a finger in the folds of the blanket Solomon sat upon.

"But I can't just take them, even if Ransom doesn't have the strength to barber anymore. We must trade for them." Solomon reached over and opened the wooden box just inside the tent, the box where Jacob's leather pack and Rosette's needle had joined the common store, but Kinley closed it firmly.

"No," he said. "No need to trade what's in there—we need that for our lot. Ransom and his lot will soon have no need for anything at all." He held out a finger as if to touch

Solomon's greasy-but-orderly hair and then drew it back. "I expect *you'd* make a fair barber . . ."

The thought of having the means to scrape up a little more food or medicine—their most precious possessions—caused a gnawing hope to grow in Solomon's heart. He said nothing more, but rose with the excuse that the flux was upon him again, and he escaped the tent.

After relieving himself in spasms that doubled him over and left his face clammy even in the heat, he crawled back into his tent, craving the shade, glad Kinley had left and no one else was inside. He touched the placket of his shirt front and felt the folded paper that he kept there in an opened seam, the paper that had once held the lump of maple candy he'd traded for food at Belle Isle. He had carried those sweets into the war for luck, a blessing of home, and he often put a finger to the paper within the fabric, to remind himself . . .

* * *

"Come stir the pans for me, Jennette," he called in his dream of working in the sugar-bush . . . And so she did, tying a kerchief over her hair to keep off the stickiness. She watched him watching her, then she turned her head coyly with a sweet smile, inviting him to sweep her into his arms. And so he did . . . All those hours patiently dripping sap into buckets, adding buckets to pans, stirring and steaming . . . *Stir, my sweet* . . . And then the crucial moments, when the thickened sap deepened to amber, then strong tea color, and finally to the moment the crystals gathered around the stirring paddle and it was time . . . *Ah! Here it is!*

* * *

He worked his fingers into the seam of the placket and drew out the paper, then unfolded it, revealing the sticky remnant of the hard, translucent candy. They had always finished the sugaring off season with a batch of candy made from a portion of the maple sugar they sold to sustain the family.

This remnant of sweetness was what he fought for, all he'd lost in being dragged away to this place of uselessness, of illness, despair, and death. He scraped his too-long, brittle thumbnail against the stickiness, feeling some gather under the edge. Closing up the paper, he put his thumb in his mouth, and he was transported by the hint of sweetness into a fevered sleep.

* * *

Solomon woke with a start when a hand grasped his upper arm. He was clutching the candy paper to his chest. "What?" he snorted as he sat up, dazed, with a powerful thirst.

Kinley loomed over him. "Why so skittish, Ramsdell? Got somethin' to hide?"

"No—just startled me," Solomon said, his voice not working right. His heart was still beating in his chest in any case. *What am I afraid of?*

"You've been out of it a day and a night," Kinley said. "Thought we might lose you. So are you ready to lift the barber things, then? It's your duty to the lot. You're the one with opportunity."

"But—"

"No shirkin'! It's your *duty*, Ramsdell!" Kinley straightened up as far as the low tent roof would allow and held out a hand. Solomon struggled up to his knees and took the offered hand to climb out of the tent.

He's kept me alive by sharp dealing. Surely it's only fair I do my part.

"That's it—square your shoulders and get on with it, Ramsdell . . . Davis!" Kinley summoned a man squatting by their tiny fire. "Give Ramsdell here some soup." Kinley turned his back, confident in his orders being carried out. As he stepped away, he put his fingers in his mouth and whistled three distinct notes to call another man, who whipped his head around and hurried over.

Solomon wavered on his feet, gripped by thirst and, behind it, the hunger that was always with him. Most of his meals consisted only of yams and cornmeal, and bits of gristle and gray fat in the dishwater they called soup. Davis crouched over the cookpot and dipped out a cupful, swirling it around to cool it before handing it to Solomon.

Ransom's good as dead . . . said so himself. Stars pricked around Solomon's field of vision as he took the hot broth into his dry, sticky mouth. *We can make better use of the scissors and such . . . and maybe I could share with Ransom what I get, not letting Kinley know . . .*

"Headin' down to Ransom's, then?" Davis asked. "You'll be needin' a stick, from the looks of ya." He stood up and drew a length of wood from their meager stores.

Solomon took it without a word—too difficult to speak—and leaned heavily on it as he made his way through the steaming drizzle that had just begun to fall. Blackness crossed his vision every few steps. He would pause to wait it out, the rain gathering on his forehead to run in cool rivulets down his nose. *Where is my cap?* he wondered for just a moment, and then forgot.

* * *

"Look at you in your papa's hat!" he could hear Jennette say. Her arms were akimbo, her head pulled back and tipped to the side. Before her, Seymour struck his own pose, chest out, looking out from beneath the brim of Solomon's bowler. *"You've got some growing to do to be equal to that one, son . . . but it suits you."* His own father appeared in his mind then, looking as he did when introduced at a political

gathering . . . Jacob Ramsdell, tall, with the silk top hat he kept pristine for such occasions.

* * *

Exhausted after his muddy trek—*How will I climb the rise again?*—Solomon sank onto a wooden crate before the slumped remains of the two tents at Ransom's encampment. *Ransom must be abed . . . he won't be needing them . . . should save his strength for the writing, anyway.* He looked about, glad at least the rain had stopped, then heard a groan from inside the tent, then a scuffling. He glanced at the opening—*Are the scissors and things in there?*—and a face appeared, small and gray, with darting eyes.

"Who are you?" the man asked. "This is *my* place now— my lot's." Then he peered more closely at Solomon and said, "Ramsdell?" followed by a low whistle.

I know this man . . . with me since Michigan, on the train . . .

"Where's John Ransom?" Solomon croaked.

"Gone with the transport." The man waved his hand as if casting hopes over the stockade fence. "Just this morning—could hardly stand up. I hear the Rebs are gettin' nervous with our forces gettin' so near."

Sam, is it? No, another John . . . John Van Wagoner . . . a grinner with a spring in his step, but steady. From Montcalm. Just a boy . . .

"And his books?" Solomon asked.

"That big fella with him—Indian, I think—carried some bundle out. Carried Ransom, too, truth be told. He was nearly ready for the infirmary line."

"Did they leave anything?"

"I expect you're wantin' the barber tools," John said with a snort. "Somebody scurried in for those in no time. You'll find a barbering operation somewhere over yonder by dusk, I warrant." He tipped his head toward the middle of the camp.

Kinley won't like that, Solomon thought, his arms growing weak with panic. *What'll he call on me to do to make up for it?*

"You were a friend of Ransom's?" John asked.

"Something like that." *Until it didn't serve me . . .*

"Well, I'm pleased to see a Michigan man again, Sol. Worked my way here from down camp—doesn't matter how." John squatted and dragged his finger through the mud. "Ransom's Indian told me they were clearing out with the transport, so I was able to claim the tent ahead of the raiders. Not much else to be had. And nobody's got the strength these days to counter the claim."

"I've been with Robert Kinley's lot, up there." Solomon gestured up the rise.

"Naw . . . I've heard things about Kinley—you went with him that first day, right? Maybe he's not so bad, then. I went with Harris, but that didn't work out." He shook his head sadly. "I'm the only one left."

Solomon shook his own head to clear it—*Not so bad?* "Transport, you said? So Ransom got free of here . . ." Solomon paused, then leaned forward against the stick and sought to rise, but the clouds spun around as his knees buckled, and he collapsed into the mud, catching his cheekbone on the stick.

Ransom . . .

Head still spinning, Solomon felt himself dragged into Ransom's old tent, then his friend left, promising to return soon. A while later Solomon opened his eyes and saw Davis peeking into the tent. He was only vaguely aware that what he then heard was Davis picking up the stick . . . and the box, too, for good measure.

John nursed Solomon after a fashion for days that became weeks, scavenging a little of this and that to sustain him, and bringing news of what was happening in the camp.

Andersonville prison was being evacuated over the course of many weeks, but hundreds of men succumbed to death before they could be sent elsewhere. When his turn came in October, Solomon had just enough strength left to stagger with John's help, empty-handed, onto a wagon at the gate. From there he went by train to Florence, South Carolina, then on to City Point, Virginia, where he was paroled back to the Union Army in late spring, 1865.

RETURN
SUMMER 1865

Homecoming

As the miles of track fell away behind him to the southeast, Solomon just stared, his mouth slack. His raggedly cut beard—the work of a kindly lady with the relief society—couldn't hide the sores on his face, and a stiff, half-laundered shirt fairly rattled around his bones. A hemp rope served to hold his trousers above his jutting hipbones.

In Virginia he had been liberated and made fit for the world—after a fashion. He jostled on the train bench like a bundle of light parcels loosely bound together, for he had no flesh to ground him on the rough board. The other silent, faded men jostled, too, some with eyes closed, some with eyes fixed out the window at the spring leaves streaking by. Steam and ash blew in and swirled around them, settling on their long, tangled hair and their collapsed shoulders.

Solomon closed gritty eyes, letting the dappled light play across his lids as he swayed on the bench.

The promise of home came back to him, carried in with the scent of honeysuckle and fresh, clean river, in rich shudders as he felt life stir in him just a little. Not fifteen months earlier he had traveled the other way. The world then was icy, thawing as he had gone east and south months ahead of the honeysuckle. The world had thawed in rolling country just like this.

He had gloried in the feel of his thighs against his favorite horse. *Hector, old boy.* That name stayed with him when others had slipped away ... his commanding officer ... the drummer boy who'd stuck to him, looking for assurance with upcast eyes. *Felix? Frederick? Freddie.* One corner of Solomon's mouth lifted, cracking the fragile skin of his lip. His eyes blinked open, and as he caught the swish of a gray's tail against spring flies in a meadow, his hand recalled the sun-warmed curve of Hector's hindquarters. Solomon clutched his own impossibly thin thigh and snorted a little puff of disdain for his wasted body. *How easily I used to offer a handful of oats to Hector, or an apple ... better yet, a lump of sugar.*

Magnificent wealth to have a palmful of oats or an apple for a horse—and just a dim memory. He wondered what had become of Hector in Virginia. *Hope those Rebs have treated you right, old boy.* Horses were more valuable than men in this world. If a man had oats enough himself, or apples—never mind sugar—he could stand and gather his strength, lay his hand upon a tool, and set about his work ... Solomon uncurled the fist that had unconsciously gripped the handle of a ghostly hatchet. His hand was bony, covered in parchment-like skin that would probably rip if he attempted a blow with a hatchet, unused as he was to wielding tools these many months.

That was as far as his mind would take him, to just the memory of sensations—a glimpse of a horse, a scent, the phantom grip of a tool. Still far removed from his ability to contemplate was his home—his farm and his crops and . . . As he swayed and bumped rhythmically with the train, he dozed off into nothingness.

White house, blue door . . . shutters flapping and banging, the wind howling through, screaming in the emptiness.

Solomon woke with a start, heart banging in his ribcage, arms aching from his thin blood fleeing to warm his bowels. A grinding pain writhed through his belly, and he groaned to his feet and hauled himself through to the next car, a passenger car with a water closet—no actual water, just a hole cut over the tracks—where two others clutched their stomachs ahead of him.

"Get some physic from the doc," one said, nodding toward the next car up. "Stills it some." When that man's turn came, he disappeared behind the door and left Solomon just one man away from relief. In the passenger car, Solomon had been able to move by gripping seat backs and supporting himself on his one good leg, but now, forced to stand and wait, he felt a grinding collapse in his bad hip. Once off the train, he'd need a stick or crutch to walk.

A flash came to mind of a brass-top cane spinning before him with a flick of his wrist, a shining-haired boy laughing up at him—

No! He shook the image out of his head, his heart hammering. *No. Not ready . . .*

Out the window he saw two boys on horses racing alongside the train, the setting sun casting their shadows long. *Jerome and I . . .* Solomon watched as if from a great distance as the riders urged their mounts with vigor and then fell away behind the train. He had gloried in strength like that just fifteen months ago, leaving much behind to do his duty. *Left the house with the blue door, the hickory, sugar-bush . . .*

Others had shirked their duty. Otis had shirked his . . . *Why that memory?* Otis leaning on his axe, spitting casually in the direction of any person nigh about him, then turning away.

But Solomon had left with purpose. He hadn't been heedless—no, he'd made every provision. He drifted off again . . . *a blue door banging in its frame, opening onto black, and then closing again. . .*

His turn came for the water closet, relieving his mind as well as his bowels.

* * *

Insensible to all but the chill, flat smell of Lake Erie filling the northern horizon outside his window, Solomon cast back to his memory of that scent, back to his infancy and earliest sensations. This train was taking him north to where he'd been born, somewhere near Detroit. His family had gone there after arriving on the barge from New York—as they'd told the story. Rosette remembered bits of it.

In the night, someone helped him out of the train and onto another. And in those final miles on the open upper deck of the train into Lowell, he relived his family's migration west across the state all those years ago. The cold wind was draining away the last of the strength he'd been holding onto for when he could fall into the arms of his family—or into the grave.

* * *

"Almost there, Sol!" Frank called cheerfully, his voice breaking as he prodded his brother's hip. Solomon groaned and gazed up into the thin blue, beyond the tendrils of cloud drawn by the spring wind across the sky. A chill trickled down from his open collar and twined around his sunken belly, then lanced into his lame hip pressed into the planks of the wagon. He raised his head, and Frank gently pulled him up to sitting and shoved some bundled quilts around him. Solomon slumped against the bale of hay at his back and looked over two sets of shoulders. His father was driving, Jerome beside him.

They had collected Solomon at the Lowell depot the evening before, and from the train Solomon had glimpsed his brothers' bright faces eager with questions. But they were subdued when they saw that sympathetic passengers were practically carrying Solomon down from the train. His father stepped forward and draped Solomon's arm over his shoulders, then nodded to Jerome to take the other side. "Frank, you can drive," were the only words his father spoke. They rode gently but none too slowly the half mile to the Ramsdells' house in town. Solomon's mother took one look at him and set about to nursing. He closed his eyes and let himself be borne on strong arms into a warm bed, his limbs bathed each in turn, broth spooned into his mouth as murmurs filtered in from the other room.

And now they were on the road north, drawing closer to Cannonsburg and the township. They'd paused briefly at what must have been Myron King's place at Vergennes, and though Solomon had not opened his eyes—the effort too taxing—he'd heard the rhythms of familiar voices a little distance from the wagon. All three families had pulled up stakes from Orange Township to come here, though Solomon intended to return to Orange. They were now further spread apart than in the days when a short walk could put the ladies together for an afternoon of mending or the men for a quick wagon ride to town, but they were still good friends. Soon the wagon had creaked and swayed as the Ramsdells climbed back up and Jacob clucked the horse on again.

Solomon jolted in the wagon in a daze, hands loose in his lap, not even trying to correct his seat when he began to slide down against the bale and a cramp set up in his slouched spine. Frank kept glancing forward at the road and then back again at Solomon . . .

It reminded Solomon of how Frank used to watch for visitors coming up or down the road by their farm in Orange. He'd scramble to the top of the woodpile, cascading carefully piled lengths of wood down the slope, heedless, excited that someone was coming.

Solomon wasn't able to return to his wife as Odysseus had to Penelope, with mastery over the dangers awaiting, in stealth. All such strength had fled him. But even though Solomon had to be trundled home swaddled in blankets, he could surely do better than *this*, so he gathered the threads of his person, then used his thin arms to arrange his legs to appear less helpless. His heart was hammering beneath the old coat of Father's that Mother had buttoned beneath his chin that morning. A hot flush rose to his cheeks—fever?

Frank patted his leg. "That's right, Sol. Almost there." The wagon turned down the quarter-mile road to the Watsons', causing Solomon to slump again. He struggled to right himself, and black washed across his vision. A dog barked in the distance. A suffocating weight settled around Solomon's shoulders and chest—his ribs threatening to fold up like a paper fan.

Suddenly the wagon swung into the yard, and above the barking, a high voice called, "Papa! Papa!" and Seymour was over the back panel of the wagon and draped over Solomon. The boy's arms nearly met behind his father's back as he clasped him with a strength Solomon couldn't answer. But the small shining head on his chest lit a warmth inside it; Solomon bent his chapped lips to the silkiness of his son's hair, felt the curve of his skull so hard and sure. The sharp scent of boy was not quite scrubbed away.

Around them the Ramsdell men quietly climbed down from the wagon, tending to things with hushed voices. Then came those small, quick footsteps, brisk and

purposeful, with the swish of skirts and little whispers—
Callie must be in her arms.

All else fell away for Solomon, leaving just this head against his cheek and the sound of her approach. His family was regathering like swallows circling back to the barn—extending their wings with a tilt and a curve, then folding them to dive through the breach to the dark, close space within—shelter. "Sy, help me climb down, son."

Frank and Jerome stepped up to help, too, lending strength. By the time Jennette arrived at the wagon, Solomon was sitting with his legs dangling over the edge, his brothers supporting his arms as he wavered down onto the box they'd brought for a step stool. The dog—*Puck*—sniffed nervously at Solomon and whined as Jennette approached.

She waited until his feet were solidly on the ground and then leaned into his chest with Callie on her hip. Solomon lifted his arms to enfold them, feeling his weight settle against her, and against the wagon bed at his back, as his brothers stepped away from him.

"Returned," she said simply, in a half-whisper, her head nestled into that place where it fit so well below his jaw. Shy, Callie reared back, straining with stiff arms against him. Jennette let her slide to the ground and patter away, Puck with her, and Solomon felt his wife's bosom press against his ribs, her hip at his thigh, her softness betraying the bones he preferred to hide. The roiling in his bowels started up again.

"Privy," he said, croaking his first word to her. "Needs must . . ."

He had gathered his remaining strength for their reunion, but the rush of momentary will was ebbing away. He half-collapsed into the supporting arms of his brothers, who led him to the privy and from there to the house, where he somehow made it up the porch steps to a rocking chair and into a nest of blankets arranged by Calista.

Convalescence

IN THE DAYS THAT FOLLOWED, Solomon was enfolded into the care of the Watson family. He gradually built up, at least as much as could be expected in the few short weeks before he had to report to Camp Chase in Ohio for mustering out—he was no longer fit for service. He began with day after day in bed. When he stirred at sunrise, the sun's glow appearing at the juncture of wall and ceiling, Jennette would be there with a mug of cinnamon tea for his bowels and to fluff his pillow and prop him up. Then the golden glow—a diffuse bright gray on overcast days—crept steadily down the wall and across where his shins lay beneath the coverlet until, finally, an hour before Sy and his Aunt Calista brought his dinner tray about noon, the glow fled to the windowsill and thence away.

Jennette brought him medicinals: tinctures to ease his rheumatism, salves for his skin. She turned him and applied a brassy-smelling grease to cleanse his weeping sores and soften the scabs. Together they focused on one part of him at a time. It was all Solomon could manage to turn his attention to—the creak of a joint or the re-fleshing of a limb—and Jennette reported the measure of his progress in each part.

"This ulcer here . . ." She traced outside its margins with a fingertip, making him conscious of how his rib protruded at one edge. "This one is reduced from last week." His body was stretched out before her so that he was reminded of a pale, sparse blueberry bush they had once stood over, arms akimbo, fists on their hips. Together they had solved the problem by gathering needles from beneath a nearby white pine to acidify the soil, and the bush had filled out and later produced summertime fruit and late-fall blazing foliage. But here he was just a mute witness, and her deliberations were with herself or with the doctor . . . or Calista.

Until he was further restored, Solomon couldn't be a proper husband for Jennette. As long as he needed use the chamber pot and leave there evidence of his frailty, as long as he couldn't climb down—or back up—the stairs to see to his own needs, he felt ashamed. It was as if he were still far away, in a field hospital, perhaps, or still on the train rumbling in her direction. He had arrived too soon to be properly reunited with her.

Calista had charge of the kitchen, and from there came comfort. Some days he was ready to eat by noon, and Sy would clamber up the stairs, announcing the dinner tray. He would bring some morsel to tempt his father—a smear of honey on a piece of biscuit, or a carefully tended spoonful of raspberry cobbler.

Solomon would sit himself up to visit with his son, and sometimes Callie would linger at the doorway, having followed Calista up the stairs. As much for his timid little daughter as for Sy, Solomon would brighten his face and infuse his voice with what warmth he could summon. On the tray Calista brought would be a meat soup, more of whatever Sy had brought up, a glass of buttermilk, and perhaps an egg in its shell. As Solomon ate, the three of them would chat a little about what Sy had done that morning—maybe followed Grandpa Watson to the barn for chores, or brought in a basket of kindling for the kitchen, or fetched some jam from the cellar . . . It was easy to talk with Sy there, and before he knew it, Solomon would have eaten most of what was on his tray. He was putting on flesh and gaining strength. Soon he must be off to Ohio for his discharge.

* * *

By the end of the second week, a week before his departure for Camp Chase, Solomon had gained enough strength to make his way downstairs, holding on to the rail. He would spend hours on the porch sitting very still, looking out to the woods and beyond, far beyond—and would startle slightly when the children ran into the yard with the dog or a stick and hoop. When this happened, he would gather his attention and turn a smile upon them for a time, but then his eyes would wander across the yard, beyond the fence, to the woods again . . . and he wouldn't come to himself until he was alone, suddenly aware that the children had gone into the house and the women were calling to them with little chores to complete for the next meal. His strength peaked at dinnertime, playing out in hearty comments to his father-in-law about the morning's work on the farm.

Callie was shy of him still, but he wooed her as best he could. "Miss Callie," he would say gently, bending his head to look around Jennette, who sat beside him at the table. Then Jennette would cover Callie's hand with her own to get her attention.

The first time he'd done this, Callie's eyes had widened and then darted to Calista, who had nodded encouragement.

"Miss Callie, did I hear there were chicks in the barn now?" Solomon asked her.

No answer—another mute appeal to Calista, another encouraging nod. Callie looked down to her lap and nodded.

"Well then, do you think you could bring me one after dinner?" he asked. "I'd like to see if it's fuzzy enough. *Are they fuzzy?*"

That sparked her. A smile deepened the dimple in her cheek. She giggled and cried out, "Fuzzy!"

Jennette sighed a little with satisfaction and released Callie's hand, giving her power over her spoon again, and then squeezed Solomon's knee beneath the table. Calista smiled, her dimple mirroring Callie's.

Solomon's knee warmed under Jennette's hand, and he suddenly became keenly aware of his wife's presence beside him. Her sleeve was still damp from the morning's laundry, but her hair had been tidied, revealing her slender neck, which straightened when she sensed his attention upon her. He fumbled his hand over hers, which she left on his knee as she helped Callie scoot back from the table and climb down.

Expectant stillness hung in the air.

Watson scraped back his chair and cleared his throat. "Sy, let's go see about that calf that dropped this morning . . ."

Calista and Sally began to stack the dinner plates and clear the table. Solomon and Jennette remained still, both looking down and inward, until it became too awkward to do so any longer and Jennette bustled up, said a few words about the laundry, and was out the kitchen door. Solomon fetched his cane—the one he'd bought in Lowell with his father in '62—and went out the front door, taking a moment to lean against the porch post and look out to the familiar woods. But he didn't take his usual seat in the rocker, nor sit on the bench Sy had set up for him with his old whittling knife and a basket of wood scraps. "In case you want to, Papa," he'd said. It had all lain untouched for weeks.

Instead, Solomon gripped the porch post with one hand and settled his cane one step down. Then he swung his lame leg from its stiff hip and, when it was firmly planted, let go of the porch post and leaned heavily on the cane, his other arm out for balance. He repeated the process with the next step and the last. Then he straightened, balancing his weight over both legs as much as possible, and slowly made his way across the front of the house and around the corner to the kitchen yard, where Jennette was cranking clothes through the mangle and into a basket.

"Can I help you with that?" he called out. Jennette looked up quickly, then smiled as she cranked a few more times to finish the garment she had in the machine.

"Surely," she said. "Just one more and I'll be ready for the hanging up."

"Probably can't manage the basket with this cane, but I can hold the pins for you."

"That you can."

As Solomon picked his way across the yard—the nearest upright of the clothesline his goal, his heart hammering with the exertion—she cranked a final shirt through the mangle and quickly swung the heavy basket onto her hip before he could offer to help. Then she handed him a cloth bag of wooden clothespins and held out her hand for one as she pulled the damp shirt from the basket.

The first pin he drew out of the bag had one of its legs splintered off. "Useless," he pronounced, and flung it toward the woodpile. The next would serve her purpose, so he handed it to her, but the third had split in its join and was too loose to hold anything on the line. He threw that one toward the woodpile too, feeling his arm jiggle where loose skin hadn't yet filled with muscle.

"Father has been too taken up with spring chores to tend to these, and I've hated to ask him," she said, nodding to the bag of pins.

"Sy is near old enough to do such work."

"But he hasn't been taught how . . ."

A wave of loss flooded through him. A small thing, the whittling of clothespins, but he hadn't been there for it. Someone banged out onto the kitchen doorstep, then came Calista's voice: "Callie, come back! Come back in here, and I'll take you to the chickens . . ." The door banged again and the little one's voice piped softly to her aunt from inside.

"I can do it now," Solomon said. "Teach him. Can't do much else, but I can do that."

"I didn't mean—" Jennette said quickly, then stopped and rummaged in the basket for another shirt like the one she'd just hung. *Then will come another, and another, shirts hung along the line like figures cut from a folded fan of paper.* And as his wife was a creature of habit, Solomon knew the trousers would come next, followed by the ladies' three skirts of the week and Callie's little dresses to balance out the line. The underthings would be similarly arranged on another line, just the way Jennette liked it. Solomon knew she'd had to do extra tubs of laundry when he'd been so ill, with his fevers and chills and his sores, and the occasional spilled bedpan. She'd been sleeping with Calista, with Callie in a trundle at the foot of the bed.

"I'm stronger now. Because of your care, and rest and good food."

"I worry for your journey," she said, then sighed. "Why must you go, only to be released again?"

"Something to do with military order." He handed her another pin. "Which can be a fine thing. When we first went, you should have seen us all in ranks on the parade ground, uniforms bright, horses tossing their manes—even my bugle was shiny! Wonder where it went after that battle . . ." He couldn't bring himself to say the word "captured."

"I think you've given enough, surely," she said, snapping a pair of trousers before reaching to pin it above her head on the line.

"I'll be back soon." Thinking about the journey exhausted him, and he longed to settle back into the rocker on the porch and rest. *Too difficult to think beyond that.*

He shook his head once to clear it, then turned his eyes to Jennette—so firm and soft at once, supple. *Like the wheat. Golden.* He planted his bad leg and maneuvered with the cane to bend toward the basket, drawing out a skirt for her to hang. When she turned from the line, she raised her brows to see him standing, the cane on the ground beside him. She smiled indulgently and took the garment from him, hanging it while he drew out another. He draped it over his forearm and steadied himself, and when she turned to reach for it, he closed his other hand over hers and drew her toward him.

Their faces close, the damp skirt twining their arms together, husband and wife remembered one another. Solomon leaned in for a kiss, and as their lips touched—the damp, clean scent of the laundry between them—they mingled breath and both sighed a hope long held in check, a sound more felt than heard. *Longing.* They held still there a moment, then pulled back and raised their eyes to one another.

"Together tonight?" he said. Jennette nodded and tucked her head into the shelter of his shoulder.

Just then Callie rounded the corner of the house, bearing a basket covered with a cloth. Calista trotted behind her. "Mind that basket, Callie!" she called.

Solomon stepped back from Jennette, who bent to retrieve his cane before taking the damp skirt from his arm.

"What have we here?" he said, bracing himself with his cane as Callie shyly held out the basket. He hooked the basket handle over his hand holding the cane and drew back the cloth with the other, and trying to crouch down to her height, he cupped his hand gently over the chick and murmured, "Fuzzy *indeed*, Miss Callie."

Forgetting her shyness, Callie poked a finger into the basket to touch the head of the chick. Calista stepped away and joined Jennette, and briskly the two of them finished hanging the wash. Solomon kept catching glimpses of them darting behind and between the garments like two birds. Jennette's uncovered golden hair was drawn up into a knot, and Calista's bronze curls escaped her bonnet as the sisters dipped back and forth, plucking things from the basket and carrying them to the line.

Before long, Calista came over and took Callie and the basket back to the chicken house, singing together a little song that blended their voices in a pleasing way. Jennette cast a knowing smile to Solomon over her shoulder, then swung the laundry basket to her hip and crossed the yard to climb the steps to the kitchen door.

Solomon drove his cane hard into the ground and leaned heavily on it, suppressing a groan as he straightened up, loosening his joints a bit as he took a few steps back toward the front porch. Once he'd made it up the steps, he settled onto the bench, picked up a stick of wood and the knife, and began whittling a clothespin while humming Calista's and Callie's little tune. Then he spied Sy by the barn and, for the first time since the war, Solomon put two fingers in his mouth and whistled for his boy.

TEMPTATION
1865–1866

<hr>

Unease

WHEN SOLOMON ARRIVED at Camp Chase, the talk was of the army mobilizing in Kansas to deal with the Indian threat now that the war was over. One man who'd seen the new frontier of wide-open grassland reported that he'd never seen so distant a horizon, and from his description, it was clear why the Indians and pioneers were at odds over it. *Farmers will do well there with wheat and with grazing cattle,* Solomon thought. But he knew it would take a new approach to farming to prosper in the West.

Solomon himself had no thought to leave Michigan. *Am I so decrepit in my thirties?* He laughed grimly to himself. *Yes, I am.* He had less strength of limb and more pain than his father, who was in his late fifties, though perhaps Solomon was sounder than Andrew Watson in his seventies. But the demons in his belly were with him constantly, so that he must always have an eye out for a place to relieve himself.

Among his old fellows of the Sixth Michigan at Camp Chase, Solomon found three sorts of men. The first sort were hale and hearty—men who had hardened in the war, who rang like brass and were just as cold. These men laughed savagely about the Rebels they'd killed and how they'd used their women. They were ready to strap on their weapons and do battle with any Indians that threatened the Kansas frontier. *Let them have at it.* Their laughter sickened Solomon, but he didn't have the strength to confront their depredations.

The second sort, consisting of released Union prisoners like him, were aged beyond all the rest—coughing, scarred, crippled. Their very presence seemed an affront to the hearty ones. It was laughable that they were required to gather here with all the rest, far from home, far from their places of suffering in the South. The army required all soldiers to appear and all officers to complete paperwork to account for their government-issued equipment. But how might a man explain on a paper that he had chewed his leather belt to keep from starving? And what of Solomon's gun and shiny bugle? There was no accounting for what had happened to those. But if he hoped to receive a pension someday when all was finally sorted out, he must be present to see to the papers and get a proper medical discharge.

Solomon collected his fistful of pay and listened to the official words—a benediction of sorts—that made him a private citizen again. Then he waited for his train home with the other debilitated prisoners. They had no heart for the old-times'-sake rollicking of the hardened ones.

The third sort of men—those who still seemed like themselves, little changed from before—drew back from both the prisoners and the hard ones. They were respectable men who'd done their duty. Some of them were signing on for Kansas, but most just wanted to settle their accounts with the government and get back to their farms and their stores, to their families. The war was over for them.

Some of those headed for Kansas were Confederate prisoners—"galvanized Yankees" they were called—men willing to make the best of their lot and take up with the victors to defend the frontier. Apparently Camp Chase had been a better host to the Rebels than Camp Sumter had been to the Yankees.

* * *

His duty done with no parades nor good cheer to finish the thing, Solomon found himself back in Cannon in late July, with improving health but a spirit palled and deadened. It was as if he'd left a part of himself behind with the regiment but hadn't noticed it missing until the mustering out. Before the journey his tenuous cheer and first glimmers of health had led to a tender reunion with Jennette in their shared bed at the Watsons'. But it had been too soon to travel, and his weakness had dragged him down in the journey to and from Ohio, and in the idle days he spent there, setting back his recovery.

In bed his first night home again, he lay stiff on his back and pled fatigue when Jennette curled her warm body around him. He felt as though he were made of pale clay from the riverbank, his flesh cool and inert. No passion stirred in him—and Jennette seemed far, far away.

In the morning Jennette groaned a little and rolled out of bed, then retched over the chamber pot. She dabbed a handkerchief against her lips and caught his eye as he lay staring glassily in her direction.

"That's the third morning I've done that," she said with a grin. "I had to have a nap yesterday before you arrived, and with so much to do . . ."

Still he stared.

"Solomon, dearest, did you hear me? I believe I'm with child."

He blinked and mechanically shifted his hand out from under the bedclothes. She grasped his fingers.

"That would make this an April baby, as I reckon it," she said. "We can get back to Orange in time for the planting, but the sugaring would be too soon for me to go. You could board with Rosette and Otis and manage the sugar-bush from there. And make repairs on the house . . . I'm sure it needs some care. Remember the loosened window frame in the children's room?"

He didn't answer; his eyes had closed again.

"But you're weary, of course. We can speak of this later," she said, then took a mouthful of water from a cup on the bedside table and spat it into the chamber pot. "I was thinking we could arrange to buy seed in Lowell on the way, as Father says the prices are better than in Ionia. Your parents could give us loan of their wagon—and perhaps one of the boys to help you with the things you can't do because of your leg—but there's time later for that." She scooted the chamber pot back under the bed and Solomon heard the sound as she pulled off her nightgown, but he did not open his eyes. She briskly put on her clothing he knew was draped over the chair. The bed creaked when she sat down to put on her stockings and shoes.

"Now you just stay there a while." She rested a hand on his shoulder. "There's no need to get up early this first day." Then she was out the door and down the stairs.

Solomon couldn't sleep any longer, but neither could he stir. A gray cloud shrouded his mind so he couldn't even consider Jennette's plans. The Orange Township farm was as far from him here as it had been in Andersonville. And the blue door he so loved was just a rectangle of wood.

* * *

Daniel returned in August—wounded, decorated, and recovered. He was uncommon cheerful and garrulous for Daniel, and the family gathered in his presence as flies to a jam jar. Daniel had a limp like Solomon's, but in his case it only added to his jaunty new character. His shooting prowess had earned him his place among men—and would likely do so with young ladies, too. In the front room in the evenings, Daniel and Calista resumed the music-making they'd enjoyed while growing up together. Jennette swooped the children around as her dance partners, one at a time, while Solomon and Sally sat gray and quiet—she with consumption, he with whatever was pressing him down. Andrew, presiding over the household, cradled the bowl of his pipe and held it out toward one or the other group, as if stitching them together with tendrils of fragrant smoke.

Before Daniel's return, Jennette had sought to remind Solomon of his old loves by bringing up books they'd discussed, new ones her father treasured but Solomon had not yet read, and agricultural journals. She'd even brought his violin to the porch one summer evening while Calista played piano quietly in the front room to soothe the children to sleep up the stairway.

"I thought you might like to have this again," she said gently, laying the case in his lap. He instinctively closed his hand around the neck of the case to keep it from falling as she backed herself onto a low stool to give him room.

Though they'd spent many summer evenings with Solomon's music in Orange, and firelit evenings with the Watsons in the weeks before he left for the war, the violin case was now an inert thing lying in his lap, like a log or a frying pan. It retained its shape and texture, its weight across his thighs, but there was no meaning in it, no purpose. The gleaming wood and taut strings latched inside the case were elements of a different existence. He could bring nothing to them.

She didn't press him.

But on an evening after Daniel's return—while all were gathered together to hear him and Calista play—Jennette brought Solomon his violin case again and held it out for him to take. He turned his face away, and she stamped impatiently and half-shoved the violin against the wall behind his chair before hoisting Callie out of her grandmother's lap and carrying her up to bed without a word.

* * *

"Solomon," Jennette said briskly one late-fall day as she presided over a bubbling kettle of apple butter while he idly turned the pages of a newspaper at the kitchen table. "Isn't it about time to go see to our house—to ready it for winter?"

"I expect it's still sound. It's overwintered twice already now without supervision."

"All the more reason to see to it, to make plans for sugaring off in a few months. For all you know, someone could have carried off your equipment."

"Didn't Rosette say Otis was seeing to it?" Solomon gestured vaguely in the direction of Jennette's writing desk. "In a letter?"

"Well, yes, but ..." Jennette hesitated, swirling her wooden spoon through the pot of browning fruit.

He turned another page, waiting for another move in their daily exchange of propose-and-deflect. She would press, he step aside. She would sharpen, he go dull.

How else could he be, collapsed as he was? *The sugarbush is a memory, not a prospect. She cannot understand.*

If he bestirred himself to answer her bright suggestions with anything approaching enthusiasm, he would be promising something he knew he couldn't deliver. *Better not to promise.*

* * *

In their bed one night in October, she'd taken his hand and pressed his palm to the place where her womb was beginning to round her belly, just as she'd done with both Sy and Callie. He'd lifted the corners of his mouth into a smile she couldn't see in the dark, and it was just as well, for it was a false smile.

He remembered what he was supposed to do, but he was reluctant to do anything before it was fully required, as if by delaying he could demonstrate his incapacity.

Here at the Watsons' he could always find some little thing to help with, to earn his place, grateful that his father-in-law—and now Daniel—had all well in hand; he certainly could not take charge. Or he'd venture to his father's saddlery in Lowell and fumble about with leather and fittings, escaping the farm for his supposed usefulness in the shop. Jennette would nod and wave him off, satisfied that he was pursuing trade, at least. Solomon encouraged her perception that it was more than it was.

The wagon shuddering over the rutted road into town jostled him into the stupor he so longed for. He would bestir himself to raise a hand in greeting as he passed the Kings' place, hauling himself upright to feign the health he did not feel. And once at the shop, his father would give him some small task, content to think Solomon needed time away from the farm to rest himself.

* * *

He was not worthy of all the good entrusted to him. Jennette would be ashamed to know he'd been willing, at the behest of another man, to steal from someone who had no way to defend himself.

Such a man should not lead a family.

Not worthy. How brash, how ignorant I was to think I could build a home for such a fine woman—and bring her to it as an honorable thing, lay claim to her as my own . . . and then venture to lay claim to a pair of scissors while the man who owned them lay dying in the mud. He retched a little behind his newspaper, then covered it with a cough.

"Speaking of letters"—Jennette tasted a bit of the apple butter on her spoon, then grated in a little more allspice—"Rosette has asked us to come for the hog killing next week, to make it a party, with the children and all . . . She wants to see you now that you're well. That would be a good time to see to things."

Solomon nodded once, not to assent but to acknowledge that she'd spoken. What could he say? It would take a monumental effort to set up a wagon for all of them, drive all those miles, and then face his sister. And Otis, who could never know what Solomon had suffered, because *he'd* elected not to enlist.

The thought that Solomon should rally himself to care for his house, to care for *anything* of his old life? It was all he could do not to lay his head on the table at the wearisome prospect.

* * *

To Solomon's relief, a flare of his rheumatism kept them from the hog killing in Orange. He dragged through November, then managed to find a small measure of cheer with the approach of Jennette's beloved Christmas. He thought perhaps he could try to take up his violin and join Calista—and Daniel when he visited from his own nearby farm—in the Christmas carols and hymns.

One uncommonly mild evening in December, he took the instrument out to the porch and privately ventured upon the strings a few lines of his own composition. The violin had lain idle so long that it had closed up, its sound tight. The sad, strained melody cried out from the violin a phrase or two at a time.

While Jennette clattered around in the kitchen with the children, making some applesauce-and-spice ornaments for the full white pine she'd instructed Daniel to bring in from the woods, Calista slipped out onto the porch. She said not a word, listening as she stood several feet away from him, but then she hummed a little in harmony with his tune, playing with the lines, adding a phrase here and there.

Solomon stiffened at first. *Is there nowhere I can be alone?* But then he realized it wasn't an intrusion, just her own meditation upon the music, as if his lines were more a memory that she played upon, of her own accord. *She has a right to that*, he thought.

So he took up his lament again, and Calista brought in the refrain at his pause, in a call-and-answer as on that first evening when he and Jennette had teased her—a lifetime ago.

"Mama Calla?" called little Callie from inside, the sound of her steps coming from the kitchen as she searched for her aunt. Calista slipped back inside as quickly and quietly as she'd come, holding the child's chatter in the house.

The spell still intact on the porch, Solomon drew his bow across the deepest note and held it there.

Revelation

ONE MORNING IN JANUARY, Myron King brought his cutter into the Watsons' yard to let them know that Solomon's mother was striken with apoplexy but lingered, and they should make haste to see her—he would wait. Jennette flew into a bustle of preparations, bending across her swollen belly as she folded clothing for herself and Solomon and calling out instructions to Calista regarding the care of the children while they were away. Calista packed foodstuffs into a crate, and soon all was ready for the journey to Lowell. Solomon was numb, just another bit of baggage loaded into the cutter.

Fear and shock were both good explanations for his blank affect, so King would think nothing of it, and Jennette patted Solomon's hand sympathetically along the way. When they arrived at the quiet house, his father was standing in the front room as Ellen, her face streaked with tears, pinned a black armband to his sleeve. Jacob's face was pale but stony, conveying stoic acceptance of his loss. Frank and Jerome sat quietly nearby, clearly stunned.

Ellen fled from her father's side to Jennette's embrace, taking comfort from her sister-in-law and favorite former teacher.

"I'm sorry, Father," Solomon said, standing slack-armed before him.

"I'm sorry, too, son, that you didn't get the chance to see her before she left us . . . It happened this morning, while King was coming for you."

* * *

In the months previous when Solomon had made his occasional trips to Lowell—ostensibly to help in the saddlery—he had spent much of his time in the kitchen with his mother while she worked to put up the harvest and complained of Ellen's marriage.

"That girl will find herself abandoned—or worse—mark my words. I knew she shouldn't have married a twice-widowed man."

Solomon was sitting at the kitchen table, idly paging through a journal he had no interest in reading.

"Your father found Rosette no better than before when he was last in Orange," his mother said. "She's so reduced since we left. But there was no help for it—needs must. Your father and I must get on with our enterprise here, and she must bestir herself to further Otis's business there."

We're a pair, Rosette and I, Solomon thought then, recognizing that he'd been drawn into the same waves of melancholy that had set Rosette adrift. Lost children at home for her, lost boys on the battlefield for him. *The pity,* he thought.

His mother had allowed his lassitude, laying all the blame on his bowels, a trouble she could understand. She always sent him home with one remedy or another to try.

Now Mother's gone.

When Jennette and Ellen and some neighbor ladies finished washing and dressing the body, Solomon climbed the stairs behind Frank and Jerome to stand at the foot of his mother's bed and see her arranged there, one side of her face slack but her hair combed smooth and tidy. For all the years he'd known her, stray iron wisps had flown around her face during her diligent labors in the kitchen. She'd been elemental in his world even when he was unaware of her. Father had been his model, Father who stood now presiding at the head of the bed, ramrod straight even with the great grief he bore.

You and I grieve differently, Father. Grief grounds you, solidifies you; you become like the monument we'll one day raise over your grave.

Solomon and Rosette, it seemed, were undercut by grief, and he by guilt to boot. *Father, you stand there, firm in your integrity. But I have none, for when I should have stood up to Kinley and his scoundrels, I dragged myself through the mud to do his bidding . . .*

* * *

When Rosette arrived with her family for the burial, Solomon searched her pale face for something he could latch onto—surely she must have guilt, too, having hurried into her marriage before she even had a house to go to. Baby DeWitt had come early, but not by too much, so there was room for doubt. Had her young marriage been diminished by the gray clouds of gossip, by questions? She'd become fretful in answer to Otis's bitterness. And she'd been dragged down by the loss of her second and third child in one terrible week years before. Rosette returned his gaze, and something in her eyes connected to something in his. There passed between them a momentary promise: they would speak of things together, later.

In the days surrounding the burial, Rosette livened up a bit in their father's home, sharing the cheer of her infant, Ella. Being surrounded by conventional grief seemed to help her somehow. While the community bustled through, following the expected forms, Rosette and Jennette were able to recapture just a little of the shared sweet times they'd known together in Orange, drawing Frank in, especially, with gentle teasing. The boy needed help to grieve his mother and wouldn't know how. Solomon didn't want to intrude on that.

"Sol," Jennette said softly beside him in bed the third night, "Rosette has spoken to me of what she thinks may be your trouble, why you have not been able to get well. She says that after losing her children, she felt in her own body the grief of her soul, and that you may be suffering the same."

Solomon didn't answer, waiting to hear more.

"She says I may be asking too much of you, wanting you up and about, if your spirit needs mending more than your body." She stroked his cheek and temple as she spoke. "Is that how it is with you?" She then rested her hand on his shoulder and looked into his eyes, hers shining in the moonlight that filtered in through the window. "*Does* your spirit need mending, Sol?"

"Something does," he said, then paused a long while. "I don't know that there's help for it, though, for what has passed cannot be changed."

"Do you mean your sufferings in the camp? The killing you saw in battle?"

"It's not right to burden you with it, Jennette. Men go to war to *spare* their women and children from its evil."

"And I thank you for that. But can't you take honor from that sacrifice and strengthen your spirit with confidence in your efforts? Or what you would have done if you'd not been captured? Surely you don't blame yourself for that?" She wrapped her small hands around his clenched fists.

"No, that wasn't my fault—just an accident of war."

"Then how can your integrity be marred?"

"Because . . . because of what the sufferings in camp uncovered in me!" He pulled his hands out of hers and turned on his back.

She propped herself up on one elbow. "But dearest, what's inside you is good, through and through. You suffered in prison, but at least there you weren't tempted to glory in killing other men—you were spared that evil of war. Much as you suffered with disease, with death all around you, surely it was not the same as striking another man down with your own hand."

"No, it was not the same . . . It was worse."

She turned onto her back and stared toward the ceiling. "Worse how?" Her question rose in a little puff of moonlit breath in the chilly room.

Now that her gaze was turned from him, Solomon drew courage. From where, he knew not exactly—but perhaps from Rosette raising the possibility in Jennette's mind that something broken within him held him back from her.

Can I tell her? Do I dare?

He drew a shuddering breath and saw, in his mind's eye, his father's regal stance, born of principle and pride, untested by anything like what Solomon had experienced. His father knew stories of war from his ancestors, from his books. But he did not know war. And now Jacob lay alone in the next room, his wife gone and the prospect of grief laid out before him. It was a landscape he knew from the ancients how to traverse, even if the cruel, cold grip around his heart might chill and pain him more than he expected. Solomon saw Rosette, too, bled pale by her own suffering. From that suffering she'd spoken words that had opened a way, a small way, in Jennette's heart.

And he saw himself, staggering down from Kinley's tent to Ransom's, where he would have stolen from a dying man the only things of value he possessed, in a camp where tools could buy a tin cup of gruel that might make the difference between life and death. Solomon felt again the iron grip of cruel savagery that had wrenched his once-warm heart from him, tearing out his humanity, nauseating him with the ugliness of his willingness to obey a tyrant, to do his bidding.

But it wasn't Kinley—it was Solomon himself who would have done the deed. When it came down to it, he could be turned to evil by such little things—a taunt or a threat from a scoundrel. His own hunger.

"In the camp . . . there I . . . I saw terrible things."

"Yes," she said. "I've heard of some of it, read it in the paper. But I didn't want to ask . . ."

"The camp showed me I have evil deep within myself, and though I've asked God to forgive me, I don't believe he has. I'm too reduced to make up for it myself, to do good in a way that will atone."

"But we never can atone for ourselves—we know that," she answered. "I've experienced rottenness in myself, too. My impatience. I've grown angry with you too many times, though I try not to show it. 'Why can he not rise up?' I ask myself, 'and be all that he once was?' I confess to you—as I have confessed to God too many times to count—that I have done you wrong in holding you to a Pharisee's measure. Can you forgive me, Sol?"

"So little to forgive, Jennette, and so easily done, especially when I consider my own wrongs."

She shook her head. "But do you see how little I was provoked and yet brought forth rottenness from within? While you . . . you have known such suffering. Can you tell me some of it, Sol? That I might bear your burden with you, and not just add to it?"

And so, long into the night, as the moon passed across the windowpanes and then disappeared, Solomon poured out to his wife the depths of his soul's sickness and took comfort from her consoling touch, from her sweet questions, her murmurs and tears.

In that quiet house of mourning, they examined, then laid to rest, the bones of death he'd carried with him from Andersonville. From time to time she drew his hand between them so he could feel the kicks of the baby in her womb, the new life that had begun with his own first stirrings of life beyond the prison.

Translation

IN THE MAGICAL MONTHS that followed, Solomon considered his armband of mourning an emblem of transformation, as if his mother's death had shaken him to life and firmly set him on his feet. Something had broken free within him—his eyes had been opened to the beauties about him. He laughed with the Watsons in the gentle humor particular to their family and became truly reacquainted with his children.

Callie was still shy, but she would blushingly sidle up to him or steal her way into his bed when he took an afternoon nap to rebuild his strength—he'd carry a little toy or rock from the field or tool from the kitchen as he climbed the stairs, then wait for her to appear. Between them they would murmur all sorts of endearments and sing little tunes, and when Solomon's nap was over, Sy would be waiting at the foot of the stairs for their "men's work" of the afternoon. The two of them were fashioning a handheld net to carry to the lake as soon as it warmed sufficiently, and Sy would chatter about the fish they'd catch and how he'd one day pole the Gargantua across the lake.

By March, Solomon was sufficiently strong and the weather sufficiently improved that he could go see to his farm in Orange. "To help Otis with the sugaring off," he told the Watsons. Solomon rode Andrew Watson's horse from Cannon to Ionia, retracing the journey that he'd taken with Hector before the war—*so very long ago!* Vast swaths of trees had been cleared for the war effort, and many farms were now neglected, like his. Overgrown fields and sagging roofs were reminders of the men who had been lost. At one homestead he saw the house standing empty and cold while smoke curled up out of the stovepipe in the shanty huddled nearby—perhaps an economizing widow was warming a smaller household now. The war had paused the prosperity of their region, but there was talk of the railroads again. And emerging from winter, the farmers who produced maple sugar were busy with that cheerful work. *It's as if the land is awakening, the people coming out of their stupor.*

His own awakening continued as he took his place beside Otis for the familiar work of his childhood, boiling the sap to concentrate it into the sugar that had profited his father and then himself. He could imagine returning to his land and settling back into his old life, rejoining his family to Rosette's. But then he would be taking Jennette from the rich hills of her father's land and her brother Daniel's farm nearby, and from Calista's sweet company. The fields of Orange Township seemed less promising than Solomon remembered, and though he felt a note ringing in his soul when he spent time with Rosette, Otis strained things whenever he appeared. Young DeWitt had none of Sy's cheerful spirit. *Would my children prosper here if we returned? Would Jennette?*

He rode the miles back to his family, debating in his mind. *What would be best?* The answer seemed suspended just out of reach, leaving him on tiptoe, barely brushing it with his fingertips.

No matter. There's time to decide. They had a baby to welcome to the family and the Watsons' crops to see to. Any decision that needed to be made could wait until fall.

* * *

Soon precious Nettie was born—named for her mother as Calista had insisted should be done. "That they might be another pair of sisters, like us." How a baby did bring joy in its wake! And sweet memories—Solomon remembered the beautiful day in Orange when Jennette had done her spring cleaning and aired the cradle in the yard, the cradle that would become Callie's, while Sy toddled along beside him in the freshly plowed fields. Now a new chapter had opened for him, and his life had been reclaimed. *Not all that's torn can be mended,* he thought, *but Providence carries us along to new opportunities for growth if we can but see them as such.*

On the strength of this new hope, Solomon climbed the stairs with a tray for Jennette one morning while the rest of the family took breakfast in the kitchen.

"What is this?" Jennette asked with a sweet smile, her hair poking out charmingly from the braid draped over one shoulder. Nettie was tucked into the crook of her mother's arm and nursing contentedly.

"You saw to it that many trays came up those stairs for me last summer, and it seemed only fitting to bring you one—and when you might not expect it." He sat on the edge of the bed and balanced the tray on his knees, peeling a boiled egg and dipping it into the little pile of salt he'd put on the plate, then offering her bites. Jennette giggled at the awkward feeding and picked some flecks of yolk out of Nettie's fine hair. Solomon handed her a piece of buttered toast and watched her eat it, and she watched him.

"You look like you have something to say," she said, squinting as if studying him.

"It happens I do," he said, offering her the cup of milk, then taking it back after she'd drained it in two long swallows.

"Must have been thirsty," she remarked. She eased the slumbering infant onto the bed beside her and closed up her nightgown, tying a pretty bow with the ribbon at her neck. "Now what is it, Mr. Ramsdell, that you have in mind?"

"Well, Mrs. Ramsdell, it has become increasingly clear to me that we should establish our own home again." He waited as the news settled in and added excitement to her smile. "I know that's what you've wanted."

"Ever so much, Solomon," she said. "I love being with my family, but I miss Rosette, and I long to have things the way we'd always talked about them. I love our home, and that shagbark you planted for us. You know how Father has been cutting marks on the kitchen doorframe for the children's growth? He made that doorpost a memorial for his family. And you planted your tree for the same purpose."

"I'm glad to be alive enough again to remember that purpose, Jennette. Thank you for your patience—waiting for me to remember. Your parents will be well here with Calista, especially with Daniel nearby."

"Maybe, in due time, Calista might come to us," Jennette said. "Perhaps we could find her a husband in Orange, or she could become our own children's teacher."

"Or both," Solomon said with a squeeze to her knee as he tidied the tray and set it on the end of the bed. "She could teach and then become a wife."

"For now, though, she is needed here, especially when we leave—and when do you have in mind to leave?"

"I was thinking," Solomon said, "that your father needs assistance with the rest of this year's harvest, and we can spend the fall and winter planning and preparing to move home in the spring, for planting."

"Home," echoed Jennette. "That sounds so good. Thank you, dearest, for deciding upon it. And thank the good Lord for bringing you so far as to be able to."

Solomon did not answer but stroked her hand, then held it in both of his.

Nettie blinked awake and looked around, and her parents gazed at her expression that embodied wonder at the present and hope for the future.

* * *

"Seymour!" Solomon called across the yard to where the children were picking July blackberries with their grandfather. "Callie! We're going fishing today!" Andrew held out his basket to receive what little had made it into theirs and waved them on to Solomon with a blessing.

Solomon was able to get around without his cane most of the time now, and he wanted to take this expedition with the children on his own. Everyone's bustling attention had been turned to the new baby, and since Calista had taken up much of Jennette's work since Nettie's arrival, the two older children were missing the amusements Calista usually made for them.

Just as Daniel had done for him almost a decade before, Solomon showed the children where the fishing things were kept in the barn, and then he engaged in much hilarity digging for worms with them, glad for the chance to have some fun. When all was ready, they went to the kitchen for provisions to take to the lake with them—apparently taking Calista by surprise.

"Oh!" she said, flustered, "you'll need a lunch." She looked about the kitchen, then hastily wrapped a loaf and a lump of cheese and laid some peaches into a basket she then hung over Callie's arm. "Be careful with these—you don't want them to bruise." She wiped the damp from her brow with the edge of her apron and said to Solomon, "I've sent Jennette to bed with the babe—she seems to be poorly this morning, with symptoms of the ague."

"Nettie?" Solomon immediately thought of Rosette's little ones carried away by the fever. His heart pounded in his chest.

"No. Jennette. Nettie is well—but could you take this tea to Jennette before you go?"

As Solomon climbed the stairs with the cup, his thoughts cast back to Andersonville and the men carried away by the ague; they'd been so reduced by hunger that they were unable to fight the fever. *But here we can care for her well.*

From the doorway he could see the bright flush on his bride's cheeks, the damp blond strands of hair plastered across her brow. He carried the cup over to her and noticed that she was trembling, curled up and hugging the bedclothes to herself while the infant napped in the cradle beside the bed. He caressed Jennette's shoulder and set the tea on the bedside table, carefully moving aside her volume of sonnets—she wouldn't be pleased should a water-ring mar the cover.

She opened her eyes and smiled weakly at him.

"Darling," he said, "I brought you some tea. And I'm taking the children fishing. I'll at least let them clamber about in the Gargantua, even if we don't take it out on the lake. Or do you need us here to tend to you?"

"No, please take them." She closed her eyes, shaking her head to refuse the tea he offered, then smiled warmly, murmuring, "I'm so glad that you can."

"If you're sure—"

"Yes, go along now. I'll dream of you all there, as it should be."

"Later in the summer we'll all go together—and make Daniel go with us to handle the Gargantua."

"Yes, that would be lovely..." She shuddered and clamped her teeth together.

Solomon tucked the blanket around her and kissed her damp temple, then slipped quietly out the door.

The children enjoyed their afternoon; they were completely comfortable with him now, calling him over to see this frog or that mushroom. Seymour caught a fish just big enough to provide a bite for each of them, but he proudly presented it to Calista to fry for supper. Since Jennette wasn't in the kitchen, the children ran upstairs, Solomon behind them, to tell her about the expedition. But all three of them halted in the doorway at the sound of Jennette moaning and the sight of her tossing her head with the headache and fever.

Solomon started in alarm but used firm hands and a soothing tone to direct the children downstairs before he approached the bed. Nettie was mewling with hunger, winding up to cry in earnest, but Jennette was not in any condition to feed her. He picked up his baby daughter and tucked her up against his shoulder. *Calista will know what to feed her—a little watered-down milk from the cow, perhaps?*

With his free hand he moistened the cloth Calista had left with a bowl of water on the floor by the bed and then cooled his wife's brow with it, shifting the baby into the crook of his arm and giving her his pinkie to suck. He looked around—what else could he do to help? Getting the baby fed was probably most needed, so with a backward glance at Jennette he stepped into the hall and hurried down the stairs.

* * *

Solomon came awake in the pre-dawn dimness of their room and stared at the ceiling. As his mind went over all that Jennette had suffered in the past few days, he was relieved at her stillness beside him now. Could the fever have passed? He blinked as he came out of that contemplation, then curved his body around her back and put his hand to her brow, which was damp but cool. A wash of relief.

"Jennette?" He whispered her name, not wanting to disturb her if she was sleeping but hoping she was waking with the dawn, too. No answer. So he lay still, knees touching the backs of hers, lips against a strand of hair on her pillow, one arm atop the quilt at her elbow.

Peace at last, a quieting of his fears.

As Jennette had struggled with the ague—sweat standing in great drops on her white brow when she wasn't shivering with chills, cheeks flaming unnaturally—fear had clutched at his throat. So had the ragged prisoners writhed—in the stinking mud of Georgia, scraps of blankets twisted in puddles of watery vomit, and worse, beneath them. They'd lain in a semblance of quarantine at the edge of the camp, while Jennette had her mother's and sister's care to keep her clean and feed her spoonfuls of tea so she had still a bit of milk for baby Nettie.

When the soldiers at last lay still after their struggle, it was sometimes the peace of illness paused, of recovery, the shadow of death having passed them over in its harvest of souls. More often, though, they were the harvest, souls snatched out of bodies that lay as if dropped from a height, limbs tangled in postures that couldn't be rest. Only the living rested with composure; the corpses were husks, cast off.

He reached back in his memory to a threshing day when they were courting. Jennette had been twirling about as he'd cast great forkfuls of hay into a wagon, dust flying through the sunlight and mingling with her corn silk hair. She paid no mind to the mess—she could comb it out later and re-plait her hair—she danced to show him what lay in store for him with her: spinning life . . . an engine of mirth and abundance.

Solomon had been terrified of losing Jennette in the chattering fever. It wasn't right that his sunny Jennette should ail so. She'd been at the center of all his longings when he'd lost the ability to remember a better world than Andersonville, and she was God's assurance that he'd heard Sol's prayers in that hell. Prison had been unimaginable, endurable only when stumbled through in a stupor. And now like Job restored, a year after his return, he had a new daughter and new plans.

The baby stirred in her cradle on Jennette's side of the bed—*Calista must have slipped her in there during the night.* The cradle creaked a bit and Nettie grunted and started to fuss, then began winding up to a stronger cry. But Jennette didn't stir. Perhaps she was just that worn out. Solomon spread his hand over her hip and rocked her back and forth a little. But Jennette still didn't stir.

Nettie was crying loudly now, but Jennette remained still upon her side. Solomon paused his rocking when Nettie's crying rose to a panicky, gasping wail. He slid his arm across Jennette's stomach, his fingers catching in her nightgown as they felt for the familiar place between her hip and ribs. But she didn't respond.

He knew. In a faraway place down the road in his mind—an open road blown by harsh winds of doubt and fear, a place far from where he lay with his bride—he knew. Her heart had flickered out from the strain of all she'd suffered with the fever, its rhythm tricked and caught by some failure of life to keep it beating. Her body had stilled and cooled beside him while he slept.

She didn't stare up at mocking stars as had the boys on the battlefield, but toward her beloved babe, with her husband warming her back. Her life had winked out oh so quietly, leaving a whirlwind at the door.

Rampage

IN HIS GRIEF, Solomon didn't fall back into lethargy; instead, he became like a wind-up tin toy. He clattered about with his cane in bursts of animation, hastily gathering crops, bruising them with his vigor. He exhausted the children with long treks around the lake on "adventures" and kept them up too long at night as he told stories Jennette would have told them, exhorting them to remember their mama. Callie began retreating to the kitchen with Calista and baby Nettie, but Sy was swept up in his papa's newfound energy, and the "menfolk" would slip away to Daniel's farm for some shooting practice whenever they could.

One storm-threatening August day, after they'd finished the last touches on a dogcart in the barn, Solomon told Sy to find Callie—"Shh, now. Don't let Mama Calla know!"—and then stole into the house to fetch sleeping Nettie from her cradle while Calista was out back rescuing the wash from the coming rain.

Callie held her baby sister in her lap in the bed of the cart while father and son hitched up the whining, excited old Puck between the shafts. Then they pulled out of the barn and into gentle rain. Nettie immediately stirred with a gasp at the shower, and Callie's eyes went wide as her hair plastered down around her skull.

Solomon turned back to the girls, calling, "Never mind the rain, little ones! We're on an adventure!"

The entourage rumbled crazily around the farmyard, Sy whooping with glee as they urged on the dog, until Solomon looked back again and suddenly stopped in his tracks and grabbed Puck's harness. The baby was rolling around in the cart and Callie was running up to the house in a great fright, calling "Mama Calla!"

What am I doing? Panic washed over Solomon as he came to himself but could not move.

Calista ran from the house and snatched up Nettie, then stood there in the rain, glaring at Solomon. Sy was suddenly sobered, too, and patted Puck's head, rain pouring off them both.

Solomon just dropped his head and walked away, and behind him Calista gave instructions to Sy to release the dog while she saw to the girls.

After that, even Sy was wary of Solomon, and when Sy refused to go along on a fishing trip, even with promises of putting the Gargantua in the water, Solomon lost his temper and shouted at him. Solomon grinned too broadly now—almost grimacing sometimes—and shrugged off Calista's soothing words as well as her rebukes.

During a week of moonlit nights in September, he started taking to the woods after dark, returning only after many hours and dozing on the porch until Andrew woke him shortly after dawn.

"Son," began his father-in-law as he handed him a cup of peppermint tea on the porch one foggy and otherworldly morning, "we're winding down the harvest here soon, and we have Daniel to help in the spring. My farming days are coming to an end. It's time you consider returning to your own place and think about what your future will be—"

"No!" Solomon said angrily, sloshing the hot tea in his cup. "I can see much that can be done about this place—the children would enjoy some goats, and they'll need barn space."

Andrew shook his head. "I'm not venturing into goats at this late date."

"In any case, I'm done with Orange," Solomon declared. "I've determined to sell up. Nothing for me there."

"What will you do, then?"

"Haven't settled on that yet." Solomon stood up with a groan and set the untouched cup on the bench where he'd been sitting. "I just want to be shut of one thing first, get that old farm off my mind. I need a fresh start."

* * *

A few weeks later Solomon returned from Orange, having made arrangements to sell the farm there, and spent long evenings in the kitchen scratching out calculations he discussed with no one.

One morning he snorted awake at the ringing thud of the stove door. Calista was in the kitchen starting the morning chores, and he raised his head from his folded arms on the table. He looked at her groggily, blinking bleary eyes, then gathered his papers together.

"What are you doing there?" she asked, nodding at the papers as she readied some things for a trip to the pump outside.

"Never you mind." He folded the sheaf in two and tucked it inside his shirt, then put the pencil over his ear.

"The Fallas family over by King's have some big plans—"

"No," he said abruptly. "That's not for me."

"Another farm . . .?"

"No!" He warded off the idea with his forearm as he stood and scraped the chair back. "I'm heading for Lowell. I mean to clear my head a while as I consider my prospects. I trust you'll care for them . . ."

"You know the children will be well here as you get settled. It's their home, after all."

"I'm no good for them in any case," he said and went to the doorway, done discussing it. "They're shy of me now, and better off without me."

Calista squared off before him, hands on her hips, cheeks flaming below blazing eyes. "I don't know *what* you mean to do, but Jennette wouldn't have you going on so—"

"Do *not* use her name!"

She didn't cower at his tone. "I have more right to it than you do. I'm the one taking care of her children in your stead." Then she added under her breath, "In spite of you."

Solomon turned his back and left the kitchen. He returned a half hour later when the children were eating porridge at the table under supervision of their grandfather, baby Nettie in the crook of Calista's arm as she offered her a bottle. Solomon leaned his cane and Jennette's old satchel against the wall, then announced, "I'm off, then, and you're likely relieved to be done with me."

The children went silent, their eyes wide and shifting from him to their grandfather. Callie looked over her shoulder at Calista.

"Father Watson, I entrust this to you." Solomon carefully placed a leather folio on the table and tapped it. "While I look out for what to do, I don't want be subject to thieves and swindlers. No, I'll make my living honestly, and eat the bread I earn."

Andrew gestured to the folio and asked, "Your farm?"

"What's left of it," Solomon said. "It'll be safe here. Which is better for the children."

"Will you go to your father, then?" Andrew asked.

"I may start there . . . and I thank you both"—he nodded to Calista and Andrew and then raised his eyes to indicate the floor above, where his mother-in-law was confined to bed—"and Mother Watson, as well. I thank you for caring for these motherless children."

Solomon went to Sy first and briefly laid his hand atop the boy's head, then hovered his hand over Callie's head as she shrank from him. He raised that hand in benediction toward Nettie and Calista and then nodded to his father-in-law. Keeping his eyes downcast, he reached for his things and quickly passed through the front room to the front door and limped down the steps. Puck followed, whining, anxiously circling him, but then—receiving no response—returned to the porch.

* * *

Solomon had established a walking rhythm by the time he left the farm lane, wielding the cane to support his lamed hip and purposefully gathering the shreds of his dignity about him.

The road was lined with frost-rimed stalks left over from the harvest. Magnificent giant hardwoods, now in their autumn glory of gold and russet, towered over the gentle hills. The first of their fallen leaves scattered over the road, leading the way. Before long, those leaves would dry and harden, crumble into the earth and be covered by snow—secretly moldering—their death somehow leaching life into the soil for the coming year.

Laboring up a steep hill, Solomon planted his cane and dragged himself after it, his hip weakening and radiating a sickening pain throughout a body that cried for rest. The sound of hoofbeats and a wagon gave him leave to stand still and look behind him, and there it was—a chance to ride. He set his bag down, drew himself up, and recalled his old gallantry with a smooth doffing of his bowler to his breast, eyes briefly downcast in greeting.

The driver pulled up with a "Whoa, girl!" to the horse. "Saw you from afar, tacklin' this slope." The man inclined his head toward Solomon's cane.

"Yes. And now that I've crested it, I can look forward to the way down."

"Looks like you could use a ride. To Lowell?"

"I'd be obliged," Solomon answered, stepping up to the wagon and putting out his hand. "Sol Ramsdell." He didn't intend to mention the Watsons.

"Bert Talbert. My pa thought he was quite a card to make a play of the name. Albert Talbert—ha!" He shook Solomon's hand and gestured to him to fetch his bag and climb up.

Just two miles of walking and Solomon was too lame to make it any farther. *Doesn't bode well for whatever work I mean to take on.* He eased himself onto the seat, wincing at the strain in his body. He knew he should say something, but he couldn't find words to begin.

"Ramsdell, you said? Don't know that name around here, but then I've been shut up in my shop—I make cane-and-fabric screens that my wife embroiders—and some carved wood screens, too." Talbert nodded over his shoulder at the canvas-covered load.

Solomon nodded back but didn't pick up the conversation. *He's a talker—will keep it up himself, looks like.*

"Baskets and cane seat chairs, that's what's wanted at Kopf's furniture store," Talbert continued. "Since the war, the ladies are lookin' about them for prettier things. And sometimes they don't know they're wantin' a fancier version of a chair, say, until they see one of Mrs. Kopf's— or a fancy screen till they see one of mine."

"Mm-hmm." *Does this fellow have any idea how trivial these things are?* The pity of it all—both the ordinary details of life and the whirlwind—set off a crazed giggle that Solomon barely managed to choke off.

"Before the war," Talbert said, "I used to see the ladies gather at the lakeside in Toledo—that's where I'm from—and watch the boats unload whatever came over from New York. From Europe, even. There we were, just knockin' together a town of rough walls, but the ladies craved the fancies. You know, a bit of lace or a china whatnot."

A slight smile tugged at the corners of Solomon's mouth. *Why not play along?* It could be a way to escape for a moment. "My sister made much of her pinned watch these years past."

"See?" Talbert said, waving a hand. "That's just the sort of thing I mean. That German, Kopf, keeps it well in mind in his store. He's got silver and watches as well as the furniture. And men like their fancies, too—ivory pipes, that cane of yours!"

Solomon curled his hand around the brass top of his cane and recalled the Grand Rapids street where he'd bought it from the peddler, his father and Daniel there, too. He pictured the leaflet about the Sixth Michigan, remembered how he'd stuffed it in his pocket . . . how it had come before his eyes in the lamplight later that night at the boarding house. He squeezed the cane's top and clenched his jaw in a flash of searing regret—*so much lost*. Then his hand went limp.

He must say something more to his host. "Yes, I . . . I got this before the war. Didn't know I'd need it so soon."

"Injured, then?"

Solomon nodded. "Prison camp."

Talbert gave a long, low whistle. "I managed to trudge through it all and then trudge back home—kept my head down. But now I've got my head up, lookin' about—and that's how I got to learnin' the cane trade and makin' my own designs for the screens. I'm good with my hands."

"So you're selling your screens in Lowell, then? I might have seen one once—"

"Yep, a screen can hide the fireplace in summer, or give a bit of privacy when a traveler has a pallet on the floor. I worked up one with little shelves that pull down on either side, to hold a dish of flowers or a whatnot. I have an arrangement with Kopf at the furniture store. 'Fine goods for finer tastes,' that's his motto. He's just bought the Cogswell sawmill and has some grand plans he's told me about."

"Sawmill, you say?" asked Solomon. "I've done my turn with lumber, spent years clearing our places in Orange."

"You farm in Orange, then, by Ionia?"

"Not anymore. Just sold my place. I'm looking for another prospect. My father has a saddlery . . ." Solomon looked away from Talbert and gazed at the trees they were passing—so many trees, the woods dense and black just behind the first few rows.

"With things settlin' out after the war, there's prospects more forward-lookin' than saddles," Talbert said. "Kopf is buildin' a new place. All the fancy goods on the first floor where the windows look in from the street, and the lumber comin' in from his sawmill at the back to be finished right there. Lesser goods, parlor furniture and such, will go on the second floor. And upstairs on the third, the undertaker's—"

"He's an undertaker, too?"

"Best line of work for a fancy cabinetmaker, don't ya think? Always business!" Talbert laughed and shook the reins to speed up his horse. "I've a mind to keep up with his plans. He's already found the means—that sawmill was twelve thousand dollars, they say! Kopf is always talkin' about how the river and train will bring in both trade and materials—and take them away." He waved his hand to indicate the trees around them. "That, my friend, means prosperity. And prosperity means more customers for his fancy stuff."

They rumbled out of the woods into a stretch with cleared fields on either side. Solomon recognized Vergennes, Myron King's place. *There already.* He hoped none of the Kings would see him passing by.

"Would you be willing to introduce me to this Kopf?" Solomon asked.

"John Kopf—though he says it was 'Yo-hannus' when he got here from Germany—and I'd be pleased to. Will you be stayin' past today? I'd be glad to give you a ride back when I finish my business."

"No, thanks, I plan to stay. I'll put up at the Franklin House. Arza King, the owner, is brother to an old neighbor of mine—we just passed *his* place." Solomon might seek work from his father, but not lodging. No sense bothering him. Or suffering his opinions just now.

"From what I've heard of the Kings"—Talbert nodded back to the farm they'd just passed—"they're a family of quality, and good luck." He aimed a wink at Solomon. "It's a beautiful farm. What's *this* brother's name, then?"

"Myron, Myron King."

"I hear Arza made out good on his investments through the war."

"Maybe so," Solomon murmured, distracted.

"I'll leave this load at Kopf's," Talbert said, "and pick up more screen frames to work up this winter. I can't wait to try out some new designs, workin' a picture into the weave." He took the reins in one hand and traced a sweeping S-curve in the air—"A swan, I'm thinkin', on a pond, with cattails on either side." He splayed his fingers out as he gestured right and left.

"Mm-hmm."

"Chinese-looking, in a way . . . the ladies like that."

* * *

Talbert dropped him off at Franklin House, promising to introduce him to John Kopf once Solomon got situated and walked over to the furniture store. When he stepped into the hotel lobby, Solomon looked around in admiration at the gleaming wood and thick draperies, at the glass-fronted cabinets showcasing leather-bound volumes, exotic taxidermy birds, and bright porcelain flowers. A slim young woman in a striped satin dress closed an ornately-carved piano, then whisked herself up the curved staircase. This was too sumptuous a place for him to stay many days, but he figured he could trade off the old family connection for an extra night or two.

Solomon rang the bell at the counter, and a paneled door opened. A clerk in a vest and shirtsleeves came out from his office, spectacles pulled down his nose.

"May I help you, sir?" he asked.

"Yes, I'd like a room—a simple one—for two nights," Solomon said, then signed the book and handed over his satchel to a boy in a bright red jacket—vaguely military— who appeared at his elbow. *Wonder if King is about . . .*

Solomon looked around the elegant lobby again as his belongings went up the stairs with the boy. Had it really been only a decade since he'd spent the evening playing his violin at the much simpler hotel in Lyons? So much had happened in that decade! Rosette had married, Solomon had built his house and brought . . . *No.* He drew himself up with a deep breath and followed the boy up the stairs.

* * *

"So, Mr. Rahms-dell," John Kopf announced in his rich, clipped German accent, shaking Solomon's hand heartily, "I would gladly welcome you to my enterprise. I mean to move much of the furniture manufacture from the sawmill to the new building, and as I have worked with your father on some things—he upholstered some pieces for me in fine saddle leather—I have no need of further references for you."

"I'm obliged, Mr. Kopf," Solomon replied, releasing the man's hand. John was a little older than himself and heartier, from not having suffered the war. It seemed a lifetime since Solomon had done business like this. He had quietly recommended himself with a tally of his lumbering, milling, and house-building experience in Orange and made a point of admiring the Windsor chairs Talbert had told him Kopf was known for, and the cane seat chairs, too.

"Yes, my Mary is clever with her hands, when she has time away from the little ones," Kopf said. "Do you have a family?"

Solomon darted his eyes away and cleared his throat. "I . . . I have two daughters and a son. But I recently lost my wife."

"Oh, I am so sorry to hear that—and regret having spoken of it. You have not so long ago lost your mother as well, I recall."

"Yes, last winter." *So very long ago.* He sought to change the subject. "I believe I met Mrs. Kopf at the house that day. She helped to nurse my mother in her sudden illness."

"No doubt she did, but I do not recall," Kopf said with an embarrassed shake of his head. "She is always to be found at the bedside of the ailing, or about the household during a bereavement."

"Her care was much appreciated, I can assure you," Solomon said. How easily he could make polite conversation and do business, when he must.

As he walked back to Franklin House, Solomon reasoned that, having just been hired at Kopf's, he no longer had any need to go to the saddlery. *I can spare myself Father's judgment. Have a new start.*

Just getting his hands on some wood at Kopf's, turning a lathe, straining his muscles at the saw—that would be a balm to his heart. Or at least allow it to scar.

RESOLUTION
FALL 1866

$$\rule{3in}{1pt}$$

Concentration

His first evening in Franklin House, Solomon put on a more gentlemanly persona to mix with the hotel visitors and enjoyed a white-tablecloth dinner while figuring in his head how far his funds would go. Only a little over a year before, he'd held back from Jennette part of his mustering-out pay, waiting until he could surprise her with just the right gift. Now he was spending those coins on himself, alone in a fancy hotel, sharing a meal with strangers. Most every meal of his life had been in the company of family or neighbors—except during the war.

As the men stood up from the dining table to gather in one corner of the lobby, the few women glided over to the piano. The young lady he'd seen earlier sat down and began to play—a simple sonata with no hesitations. *Not bad,* Solomon thought idly, then she caught his attention with the next piece, the more difficult *Moonlight Sonata,* with clever ornaments. *She knows the instrument!* He excused himself from the men's conversation and wandered over to the piano. It was a pleasure to hear a piece played that well.

Then the music was done and the young lady was in conversation with another lady. Solomon found his way back to the men, who were speaking of the business they hoped would be coming to Lowell and the swelling prospects they envisioned and planned to finance themselves.

By the end of the next day, Solomon was covered in sawdust and soaked with sweat, no longer fit for such polite company. He took his meal in his room and determined to board in town, closer to the furniture factory, as soon as he could find a place, especially since Arza King seemed to be away and Solomon couldn't ask for a discount on the room.

John Kopf had introduced him right away to the stages of constructing Windsor chairs—an English craft—and explained that he had lured two New England artisans to his new factory, where he intended to set up large-scale production of the fine specimens that had traditionally been completed one at a time. According to Kopf, Solomon's experience with military order and his civic efforts to build roads and homes in Orange, shifting from logging to transport to milling to building, made him just the man to organize these temperamental craftsmen into producing with more efficiency, and more profit.

"I have an eye for a good man, Mr. Ramsdell, and I find it fortuitous that you have arrived just as I need an intermediary for these two. They need delicate oversight."

Even in that first week, Solomon found a place in his being that could respond to useful work; turning his mind to the task at hand, he could close off the rooms in his memory that held such wrenching pain, such darkness. The men he worked with knew him only by the words and actions he presented to them, and there was simple satisfaction in that. George Porter and William Campbell had different ideas about what constituted the best way to produce Windsor chairs, Porter specializing in the newer compact bow-back and Campbell in the grander armchair design. Solomon had seen right away that flattering each in his specialty was wise, and that the common preparatory activities could be accomplished by other workers. For the time being, though, he cultivated each man's crotchets and carried out each one's bidding, scurrying around to learn the fine points of how their work differed.

So far, this life suited him. Each morning he entered the workshop to confront new problems: How should they transport the four different hardwoods Porter and Campbell had agreed were acceptable? Were there other varieties that might be worth experimenting with? The craftsmen required freshly cut logs from which to fashion the sleekly curving or smoothly straight components of their chairs, but there was no reason the bark couldn't be removed and the lengths rough-split at the sawmill before being delivered to the workshop, providing the craftsmen with clean materials and generating less waste. In service to their art and to Kopf's economies, Solomon disappeared behind the work.

And at the end of each day, he'd return to a tiny house two blocks away, bringing back the dinner pail old Mrs. Montague prepared for him each morning as he ate his porridge. He was the only boarder, and Mrs. Montague very timid. She shied from his first efforts at conversation and he found that just as well. She didn't eat supper herself but left a plate for him on the kitchen table, and each evening he lifted the clean, embroidered cloth, creased from ironing and folding, to reveal the plain but wholesome supper she judged adequate for his needs. It was.

He and Mrs. Montague exchanged a few practical, pleasant words each morning. He'd ask if he could split more wood for her—if a new load had been delivered to the back porch—or he'd offer to make a repair, like patching the spot in the roof that was no doubt the source of the growing stain on the ceiling at the top of the staircase.

Bright spots bloomed on her cheeks when they spoke, probably the only words she shared with anyone most days, and he felt he was doing her a kindness to speak with her. Her shyness kept him subdued as well, and the quiet of the little house held him tight, containing the swirling storms that had so frenzied him back at the Watsons' last summer. Whenever the memories sneaked up to twine around his temples, he would shake them out of his head.

* * *

One day in early November, two weeks after he'd come to town with Bert Talbert, a still presence drew Solomon's attention as he prepared to enter the workshop. His father was standing before him, his top hat magnifying his height.

"Solomon! What are you doing here?" Jacob asked, his brow furrowing. "Daniel was in town a few weeks ago and said—"

"Oh! Father, how are you?" Solomon switched the dinner pail to his left hand and extended his right. *What might Daniel have said? Must make the best of it.*

His father faltered at the question. "I . . . well, I wonder how *you* are . . . Where are the children? What—?"

Solomon flushed, but attempted to rescue himself with a firm stance and a bold reply. "They're at Watsons', in good care. I thought it best to remove myself for now . . . To look out for a new enterprise." Solomon looked levelly at his father.

"Rosette wrote last month that you'd sold the farm," Jacob said. "Calista had written her, I believe. Are you looking for another in this area? King would know what's available, or his neighbor Morgan Lyon. It wouldn't be hard to get into fruit production—have you seen his evaporation works?"

"No, Father." *No need to say more about that.* "I'm setting up John Kopf's new workshop here, for Windsor chairs. He has in mind making them more profitable with faster production." *Father should appreciate that.*

"He certainly is one for experimentation. We've worked together on some leather pieces."

"Yes, he told me that when we met. Your reputation secured me the position, so I thank you for that." The top hat indicated that his father was there for some official occasion. *I'll likely never have call for such a thing—my bowler will do.*

"Your own work should recommend you," Jacob said gallantly. "I'm sure he knows that by now. Would you like to come to the house for supper tomorrow? Ellen is with us and would be glad to see you."

"Why is Ellen with you? What about Charles?"

Jacob shook his head sadly. "Her husband has put her away, it seems—just the sort of calamity your mother feared. Frank is still at home, of course, always in the books as you used to be, and Jerome is working as a tinner in Grand Rapids—"

"Very well, Father," Solomon said. "I'll join you. Now I must be on with my day." He raised his dinner pail and continued in to Kopf's.

* * *

That evening after supper, Solomon decided that, rather than climbing to his cramped room huddled at the top of the stairs to run his eyes across the book he'd borrowed from Kopf—his routine of rest and inattention—he would go for a walk. He was restless, and the pain in his hip had improved lately. He looked out the tiny window, wiping away the fog of his breath, and saw the moon bright upon the few inches of snow that had fallen the previous night.

The afternoon's drizzle and freeze had glazed an icy sheen across the landscape.

Solomon pulled his outdoor clothes from the peg at the bottom of the stairs and put them back on, then picked up the rough walking stick he'd fashioned at Kopf's—a little shorter than his fine cane, to better bear the weight of his limping pace. He quietly let himself out, not wanting to disturb Mrs. Montague but expecting she would hear him anyway and watch from the upstairs window. He set off toward the river, looking for a path not churned up by horses or wagons or foot traffic. He settled on a stretch between the railroad track and the river and set his eyes on a bend a half mile away where the moon seemed cradled just between two stands of trees, its gleam cast across the snow. His booted feet crunched solidly through the inch or two of crust to the firm ground below, his stick planting beside him to leave a track, as if a tiny toad had leapt from spot to spot. *Callie would like that.*

Sy would have run ahead and doubled back, breaking a stick from a tree and dragging it across the railroad ties or finding some odd bit of iron bar to make the rail sing. But the children were surely tucked up in bed by now, sleeping at peace in the calm of their grandparents' home, Calista near at hand, an echo of their mother to comfort them.

I can't bear to see again the fear that I brought—even to Sy's face! Solomon drew his arm across his own suddenly flushed face, hot and damp despite the chill. A hollow place opened up inside him as he trudged on; he felt like some tin soldier with the wind whistling about and through him.

However, there was solace here. He could do more for the children by sending them money, and Calista would know better how to spend it. He could shop for them in the Lowell stores—how delighted Callie would be swinging about in a hooded cape like he'd seen one of the Kopf girls wearing.

A little cheered by the thought, Solomon relished the numbness creeping up and in from his toes and fingers and face. He labored along with the stick, his efforts keeping him warm, until he reached the half-mile point—the bend in the rail along the river—where he found that he was more or less moving with ease and was ready to head back. As he retraced his steps, making a matching toad-hop track along the other side of his path, the moon that had been shining before him now cast his shadow ahead of him.

His bowels hadn't pained him so much these weeks in town, and he'd hardly noticed the change. Perhaps he was finally healing. He was still doing purposeful work directed by someone else, but he had chosen it. It wasn't just expected of him. *The Watsons were always watching me, each pair of eyes bearing questions for me every day. It's a relief to be away from there.*

Just as he thought that, he came to the house and looked up. Mrs. Montague's window was dark—no waver of a candle behind the gauze curtain. Solomon sighed. Tomorrow he must face his father and give account of himself.

* * *

Solomon climbed up the steps on the side of the Ramsdell house, knocked on the kitchen door, and waited.

Ellen opened the door. "Sol! Father told me you were coming! But why knock?"

"It's been so long, it didn't feel right."

"Well, come in and get out of your outdoor things . . . " She stepped back and he came into the kitchen and took off his hat and coat. "Still can't believe Jennette is gone," she murmured after taking his coat, absently stroking the soft wool.

"Much has changed," he said. "And for you as well, I understand?" He searched her face.

"Well," she said with forced lightness, "I suppose Rosette and I both have known disappointments in our marriages." She smiled bravely but blinked away tears.

Just then, their father and Frank banged through the front door, so Ellen turned back to the supper preparations and Solomon went to greet them.

The table was uncomfortably altered without his mother, without Jennette, and with the addition of Ellen, who shouldn't have been there. Solomon hardly recognized his family in this new form. Each person tried to raise a topic of conversation, but none seemed to have the will to see it through. The meal complete at last, Ellen escaped to the kitchen and Frank got up, too, saying something about meeting a friend.

Jacob followed their retreat with his gaze, shaking his head, then turned to Solomon. "So we expect Charles Lewis to complete the divorce soon."

"Is there no hope for it?" Solomon asked.

His father sighed. "Like her sister, Ellen was determined to follow her heart . . . But speaking of doing better, would you care to explain your plan here in Lowell—with your family left behind?"

"It's not what you think, Father," Solomon said. He'd been expecting such a question, and he went on to explain his part in Kopf's business and repeated the speculations he'd heard at Franklin House from men of business.

"Be that as it may, son, you are not in the position of a single man. Unlike Jerome setting off for Grand Rapids, or Frank applying himself to the law, you have duties."

"I have *done* my duty, Father—given all for my country, and had the only thing left to me taken away, too."

"I know your grief—" Jacob began.

"No, you do NOT!" Solomon slapped his hands on the table and knocked over the chair as he stood up. "You do *not* know the loss of your partner before you've even begun. You and Mother had *decades* together, and even when I came back from the war, I was not myself for Jennette. I had only a few short months—"

"And now, son," Jacob said quietly, "you must rally yourself for the next duty."

"Don't tell me of my duty . . ." Solomon leaned toward his father, clenched fists bracing his stiff arms on the table. "I have given Lincoln's 'last full measure' and have nothing left. You have not known what I have known, and you have *no right* to instruct me in this."

With that, Solomon lurched out of the dining room, leaving his father sitting alone at the table. He grabbed his coat and hat from the pegs in the kitchen, raised a quick hand to bid his sister goodbye, and—insensible to the cold—returned to Mrs. Montague's.

Thanksgiving

SOLOMON WRAPPED UP some German sausages and some cookies that John and Mary Kopf had given him for his family. Bert Talbert was going to be at Kopf's tomorrow, the Tuesday before Thanksgiving, and might agree to detour on his way home to deliver a parcel to the Watsons. He'd enjoyed chatting with Bert on his occasional trips to the shop, and Solomon was glad now to call him a friend.

* * *

"You'll be going back for Thanksgiving, of course," Mary Kopf had said, holding out a cleverly fashioned cane basket with two handles. She was a pretty woman, happily in control of the three children who came with her to the shop.

"Well, no, ma'am," Solomon answered. "Mrs. Montague, the woman I board with, is taking the train to visit her sister's family, and I agreed to keep watch on the house for her for a few days. So I'll be here."

She frowned. "That seems a shame. Will you be taking the feast with your father, then?"

"No, I haven't spoken with him recently." Solomon felt a bitter tang in his mouth. Frank had stopped by the workshop last week to talk about smoothing things over with their father, and Solomon's coldness had provoked some biting words from his brother.

Best to keep all of that at arm's length.

"Well," she asked, "would you be willing to join us? We have plenty of room at the table. John made it to accommodate all the children he expects us to have!"

"I . . . I don't know. I was planning to work on the rocking horse I'm making for the children."

"Oh, that's so delightful! John told me of your plans. You should work up a herd of them for the store."

"It's just something simple, for Christmas."

"Surely you could spare an hour or two for us," she said, pressing. "I expect Mrs. Montague is not leaving you a feast for when she's away."

"Perhaps an hour, then," he replied. It was important to keep up good relations—and he would have most of the day to himself, after all.

* * *

With the parcel paper lying flat on his bed, and the basket-tray in the center ready to be done up with string, Solomon took up a pencil he'd borrowed from Mrs. Montague and wrote a note on another sheet of paper. *Best keep it quick and short,* he thought.

> Dear Children,
>
> I'm sending these things from the family who have hired me in a shop where they make chairs

and other furniture. Mr. Kopf is from Germany and these sausages are a specialty there. I've had some myself and think they'd go well with apple pie, so you should ask Mama Calla to make some. The little cookies are called a German name that sounds like "feffer-noose." Mrs. Kopf makes them, though she's of English heritage.

What to write next? Exhortations to care for one another? No, he didn't have the right. Nor to tell them of the duties of giving thanks. *Watson will see to that.*

Instead he simply added a signature line:

Your Father

Solomon folded the paper and tucked it into the basket-tray, then did up the parcel with string. He set it on the tiny table in his room, to take to the shop the following morning.

* * *

"But why do ya need to send by way of me?" Bert asked, contemplating the parcel in his hand, one foot up on the wagon board. "Won't your little ones be wantin' to see their pa?"

"I have just the one day, and they're with"—Solomon cleared his throat—"with my late wife's family."

Bert cocked his head to one side and squinted at him until Solomon, feeling guilty, finally looked away. "Are you not welcome with the folks, then?" Bert asked. "Did they send you packin' that day I found you on the road?"

"No, nothing like that. They're good people." Solomon gestured up the road to Cannon, changing the subject. "Now, when you get to a half mile past where you picked me up on that hill . . ."

* * *

On Thanksgiving morning, Solomon got up as if he were going to work and went to the shop, letting himself in. All was deserted, as everyone had the day off, and he started the wood stove to take the chill from the air. From a shelf reserved for the wood he'd been gathering, he selected some pieces and took them and his pattern to the workbench. It would be a simple rocking horse, but with rockers fashioned with the bentwood technique he'd learned from George Porter, two "U" shapes with the arms cane-bound together for sturdy rocking and crossbars on front and back for an additional child to stand on. He'd finished those a week earlier. The horse would be big enough for Sy for a year or two more, but then he'd outgrow it. *He can help his little sisters ride.*

He sawed and planed and sanded, frequently checking his pattern and testing the extent of the rocking. He found that his original design pitched the horse too far forward on the rockers, but he needed to be careful not pitch it too far backward, either, lest Callie be frightened. He felt a pang in his chest as he recalled her face the day of the dogcart debacle. The horse must rock gently.

Determined to make the toy the best he could, he wrapped a scrap piece of leather around some muslin he'd stuffed with sawdust. The whole thing would wrap around the wooden form of the horse's back, fastened with fine brass tacks to form a comfortable seat. He would fashion the mane and tail from long strips of leather, and the rest of the features he could paint on.

But all that would come later. It was time to go to the Kopfs'.

* * *

One of the Kopf boys opened the door, letting out a gust of warmth and the tantalizing scents of meat and spices. Solomon was standing on the porch with the bare wood rocking horse under his arm when John Kopf came up behind his son and welcomed Solomon in.

"I do not know if we have food for the horse, Solomon," said John heartily through his thick German accent, relieving him of the horse and ushering him inside. "But perhaps Mary can find a bit of hay . . ."

"No need," Solomon answered in the same spirit, unwinding his scarf and removing his coat and handing them to the boy who had opened the door. "I brought it only for a riding trial. I expect you have enough different models of children to test its suitability for each."

His host led him into the front room and offered him a chair. "Now that you are here in our home, please call me John. Mary should be calling us to the table soon—our work of the morning has been to keep out of her way."

While they were speaking, two smaller children had gathered and were jumping up and down with excitement at the rocking horse.

"Now, this is not for you to keep," their father warned gently. "Mr. Ramsdell is making this for his own kinder."

Solomon helped the daughter settle herself on the board that would hold the seat and placed her hands on the ends of the rod that passed through the horse's head. She began to rock, sliding back and forth a little on the sanded board.

As Solomon watched her operate the horse, he was pleased that it rocked neither too far forward nor too far back. "With the leather seat it will be easier for the rider to stay in one place," he said, "but this is a good size."

He turned to the older boy, who looked about nine. "Young sir. Would you try as well?"

The boy seemed reluctant, as if it were beneath his dignity to ride a rocking horse.

"Is Martin the size of your boy, then?" John asked.

"Sy's big for his age—nearly eight."

"Well, he will need to teach his sisters how to ride it, in any case," John said. "Go ahead, Martin. You see how it is."

The boy relented and gamely straddled the horse, then rocked it a bit manically before standing up again, to show he hadn't enjoyed it much. His little brother clambered on right behind him and rocked wildly himself, a smaller version of Martin.

During the meal Mary plied Solomon with all manner of German specialties she said she had learned from John's mother. He was relieved that there wasn't much that reminded him of his own family feasts—especially Christmas. Lincoln had only recently proclaimed that the last Thursday in November be a celebration of Thanksgiving—in the midst of the war—but the Watsons had made much of it last year when Solomon was slowly healing and Jennette first showing with the babe that would be Nettie.

No! Don't think about that! Solomon gripped his knife and fork to steel himself and returned to the present.

John carved an enormous pork roast, and Mary served it with sauerkraut and apples, and for dessert there were cookies like the ones he had sent to the children two days earlier. Sitting at this large table surrounded by people he didn't know well, eating foods that didn't dig at his memories, was a pleasure he could enjoy for its own sake. He ate heartily and even entertained the Kopfs with a few funny stories of his own.

When they stood up from the table, he found himself looking around for a piano, even—unaccountably—for his violin. But the Kopfs were not a musical family, and instead they went to the parlor to play charades. It soon became evident to Solomon that little children must be enjoyed on their own terms, not as successful partners in a game.

After an hour of these amusements, Solomon felt it was time to go, so he began thanking everyone for their hospitality and rose. The family escorted him to the door.

"Solomon, I believe you have earned the title of 'Uncle' in our family today," Mary said warmly as she held out his coat and hat and cane for him—he'd brought the good one today. "The children don't have close relatives here—John's are all still in Germany, and mine in New York."

"My people are from New York, too," Solomon said, then stopped. *Don't want to dig at that just now.* He smiled at the Kopfs as he donned his coat and jammed his bowler onto his head. Then John handed him the rocking horse, which he tucked under his arm before taking his cane from Mary. He went down the steps lit by the setting sun and along the snowy road to the workshop, to store the horse until he could work on it another day.

Interlude

As the cold clamped down in early December, snow on the ground, Solomon realized he hadn't packed enough warm clothing to see him into deep winter. Unused to buying clothes since the Ramsdell women had always provided his, he purchased a rough wool scarf at the mercantile; it felt like burlap against his skin but shielded his breath, the warmth held in by the brim of his bowler.

The work at Kopf's was going well, and Solomon was well paid and thriving, glad for the opportunity to be a part of making something tangible and beautiful and useful. Even though each chair they produced had the generous embracing arms of Campbell's design or the spare elegance of Porter's, and bore the burned-in brand of Kopf Furniture under the seat, each one also had something of Solomon's craft in it—a stain or an angle of the legs. For a while this was enough, but as the days passed, he found himself longing for something of his own—a little something more.

In the dark of an early evening, Solomon took a longer way back to Mrs. Montague's, enjoying the cozy sight of lanterns in house windows and the warm smells of supper—wood smoke, ham, cabbage, some deeply spicy stew from an unfamiliar part of Europe. From the second floor of one house, a harmonica sent plaintive chords out into the icy air, where they hung, suspended. Solomon looked up and wondered who was the source of the sound: maybe some boy whose family shooed him and his noise up and away from the din of the kitchen, or maybe a grandfather who sought solitude to remember old jigs and love songs . . .

As he rounded a corner, he heard the clatter of dishes as tables were cleared at Franklin House and spied men through the lobby windows, gathering for smoking and conversation. Then the piano clashed insistently with the opening chords of a march, stilling the chatter, the music then spinning into playful arpeggios that invited women's giggles. A couple of men men drifted over to the piano at the longing strains of "Tenting on the Old Campground."

Just outside, on the carefully swept wooden walk, Solomon stepped closer and watched from the dark, invisible to those in the brightness, stamping his feet and beating his arms against himself to stay warm, hitching the scratchy scarf up around his ears. It was the young lady at the piano again, in a white dress—likely a King relation. She looked around at her audience and then launched into another tune, the exuberant "When Johnny Comes Marching Home." One man twirled a woman once, but the rest of the hotel guests seemed reluctant to dance, the gathering too stiff for such frivolities. Solomon's fingers itched to add a violin line and swing the dancers around with his bow.

The pianist took the measure of the room and subdued her playing, switching to some idle melody that stayed in the background as the guests took up their conversation again—and when her head bowed over the keyboard, Solomon, too, knew the moment had passed. He huddled into his coat and scarf and stamped a bit before leaning on his cane and heading back for a cold supper and a book in his room.

The next evening, he lingered after work again and then wended his way home via Franklin House. He saw through the windows that there were fewer people than there had been the night before. Thin, quiet melodies scattered pleasant notes around the lobby and wafted up to the ceiling. With a boisterous story from one of the men, the music was drowned out altogether, and the girl quietly closed the piano and went upstairs. *She needs an audience,* Solomon thought. *Too bad she doesn't know I'm out here.*

At breakfast the next morning, a Saturday, Solomon told Mrs. Montague he would be taking supper elsewhere and would not need her to cook for him. She nodded with resignation.

"I'm appreciative of your care for me," he assured her. "I have another plan for this evening—that's all."

She added a thin smile to her nod, then disappeared up the stairs.

Solomon took with him to work that day a folded, clean shirt that he tucked into his jacket, and he chose his good cane and brushed off his bowler. After the others left the workshop late that afternoon, eager for their Saturday night revels and Sunday rest, he washed up and put on the clean shirt, then slicked back his hair with wet hands as he peered into the glass of a curio cabinet in the workshop.

He made his way to Franklin House and, just outside, looked down and noticed his dirty boots. He swept the sawdust away with one end of his coarse scarf and then drew himself up, shoulders back, ready to go through the doors into the warm, bright hotel.

Several people were already gathered at the tables covered with white cloths. Solomon was shown to a place across the table from Arza King and his wife; the pianist was on King's left.

"Welcome, sir," King said, half-standing and extending his hand. "I believe you're a Ramsdell—am I right?"

Solomon took his hand and shook it. "Yes, sir. Solomon."

"Glad to have you with us at Franklin House. Mrs. King"—he inclined his head toward his wife—"you remember Solomon Ramsdell, son of Jacob, neighbor to Myron when he was in Orange?"

"Yes, of course," she answered, extending her hand so Solomon could grasp her fingers from across the table.

"And this is my young cousin, Lillianne Baker." King indicated the pianist, who nodded but kept her hands in her lap.

"Miss Baker," Solomon said, "I enjoyed your playing when I stayed here earlier this fall."

She smiled up at him with pleasure, and King said, "Oh, that must have been when we were away, seeing to some business in Detroit. Will you be staying with us tonight, then? Are you here from Orange?"

"No, I've been here in town working for John Kopf, with his chair manufacturing. I recently sold the place in Orange."

"We were sorry to hear of the loss of your wife, Mr. Ramsdell," offered Mrs. King, "and so soon after your mother. Such a blow."

"Yes, it was."

Solomon politely answered inquiries about the children and then fell quiet as the Kings turned their attention to a couple sitting beyond the empty chair beside him. He welcomed the heartier portions and richer fare than Mrs. Montague provided, surprising himself with his eagerness to tuck into a thick slice of beef; he was buttering his third piece of bread when he came to himself, aware of Miss Baker's eyes upon him. Embarrassed, he looked up.

"Pardon me, miss. I'd forgotten where I was. I've grown accustomed to dining alone these weeks."

"There's no need for pardon. You seem to be enjoying your supper so . . ." Her blue eyes slanted upward as she smiled.

Charming, he thought. Hair sleek and light as *hers* . . . No pang this time, but something inside him chimed softly at the touch of familiarity, like a bell.

He cleared his throat. "What brings you to Lowell, Miss Baker?"

"Cousin Arza is teaching me the hotel trade, so that I might manage a place for my father—an investment."

"Most young ladies I know set up as teachers," Solomon said. "My sister, for one. Well, it's actually a family business in a way, for my father was a teacher, too, and then I married a young teacher who came to Orange after my sister got married."

"I'm sorry about your loss—what was her name?"

"Jennette." *How long since I've spoken that name?* The bell within him sounded deep and full, summoning her back to his mind. *Jennette! You've been so far from me, all these frenzied months . . . I felt only a void, and I needed to escape it.*

Now he saw her standing there, in his mind's eye—as always, in command of the room. The mirage Jennette gave a simple nod, which stroked the bell as he'd once seen a percussionist stroke a cymbal, or boil up a distant thunderstorm from a timpani.

He shook his head to rouse himself from the vision, and he took a sip of water. "Excuse me, Miss Baker. What was that you said?"

"I asked what sort of person she was."

"The best sort," he replied. "She was sunshine in a room, drawing others to her not by power, but by lightness of spirit."

"Did she play piano? I noticed you lingered near the piano when you were here this fall."

"Oh, you remember that?" Solomon said. "You didn't play for long, but you played well—the *Moonlight Sonata,* with embellishments I haven't heard before."

"My own piano master taught me that, from Franz Liszt. Have you heard of him?"

"Yes. A genius, I understand."

"Ever so." She sighed. "He was a student of Czerny, who was a student of Beethoven."

"That's quite a pedigree! From him to your teacher to you, and thence to me."

"I'm glad you took notice of it," she replied. "Was . . . was Mrs. Ramsdell musical?"

"No!" he said with a laugh. "But her sister is. We had a funny meeting over that, years ago—"

"So it seems," King interjected, "that you have discovered your mutual interest in music."

When Miss Baker looked at Solomon in surprise, King added, "Mr. Ramsdell is quite the violinist! I heard him at Myron's place back in '58."

She turned to Solomon. "You didn't say!"

"I don't have my violin with me here in town," he explained. "But I would enjoy hearing you play after supper, if that's possible."

"Of course. I always do. They don't always listen, but I try."

"I know." He caught himself, then decided to continue. "I've passed by here once or twice and heard you."

Custard was served and cleared, which signaled to the hotel guests that it was time to take their usual places. Lillianne went to the piano and paged through her sheet music, and Solomon lingered at the outer periphery of the men's circle by the windows, declining the offer of a light with pats to his pockets to show he had no pipe with him.

He struck up a conversation with a man he'd seen at Kopf's and learned he installed the clockworks for the beautiful grandfather clock cabinets that Kopf hired master woodworkers to embellish. Kopf wanted to introduce Michiganders to the cuckoo clocks of his homeland, small wall-hung clocks regulated by pendulums, with pinecone-shaped iron weights suspended from the bottom.

Drawn in by the prospect of such an addition to Kopf's line, Solomon was entranced at the idea of the little birds popping out to indicate the hours. But he was taken by surprise that Miss Baker's unobtrusive tinkling etudes had given way to the *Moonlight Sonata,* once again embellished by trills and arpeggios. He couldn't help himself—he wandered away from his acquaintance and found himself with the women around the piano while Lillianne Baker bent to her art. She was so swept up in the music that carried her hands up and down the keyboard, and she so inhabited the scene she was creating that her body rocked from side to side. Beethoven fell into conversation with Liszt, whose ornaments she reproduced, or imitated, or perhaps invented herself. Then Liszt—or Lillianne—fell away, and Beethoven commanded the room.

Her playing took center stage and the conversation died around it, all the guests drawn to the piano. And when she finished, she was panting and flushed. She cast her eyes toward Solomon, who found himself grinning as he clapped with the others. After a moment to catch her breath, she returned to playing, this time a playful ditty, and he turned back to the clockworks dealer to ask about the crafting of those weights and to learn more about the little birds.

As he left the hotel a half hour later, Solomon noted that Miss Baker was no longer downstairs, and he regretted that he couldn't commend her performance more personally. But altogether, his heart was light. He found the bitter wind outside refreshing, and he was glad he'd sought the company of others for the evening. Surely this was a good sign. Perhaps his burden was lifting.

* * *

The next morning, while eating his porridge, Solomon offered to walk Mrs. Montague to church. It would be his first time at worship since he'd come to Lowell.

"I'm generally a Congregationalist," he said, "but I'd be pleased to be a Presbyterian today for your sake." He wanted to make up for having been away the previous night.

Mrs. Montague was not such an old woman, though she dressed like it and bent herself like it. This morning, though, she skittered around the house a bit before tucking a fancy hat into her bag and wrapping her usual scarf around her head. Once outside, she took Solomon's arm, at first tentatively and then proudly, and he gallantly drew himself up and flourished his good cane, enough to draw curious eyes. He sat with her in her usual pew, as if he were a family member, and sang the hymns in a rich baritone the small church didn't usually have opportunity to enjoy.

Jennette would like this, he thought. She'd nod at his kindness to Mrs. Montague and smile at his gusto in the singing.

That afternoon, as he lay in the thin light that shone weakly through his bedroom window, he felt the warmth drain away from him, and grief gripped him in its claws again, piercing him around his ribs, raising his gorge a little.

But with a series of steady breaths—one hand on his belly and another on his chest as Jennette had soothed him in his panicky nightmares after the war—he stilled his heart and calmed his clattering mind; he even managed to drift into the upper reaches of sleep, a sleep so light he could hear Mrs. Montague banging about the wood stove and boiling a kettle for tea, so light he could hear the bells of a sleigh passing by on the road.

PROSPECTS
EARLY DECEMBER 1866

$$Gifts$$

MONDAY IT WAS BACK to work, and Solomon was alert, scanning the deep-rose dawn on his walk to the workshop that morning—*Is there a storm on the way?* An overnight rain had cleared the world of snow and ice, but there hadn't been enough to create the muddy slog of a false spring.

Midmorning, John Kopf took his usual tour through the workshop and clapped Solomon on the shoulder, saying, "I have heard of the 'brown study' that some fall into, my friend. The heaviness falls upon them, and they must dig their way out. But you have a look of a *green* study, I am thinking." He tapped his own temple with a forefinger. "Something is growing in there."

Solomon smiled and waved away the thought, answering lightly, "Just working through these figures." He held up his pencil.

"Very well. I will not press you." Kopf moved on to greet another worker, then had his usual audience with

Porter and Campbell in turn. The artisans must be kept contented—for their excellence made the difference in his goods. Today, though, he spent longer with Campbell, their voices rising and falling, the tones alternating between questioning and declaration. With a final note of surrender, Kopf came out of Campbell's private work area and left the shop for his office. The workmen glanced around at one another, but Solomon trusted Kopf would sort it out. He could learn later what had happened.

Suddenly restless, Solomon stood and went to the shelf where he stored the horse. He rocked it a little, stroking the fragrant strips of leather that made up the tail, gathering them in his palm and releasing them. Suddenly it came to him—*her birthday!* Callie had turned four just days after he'd left the farm, and he hadn't marked the day. Tears pricked behind his eyes. *How am I remembering only now?*

When dinnertime came, he wolfed down the bread and meat in his pail, then splashed through the remaining puddles to the mercantile, where he went right to the textiles and scanned the array of ribbons. A broad blue-and-white plaid ribbon caught his eye, and then a thin gold one edged with tiny loops of thread. When the proprietress joined him at the display, he placed his order—including some red satin ribbon for the horse's neck and tail—gesturing the lengths he wanted.

Christmas, too . . . He turned to the other displays as the woman wrapped up the ribbons. *A tin whistle for Sy, yes, and a top—or I could whittle one for him . . . or with him.*

Solomon felt the tears again and gulped them back. "Something for a little girl, ma'am. Just four years old . . ."

She directed him to a shelf where three dolls were sitting. The china baby doll with the soft body was clearly the one.

"Yes, this." He cradled it down from the shelf with one hand, just as he'd held newborn Nettie last spring: head nestled in his palm, body extended along his forearm, tiny legs draped on either side. *Something for Nettie, too . . . Is she sitting up yet, I wonder?*

"And for an infant?" he asked.

The woman picked up an iridescent flat ring with a silver bell attached, shaking it a little to demonstrate its sound, saying, "A mother-of-pearl rattle for a little one."

"That's pretty stuff, but I know it as nacre"—he grinned—"on my brother-in-law's best pistol . . . While I'm here, I'd best get a few other things." Sy should have more, though perhaps the whistle was enough if they made the top together. *Odd how spending money on little things can boost the spirits.*

Solomon found himself longing for his children. "Do you have some paints, small ones, suitable to paint a wooden toy?"

She showed him a set in a tin tray, six colors, and he bought a sheaf of paper as well. *He can try his hand at pictures . . .*

He went back to the mother-of-pearl display and found a small round mirror for Calista and then some rose water for Sally Watson, and nearby a mechanical pencil for Andrew. He then thought of the Kopf children and got them paints and paper as well.

Carrying his parcel, Solomon stepped out into the street, right into a mighty gust of wind that took his hat right off his head, and when he looked in the direction it had blown, there was Bert Talbert standing up in his wagon, the bowler clutched to his chest.

"Lose something?" Bert shouted, then gestured for Solomon to climb up into the wagon.

Once Solomon was seated beside him, Bert asked, "Goin' back to Kopf's?"

"Yes, and thank you kindly. Looks like a big storm—" He was cut off by a snow devil that lashed all his exposed skin and made the horse shake her head and snort.

Bert shook the reins. "On with ya, then, nag!" he called, then added affectionately, "There'll be an apple in it for you." To Solomon, he said, "Might not have judged this trip quite right. Soon only a cutter will make it. But I wanted to make these deliveries and get supplies for the winter at home."

In two short blocks they were at Kopf's. Solomon hurried inside to put his parcel on a shelf and then helped Bert unload his screens, which were light but unwieldy, especially when the wind caught at the screens and twisted them in their hands. The two men brought in a few other bundles and boxes, then took shelter inside and pulled off their hats and coats and gloves.

"Will that be all of your trips to town, then, at least for a while?" Solomon asked, looking about the nearly vacant shop. The deaf old man was sanding with a meditative air in his usual corner, but there were no sounds of activity from Campbell's and Porter's work areas, which were usually busy with the comings and goings of men and boys.

"Don't have a cutter m'self, so that's how it settles out."

"Thaw here a bit with me." Solomon waved a hand toward a short stool near the stove. "And then you can settle accounts with Kopf."

"He's done good trade in America, I'm thinkin'," Bert said, knocking a knuckle against a gleaming Windsor chair hanging on the wall beside him. "No wonder he fancies going from Johannes to John."

Solomon braced his hands on his thighs and stood up. "Since you're here, I was wondering if you'd be willing to take some more things to my family for me—for Christmas."

"Glad to." While Bert held his hands out to the glowing potbellied stove, Solomon fetched his parcel, then sat back down and opened it on his lap. He drew out the paper-and-string-wrapped items one at a time and explained each one to Bert, setting aside the paint and paper for the Kopf children, and then did up the parcel again.

"Y'know," Bert said, nodding toward the package, "your kin would likely favor a word or two from you in there." He gazed into the flames behind the iron slats of the stove. "Miss Watson fairly ate up your words with her eyes when I handed her that note you gave me with the last parcel." He squinted up at Solomon. "Then she sat right there on the porch step in the cold and gathered the boy and the girl to her lap and read it to them, explainin' a word or two to your little girl—Callie, is it?"

"Yes." Solomon gazed into the flames himself, knowing just how that scene on the steps would look. "Callie, named for her Aunt Calista—Miss Watson."

Bert went on to relate how the Watsons had invited him in to their dinner table, and that before he'd left, Calista had produced some things for Bert to take to Solomon on his next trip to Lowell. Bert got up and sorted through the items they'd brought in earlier from the wagon. "Ah! Here it is!" he said, producing a burlap-wrapped bundle he then cradled in both arms. "She fair got stern with me about how to treat this in the meantime—no damp, not too close to a fire, and so on."

Solomon untied the string around the burlap and opened it to reveal the old green-and-brown diamond quilt Jennette had always layered under their best quilt. Inside it—he knew—was his violin. Underneath the layer of quilt, the case was further wrapped in the two-tone blue chevron scarf that Jennette had always said matched the blue of his eyes. Forgetting Bert's presence, Solomon breathed in the scent of home, the tang of their cedar chest, then meditatively wrapped the scarf twice around his neck and rested his splayed hand against the familiar case of his violin.

"Seems you're readin' a letter there, too, my friend," said Bert, "even without the paper 'n' ink."

Solomon thumped the case twice. "Been missing this, though I hardly knew it."

"Watson told me that story of your first meetin' the family at his farm, when you fooled them with that thing," Bert said. "Had to say I was surprised—ya hadn't struck me as a prankster."

"Jennette and I were just courting at the time, or about to, and it was her idea—both of ours, actually—to torment Calista. Miss Watson. She's particular about her music."

"I see. Well, she seemed to know you'd like to have that." He nodded at the case in Solomon's lap.

Solomon shifted the violin case to one hand and stood, letting the quilt and burlap fall to the well-swept floor. He swung open the stove door and added two knots of wood from the nearby pile and clanged the door shut again, then slid the violin case onto his shelf and withdrew the rocking horse.

"Since you're unloading on this end," he said, "I hope you might have some room to take this to the children as well—just need to add the ribbon. I'd be obliged."

"I'll stop by for that and the parcel when I leave in the mornin'. I'd rather make the trip here and back all in one day like I can in the summer, savin' on the lodgin', but with short days and this storm kickin' up ..." Bert got up and went to the door to look out. "I wonder if Mr. Kopf would let me stay here and watch the place, keep that stove goin'."

Just then Kopf himself came into the workshop, and after peeking into Campbell's work area, walked over to where Solomon had begun working figures at his table that caught the best of the weak afternoon light. "Mr. Ramsdell," he said after a nod to Bert, "we have a situation that is altering the course of our business here—you will see I've dismissed the workers for the afternoon. Mr. Campbell is insisting that he must leave work for several weeks, go back to New England to see to concerns there. Not to be outdone, Mr. Porter learned of it and has said the same, and the result is we must leave off our chair production until such time as they return."

He paused to let that settle in, then said, "Mr. Talbert, I am glad to see you—a delivery of screens today?"

"Yes, sir," Bert replied, "and some other fancy-work my wife thinks might catch the eye of ladies lookin' to spy out some pretties at your place."

"I'd be glad to see them, then. Frau Talbert has a way with the beads. Frau Kopf will be eager to see them, too."

He turned his attention back to Solomon. "I do not think we can proceed without the artisans, but I will leave it to you to consider the best use of the workers—I want to keep them in my employ if I can, for you have trained them well to carry out the tasks, but you see how it is . . ."

"I need to consider how best to proceed," Solomon said. "Could I have an hour to think on it?"

"Of course! Of course! Now, Mr. Talbert, would you be so kind as to show me what you have for me?"

With Kopf absorbed in the inventory of Talbert's goods, Solomon started a new sheet of figures, licking his pencil as he considered the problem. A little later he took his pages to Kopf's office, passing a shop boy helping Bert move his screens and other goods into the store.

When he returned to the shop, having delivered his counsel, Solomon told Bert that Kopf and his wife had invited Bert to enjoy their hospitality that night, sparing him from having to find lodging.

"You'll have a warm welcome in their home, Bert," Solomon said, "as I did a few weeks ago for Thanksgiving. Before I leave here tonight, I'll make up tags for the gifts for the children, and I'll tuck them into the parcel for you."

After Bert left, Solomon carefully cut lengths of the red ribbon and tied them into bows on the neck and tail of the rocking horse, saving a piece that he then split into narrower ribbons to secure name tags to each of the gifts. He used a bit of the red paint in the tin to letter "Happy

Christmas" on a large tag which he hung from the leather ear of the horse. Then he penned a small note to Seymour, promising to make a top with him when next he saw him. "And not too long from now," he wrote. Solomon hoped the offerings would help the children to remember him.

After wrapping the parcels in the burlap Calista had sent and setting the package next to the rocking horse—in case Bert started back before he arrived at work next morning—Solomon spied his violin on the shelf, and he put out his hand for it.

<h1 style="text-align:center">Lillianne</h1>

MRS. MONTAGUE HAD HOT SOUP on the stove for Solomon that evening. "Against the chill," she said before retiring to her parlor while he ate. *A veritable luxury,* he thought, tallying it up with the other blessings he had recently known. *And there's a thought—counting blessings. For your sake, Jennette.*

After his supper, Solomon called to Mrs. Montague that he was going out for a while. She came to the parlor door to see him out, her shawl wrapped tight around her, and when she noticed his violin case, she raised her eyebrows.

"Yes, I play a bit, and I mean to do so tonight." He buttoned the violin case inside his coat, then wrapped the blue chevron scarf twice around his neck and tucked in the ends. He tugged his bowler down tighter on his head and stepped out.

Leaning into the wind, his breath fogging the familiar cedar scent up around his face, Solomon watched crazy whirlwinds of snow play across the road and lift over buildings as he trudged through town. No one else was about, but the Franklin House windows were aglow, and the steps recently swept but snow-drifted and scoured by the wild storm. He stamped the snow from his feet and dusted off his violin case once he reached the sheltered entrance, then pushed open one of the doors and entered the lobby just as the guests in the dining area were splitting into their usual groups.

Small crowd tonight, he thought, noting only six people besides Miss Baker—three men and two women and a little girl. And no Kings to be seen.

Tonight she wore a soft lilac shawl over her shoulders against the cold, and as she crossed to the piano, she nodded and lowered her eyelids in greeting. He hastily stowed his things on a hook by the door and followed her, holding his violin case behind him.

She began with a lullaby, and the little girl, recognizing the tune, looked up at her mother with delight, bouncing on her toes, then creeping closer to Lillianne to watch her play. Then came the familiar lines of Haydn's *The Creation*, and while one of the ladies mouthed the words from the hymn—"blue, ethereal sky"—the child spun and stamped to the march-like beat. Not waiting for permission from the pianist, and behind her back, Solomon opened his violin case, very quietly tested the A and then the other strings, then insinuated himself into the melody.

Half a year neglected, the violin had closed up its sound; Solomon would have to coax it back to life. *It will take much playing to return to itself.*

At the unexpected sound, Miss Baker looked over her shoulder, mouth agape, then smiled and nodded encouragingly at the dancing little girl as her mother took her hands and whirled her around on the polished floor. Solomon played plainly at first, then worked in his flourishes as Lillianne responded. When the Haydn was done, she started *Moonlight Sonata* again, and Solomon, remembering her additions from her Saturday performance, joined in and took them up himself. Thus they had a musical conversation while the small crowd, perhaps unaware of the extent of the artistry in their midst, simply enjoyed the music.

With the long, deep notes, Solomon felt the strings' reverberations travel up through his bow arm and into his chest, while the percussive bass from the piano thrummed up through his feet. This was how life flowed into him, and he tried to remember the last time he'd known this feeling—in June, perhaps, before Jennette fell ill.

Half a year, two seasons come and gone. And she missed the golden harvest she so loved . . .

When Lillianne left off Beethoven and went back to a hymn, she chose Wesley's "Hark! the Herald Angels Sing," and Solomon felt a catch in his chest at the thought of the Christmas Jennette was missing, too. *Her Cratchit home comforts,* he thought with a sad smile as he played his way up to the high "glory" then carried it back down to the final "newborn king."

"Now there's some Christmas spirit!" cried one of the men from across the room, pipe clenched in his teeth. At that the little girl's mother spoke quietly to her, thanked the musicians, and led her daughter up the stairs. The other woman, who was elderly, took a seat nearby in a plum velvet wing chair.

"Thank you for joining me, Mr. Ramsdell," Miss Baker said breathlessly, her fair hair escaping a little from the knot at the back of her head and one wave clinging to her cheek. "I was glad to hear you play—I may have inquired a bit into your reputation." She drew that tendril behind her ear and looked directly into his eyes.

"It was a pleasure," he answered. "I haven't played since—"

"Since the summer, I expect, before your loss." She didn't demur, and he took courage from that . . . so he must be able to speak of it.

"Yes, I was thinking I last played in June."

She absently played a little etude that called for no attention, and continued the conversation. "I'm glad to see you play—it changes you," she said.

"Or rather, its absence changed me." He held up the violin. "I feel more myself with this." Then he plucked a few notes that matched hers on the piano. "You're very forthright, Miss Baker, for someone who was so quiet at first."

"I find it is best to be one or the other, according to the occasion," she said. "For example, in forthrightness, I will ask: have you considered yet what your future will be? Your children's?"

Taken aback, Solomon stammered, "W-well, yes, in a manner of speaking. I'm here to do business for their good, learning the furniture trade with John Kopf."

"Do they understand that this is for their good, then? Do you mean to set them up in a house in town, or do you mean to raise them on a farm . . .?" She laughed. "Yes, I know they're with your in-laws." She flew her fingers up two octaves and then back down. "I generally find children are more aware than we give them credit for."

"And that's exactly why I left, to be frank," Solomon said, marveling that he spoke so plainly to this young woman. *So be it.* "I was beginning to be pulled under by dark storms in my soul, and I didn't want to take the children with me. I was angry, and even a little crazed at times. I feared for them . . . for myself."

"We should probably leave off this close talk"—she leaned her head toward the elderly woman in the velvet chair—"especially with my cousins not here."

Solomon lowered his bow hand to his side and looked about; he'd forgotten all about the people in the room, and he'd forgotten himself as he told more of his soul than he'd revealed to anyone since Jennette.

"Of course," Lillianne added, "if you'd be interested in taking up this conversation again, my cousins have been deputized by my parents to act in their stead in these matters." She smiled at his gaping in surprise and said, "I can see you're not used to such plain speaking, but you're a man who needs a mother for your children—and even if you don't realize it yet, a wife for yourself."

Yes. I've begun to realize that. Solomon thought back to that restless Sunday afternoon in his room.

"And so," she continued, "I wouldn't be averse to such a role, though you should know that I intend to be in the hotel business. Any man that seeks my company needs be apprised of that."

When Jennette had taken charge, she'd done so more subtly, so it had seemed more his own idea. This boldness was unfamiliar—but not unpleasant. A house in town, a business in town . . . *I could manage that,* he mused.

They played a couple of Stephen Foster numbers, and after that, he thought it proper to take his leave, especially with the Kings being away. So Solomon packed up his violin while she tossed him an offhand wave and gathered her skirts to climb the staircase to her room.

The storm at his back required Solomon to focus on keeping his footing and hunching up his scarf and collar around his neck, but once in his chilly bed under the eaves at Mrs. Montague's, he mulled over his evening at Franklin House, and he found himself humming snatches of the tunes under his breath and recalling the brilliant play of Lillianne's fingers across the keys. The shine of her hair, the flash of her eyes when she first heard him playing with her—excitement surged through him, banishing sleep.

What would life in a hotel be like for me, for the family? Sy could chase a hoop with a stick down the boardwalk, Callie could curtsy to welcome guests and sing for them . . . *But could she be so forward?* Callie was Calista's shy shadow even before Jennette took ill.

"It's best this way," Jennette had told him one day in the spring while she was nursing Nettie in the kitchen. "In some ways, Callie is more Calista's child than mine—she draws comfort from her very presence." After a moment she'd added, "As do I."

Jennette had always been taken with the outward flair of things—the bustle of cleaning, flashing smiles at guests, arranging all the effects just so. And Calista, except when she took charge at the piano, had been more about the atmosphere of the home, quietly concerning herself with the substance of what needed to be done. How many times had Callie curled up in her aunt's lap by the fireplace or the kitchen stove, tucking her rosy cheek against Calista's encircling arm?

How could I take Callie from that refuge? Solomon shook his head side to side on the pillow in answer to his own question. His eyes were wide and unfocused, more imagining than seeing the dark planks of the ceiling.

It would be more expected that I take Calista. Marrying within families was common among the first settlers: Myron King and his brothers had married three sisters, Otis Churchill's mother being another sister of that family; Myron King's neighbor, Morgan Lyon, had married his first wife's sister after his first wife passed. *It makes sense,* he thought. *Familiar ways . . . even the cooking.*

There would, of course, never be another Jennette, and it was just as well Calista did not favor her. There Lillianne shone—she combined Jennette's features with Calista's musicality.

Poor, tone-deaf Jennette—he sniffed out a little laugh—*and so good-natured about it.* The music called out to a part of him Jennette couldn't reach. Long months had his chest been clenched around his heart, but Lillianne's playing, and then his own, had opened him into remembrance of life, the beats and melodies and rich chords coursing through him, well-being growing from within.

Calista has the music, too.

And Calista was fetching in her own way—just a girl when he'd first met her a decade before, but now a woman. *I've hardly noticed,* he thought, reaching into his memory for an image of Calista as she was now. He couldn't picture it, instead recalling how she looked the day they'd first met, when she had taken pains to arrange Jennette's smooth blond hair in the latest fashion, for him, the suitor. Calista herself wore a sprig of meadow flowers tucked into her curls, an afterthought.

It would be such a sensible thing to take Calista as his wife, to accept what nature seemed to offer. Surely Watson would see the sense in that—and would gladly see them settled nearby in the rich Grattan land. *Fruit trees have promise . . .*

Callie would then have her secure companion, Sy the familiar scenes of his boyhood, and poor Nettie the only mother she'd ever really known. As for Calista, she'd likely see the sense in it, too. *She's that sort, and since the war there've been few suitors available.* But it was too much to assume.

Lillianne had a great deal to offer as well, including a chance at a whole new life.

Perhaps there's a future for me, after all. Could it be, Jennette? The chilly quiet of the room assented: peace, possibility.

With a smile and a sigh, Solomon turned on his side and, for the first time in months, fell into a comfortable slumber.

Reaching

HE SENT HIS GIFTS with Talbert the next morning. The storm had quieted and fat snowflakes were drifting down, creating the first layer of the enduring blanket that would keep Talbert home all winter. Solomon set to some mindless sanding at the shop and considered what should be done. He'd found a useful mooring at Kopf's during these months, working steadily at a business with fewer vagaries than farming had. As long as people had the means, their taste in furniture could be indulged, even as their whims changed. But there was no mistaking the order of things. Kopf was surely the one in charge, and Solomon just a worker. He'd taken solace in that arrangement these many weeks, but a man needed his own enterprise.

Could hotel-keeping do for him? In order to pursue Lillianne, he must be all in for the hotel business—she had made that clear. Lowell was growing and trade should be good for a long time to come. Or maybe there was another good town along the railway, where they could have a fresh start without the eyes of Watsons and Ramsdells upon them. *Lillianne said her father had investment in mind . . .*

Tearing his roots out of the soil where Jennette had been buried—that would be one way to rid himself of the clutching grief that dragged at him. Town life—hotel life— might be a lovely new start for the children . . . even Nettie once she was older, old enough for school. Perhaps Calista would want to keep her until then.

If I prosper in the hotel business, Solomon speculated as he ran his hand over a turned table leg, *maybe I could even travel with Lillianne and the children—back to my ancestors' places in New York, Massachusetts . . . maybe England itself!* A farmer's life allowed for no such mobility, but even in the short time he'd been in town, he'd noticed that the Kings went away for weeks at a time, their business set to run itself without them. Yes, that would certainly be something—no need to tend livestock every day, or to stay one step ahead of the weather or the pests. *Father gave up farming for business, too.*

At midday, he stepped out into the fluffy snow that was drifting down over the town and shuffled through ankle-deep drifts to Franklin House, thinking he'd have a bowl of soup while considering his prospects. While removing his gloves and coat in the lobby, he saw her behind the counter, brow furrowed in concentration as she wrote in a ledger with a mechanical pencil, the same sort he'd gotten for Andrew. Lillianne—Miss Baker—did things with flair.

Solomon approached the counter and quietly touched three fingertips to the polished wood—a gentle movement, hesitant but inquiring—and she raised her head, blinking twice before smiling.

"Mr. Ramsdell!" she said with pleasure, "I'm not used to seeing you in daylight . . . such as it is." She waved her pencil toward the muted light coming through the windows, screened through the myriad snowflakes coming down outside.

"Miss Baker," he said, and that was all. The seconds ticked by on the large clock on the wall behind her, the second-hand climbing its way up from seven to eight to nine.

As if she knew she'd gone too far ahead of herself the night before, she waited for him.

Solomon, drawing some power from those moments, felt purpose enter him. He cleared his throat and began again. "Miss Baker, when do you expect your cousins to return from their journey?"

She colored a little, her forehead first and then below, a veil of pink being drawn down her face. *Jennette's own blush bloomed on her cheeks first, instead.*

"Oh, um, any day now," she said. "Before Christmas, in any case." She looked him in the eyes, but not as directly as last night. Instead, her gaze flicked back and forth, as if searching for something.

As am I, he thought, taking in the sensation of her attention. *Such a substantial, purposeful young lady.*

"Well, then," he said, tapping the counter with the three fingers that had been resting there all those seconds, "I will see Mr. King then, whenever it might be. If . . ."

"If?" she asked, her eyes still searching. Her hand holding the pencil lowered onto the counter just a short distance from his.

"In case"—he nervously moved his hand to grasp his lapel—"he is willing to discuss the hotel business with me."

"Oh, I see," she said, taking up her sureness again with a mischievous smile. "Well, I can heartily recommend it myself!"

* * *

Mischief, he thought later, after catching himself whistling a little tune while gathering the ledgers for an afternoon in front of the wood stove. *It would be mischief to rush along with her so quickly. Though she seems willing enough . . .*

Over the course of the afternoon, he reconciled the accounts and felt the satisfaction of the balances, the approving judgment right there before him of work well done and profits made. But then the crackle and thump of wood in the stove would remind him of elemental things, pulling him back to earth.

As the late-afternoon dusk crept through the workshop, Solomon the last one there, John Kopf came in from his office.

"Solomon, I have considered your counsel about the workers. As Christmas is on a Tuesday this year, I have decided they—and you as well—may leave off work at noon on Saturday and not return until Thursday."

"I think that will cheer them, certainly," Solomon answered.

"And I will give you the privilege to tell them so, in the morning." Kopf lightly slapped Solomon's worktable and turned to leave with an upward swirl of his hand that said, "Finish up now."

As he began closing things down, securing the windows and wrapping himself up against the cold, Solomon wondered what this extra time off might mean for him. Could he even find transport and surprise the children?

Would they welcome me? Or fear me?

Before he could even consider Lillianne as a mother to his children, he must be sure that the life she offered would suit them, and if they were to trust him in that, they would need to trust him as a father. He winced in pain as he recalled Callie's skittishness, and how even Sy had become tentative with him after the dogcart incident last summer. He must reclaim his place as their father, so they might trust him again and wish to join him in a new life.

And to do that he must go to them.

RESCUE
LATE DECEMBER 1866

Proposition

A FEW EVENINGS LATER, Solomon returned to Franklin House with his violin. From his place behind the registration counter, Arza King put a forefinger to his temple in greeting. As Solomon hung up his warm things and took his violin from its case—preparing to join Lillianne at the piano where she was toying with some cheerful melodies—King approached and put out a hand to shake Solomon's.

"Mr. Ramsdell—Solomon—I understand you've been adding to the entertainment of late."

"Yes, sir. It's been a pleasure returning to my old friend." Solomon released King's hand and gave his violin a pat. "I do hope it's all right with you. I used to provide the music for all manner of dances, and in a hotel back near Orange—in the Lyons American Hotel, to be exact."

"It's quite all right. In fact, I'm looking forward to hearing you play. I remember you added much to the entertainment at Myron's."

"Thank you. So many good times before the war," Solomon said.

"I recall you were a newlywed at the time."

"Yes, Jennette and I married in the summer of '57. We had the place with the blue door within sight of your brother's place."

"Much has changed since those days . . ."

"Yes, it has." Solomon straightened up and squared his shoulders. *As good a time as any,* he thought. "And for me, the time has come for another change. I must look to my family."

"Yes?" King nodded encouragingly.

"And to our future," Solomon continued, feeling like a callow youth instead of the old war veteran his bones and bowels told him he was. *Why so jittery?* he wondered. "What I'm getting at—I understand I'm supposed to speak to you about this matter—is that I would like permission to court Miss Baker."

"I thought that might be the case." King smiled and put a fatherly hand on Solomon's shoulder. "But I'd like to discuss this further. Can you meet me at your dinner hour tomorrow? I'll provide the meal and we can take it in my office." He gestured toward a door behind the registration counter.

"I would be honored," Solomon said, then shook King's hand again before the man turned to the other guests. Solomon whistled a little as he rosined his bow, then swung his violin to his shoulder and took his place beside Lillianne.

* * *

After they finished their chicken stew and light rolls served on slender-legged trays in Arza King's office, King folded his napkin and placed it on his tray. Solomon followed suit, and they both sat back in their wooden chairs.

"Lillianne," King began, "has told me of your recent meetings over music—and of her expectation that you would request this meeting."

"I'm glad to hear it," Solomon responded, staking his claim to some of the authority in the room. Arza King might be old enough to be his father, but Solomon was a father three times over himself, a widower, a veteran, and well into his maturity. He deserved to be taken seriously. "I find her an accomplished and enterprising young woman, and I would like to have the opportunity to get to know her better, to see whether she would consider becoming my wife."

"She's amenable to the idea, and that's important to me. Your family's reputation and your own commend you. But I understand you haven't had much to do with your father's household while you've been in Lowell . . ."

Solomon rushed to explain. "Well, I've been much occupied at Kopf's—"

"No doubt. But you've had time to spend at Franklin House, and to be frank, your father is somewhat concerned—"

"My father! What has he to do with it?" Solomon took a deep breath to calm himself. "I have simply been pursuing business—"

"It concerns me," King said coolly, "that you, a family man, have detached yourself from your own family and even from your kin here in town. It causes me to wonder what your intent is, your disposition toward your future."

"Well . . . I intend to establish a household for my own children again, certainly, and that was the intent I had in coming to Lowell in the first place—to explore a trade, some business." He tapped a finger into his other palm before him. "As my own father did. He gave up his farm to start the saddlery here." Solomon, having come to the edge of his seat in his vehemence, now relaxed back into the chair. *I must control myself—maintain decorum.*

"Obviously, I value business." King lifted a hand to indicate the dark wood paneling in his office, and the satin-stripe wallpaper above the wainscoting. "And that brings me to my other concern."

"Yes," Solomon said, perhaps a little too fast. "I'm aware of Miss Baker's—and her father's—desire for her to be in the hotel business. And I'm more than willing to consider this sort of establishment myself. My mother taught us homestyle hospitality in my growing-up years."

"Yet you are in the furniture trade here at Kopf's—"

"It's as important to find the right wife as to find a line of work, and my interest in Miss Baker has also kindled my interest in the enterprise that she is set on."

"Do you mean that, really? It seems to me a man must know his own mind and calling before calling a wife to join him there." King stood and walked behind his chair, holding the back as if it were the ledge of a lectern.

Though Solomon longed to rise as well, to establish himself as King's equal, he thought it best to stay where he was. He forced himself to relax into a convivial attitude.

"Mr. King. Arza, if you don't mind." *There's a calculated risk!* "You know of my family's work as pioneers—my departed sister Diana was the first child born in Kalamazoo County. Our intent has always been to build a civilization here in Michigan. We have, many of us—including you Kings—come a generation ago from New York, and a generation before that from Massachusetts, and a revolution and a century before that from England. Though we started out as farmers in Orange—after Father laid out the streets of Kalamazoo—we couldn't even do that until we'd cleared the land there. Year after year we made our mark on the land, but my father had grander visions than that. As I do now.

"Yes, we've been farmers," he continued, "but we never dreamed of staying farmers. Thus Father's saddlery, and thus my interest in other modes of business." He paused to see the effect of his words.

"Your point is well taken, Solomon. There is certainly no harm in a man seeking other ways of living than the one he was brought up in. After all, we've advanced from the guilds of our forefathers in Europe. I myself mean to move on from this small hotel to build another here in town, a grander one, for the trade I believe is coming soon . . . from lumber, in particular."

Solomon nodded. "The river and the railroad are, for me and my father both, what attracted us to this area before the war. Of course, the war has changed much in our country—for us veterans, especially." *Would he contradict one who has served in the war?* "So I hope you can see that you and I are of one mind after all—open to possibility."

Solomon stood and offered his hand to King. "May I, then, have permission to court Miss Baker? Or should I write her father?"

"Baker has entrusted me with his daughter's future, but there's another matter I would like to discuss first." King did not take his hand but indicated a leather swivel chair opposite his desk, then moved to his own larger chair behind the desk.

More, then? Solomon wondered as he sat.

"Solomon . . ." He put his elbows on the desk and put his palms together as if in prayer.

"Yes, Arza?" *Just to remind him.*

"I'm concerned about your children. I know Andrew Watson and his wife and daughter have been caring for them in your absence, and I expect it will be quite an undertaking to remove them into your care."

"I wouldn't do that until I was married," Solomon said, "and the little one—Nettie—I'm considering leaving her with her aunt until she's of school age, or near to it."

"The details may, of course, be left for further deliberation later. And if you marry Lillianne, it will be your concern at that time and none of mine—besides family interest. But your children haven't lived in a town, and they lost their mother just months ago. I presume they're close to their grandparents and aunt . . . and isn't an uncle nearby as well?"

"Yes, Daniel is establishing his own farm nearby."

"It is a concern not only for the children's sake but for Lillianne's—she is quite young, you know, and desirous of applying herself to business. I imagine she'd want to engage a nanny, a governess . . ."

"But no one I know has a nanny!" Solomon was taken aback; in the homes he'd known, only mothers or older sisters or other female relatives ever held such a role.

"In the cities they do," Arza replied. "And in a grand house, which Lillianne would aspire to in the course of things, it would be expected."

"I suppose we could consider it . . ." Solomon's mind was racing. *A nanny, governess, boarding school—Jennette would not countenance it!* Surely Lillianne would want to be their mother, a true mother, not just in name.

"As your sister-in-law has been caring for the children since Mrs. Ramsdell's death, I wonder if she'd be willing to continue in that role."

"What? No, I can't see it. Calista has been a second mother to the children—even before we lost Jennette. But she's of an independent mind herself. She has musical talent like Miss Baker's. She's been a teacher. I wouldn't ask her to do such a thing."

"Well," Arza said with a shrug, "I only ask because it would make the change smoother for the children. I thought she was essentially their nanny now. If you're to take them from the farm they've grown up on, and into a town, it might be good to provide them with some familiar comfort."

Solomon felt his cheeks flushing at the implication that he'd not thought of the children—at the accusation. For it struck home. He didn't speak.

"Perhaps you should spend some time at home to discuss these things with your family, with your in-laws."

"I was hoping to find a way to visit," Solomon said, his only defense in the moment.

"The snow has come in earnest now, I do believe, and no wagon might make it." Arza stood and stepped to the window and gazed out. "As I have no intention of traveling until the New Year, I would be willing to give you the use of my cutter and bay if you'd like, to make the visit for Christmas."

"That is very kind of you," Solomon replied, wondering just what was behind all these vagaries of demeanor. King was alternately warm and steely, dubious and encouraging.

"Before you begin courting my cousin, I'd like to be sure you have your own affairs in order, and know what you're willing to do for the sake of the young woman who's in my care. Therefore, I believe it's in the interests of us all that you spend some days with your children and your in-laws." Arza picked up two ledgers from his desk, then tucked them under his arm, as if to announce he was now moving on to other matters.

Solomon stood, too, a little bewildered but excited at the prospect of taking a cutter home. *And it IS home, after all, for it's where all who most loved Jennette are gathered.* "I thank you for your generous offer. There are several days that Kopf's will be shuttered that I could make the trip."

"It's settled, then." Arza escorted Solomon to the door.

Solomon absently gathered his hat and coat and blue scarf and trudged through the drifts to Kopf's. It felt almost as if Arza were loading him in the cutter and pushing him toward home—as if he hadn't already decided on his own to get there somehow. *So be it,* he thought. *It's not like I have much pride left, anyway.*

Cutter

As Solomon traveled north from Lowell, the afternoon sun shone from just behind his left shoulder and sparkled upon the high drifts on the east side of the road. The day was perfect for a cutter ride, and the agile vehicle sped along the snowy roads much more elegantly than the lumbering old sleigh that he and Jennette had taken out just before the war. This was more like the cutter his family had fashioned a decade before, the one Otis and Rosette took on their wedding journey. *How that thing could fly!*

Solomon hadn't been able to set out until after midday, but he wanted to arrive before evening. Only an hour or so was left before dark. Since he'd already sent his gifts by way of Bert, he had little to offer, but he brought his violin, a jar of kraut and a jar of beet-pickled eggs from Mrs. Kopf, and a gold-rimmed china dish with dainty teacakes Lillianne had procured from the hotel kitchen.

"The chef is serving these on Sunday," Lillianne had said when she'd brought the dish to Solomon at the stables.

"They're a foretaste of Christmas, and I thought the children would enjoy them." A fur wrap about her shoulders, she had carefully perched at the edge of the brick pavement, holding the plate out to avoid venturing into the mud of the stable. A jeweled comb held her upswept hair at an angle over one ear.

Delightful, he thought. The life she offered promised ease and pleasure. And he could, with some tutelage from King, quickly catch up on the hotel business and have something of substance to discuss with Howard Baker when it came time to negotiate the investment.

As Myron King's place came into view, a knot of emotion caught in Solomon's chest. Growing up, he'd been in and out of Lucinda King's kitchen back in Orange, tromping the fields with the King boys and learning to snare small game. Now, like Solomon's own father, Myron King presided over a finer house, but emptier, this one marking King's claim in the rich land where the old flood plain gave way to northward hills. Solomon slowed the bay to survey the place. No one seemed about in the yards, but thick smoke curled cheerily out of the two chimneys—one the kitchen, no doubt, in preparation for the holiday.

Once Vergennes was behind him, Solomon peered down the eastbound road toward Fallasburg, where—to judge from the condition of the road—the Fallas brothers were busily establishing a town to rival Lowell in trade. *River or railroad?* Solomon wondered. Which would be more promising in the years to come? The Fallas family had invested in the barge trade, but though the Ramsdells had made a family enterprise of new developments, Solomon felt too old for that level of risk. *My endurance does not measure up to high hopes these days.* But a hotel seemed like a sure thing—especially with the reputation of the Baker and King families to recommend it.

As the cutter descended a steep hill into the twilight gloom of late afternoon, Solomon took one hand at a time from its leather glove and blew on it within the shelter of his scarf, the numbness aching away from his fingers as they thawed. He encouraged the bay up the next hill; the horse's shadow and that of the cutter stretched long and blue up over the snowbank as the sun approached the horizon.

At the next steep descent, he recognized the hill he'd been climbing last fall when Bert Talbert had overtaken him and offered a ride. Solomon twisted a bit in his seat to ease his back. He'd strengthened substantially since that time, putting on flesh even with Mrs. Montague's plain fare. The work had kept him ahead of the brooding that had stunted his appetite before.

Town is good for me, he thought with a nod. Regular hours at Kopf's, work set by another man but with scope for innovation, and now the heartening prospect of another line of work and a spacious and rich home for his children, with a lovely new wife and mother—and servants! He shook his head to clear it, with a smile and a little snort— *Who'd have thought?*

Wait, was this the hill where I took leave of Jennette? He pulled back on the reins with a "Whoa!" then looked about him as the sun touched the horizon in a swirl of lavender and pink and its own clear, cold yellow.

Was it really just three years ago that they'd taken that sleigh ride together? A thousand sunsets, and how many had he watched in that time? The ones behind him as he journeyed east to war, casting a long shadow before him. The pinkish haze that cooled the Andersonville swamp for just moments before battalions of mosquitoes swarmed in to redouble his misery. The angry red that threw the trees into silhouette as he thrashed through the woods in his madness of just months ago. But there had been others, too: the sweet deep-blue-and-lavender dusk when he and Jennette cooed over their Nettie on the porch while Calista read to the children upstairs before bed. Even at Kopf's the ray of gold through the window fell across his desk as if to say, "A day well spent—now you may rest."

In the last blue-gray of twilight, Solomon found the lane to the Watson place from the main road and was able to follow its curve, the horse breaking through new snow as they passed between the trees, Solomon's eyes fixed on the glowing panes of the farmhouse windows. He pulled up where he'd stopped the wagon with Jennette his first time visiting this home nine and a half years earlier. The horse was snorting and blowing, but it was only when he climbed out of the cutter that he heard the dog barking from inside—*Not Puck!*

The door creaked open and Andrew Watson appeared in his shirtsleeves, silhouetted, gripping the dog by the collar, no doubt ready to let the creature fly to the family's defense. The yellow hound strained against the hold, then squared its stance, teeth bared, and Solomon saw Andrew's shotgun loosely held, butt down, beside him. His father-in-law peered out into the darkness, then set the gun against the house and pulled the door closed at his back.

"So," he said, after shushing the dog. "Sol, is it? Have you come back, then?" The question held judgment, and caution.

"Yes, sir," Solomon said, holding his bowler to his chest, head slightly bowed. "I have a few days off from the shop and was offered the loan of this horse and cutter"—he reached out to pat the bay's neck—"to see the children."

Andrew stood still on the porch. The dog wove nervously between and around his legs and he bent to comfort it—"There, there, Penelope." Then to Solomon, he said, "How does it fare with you, then?"

He's wondering if I'm in my right mind. "Well, sir. I've been learning the furniture trade, but I'm looking at other possibilities as well. My . . . my health has improved, too."

"That's good to hear," Andrew said, his tone tentative. He half-turned to the door. "I'll get my coat and help you put the rig—"

"I'll do it, Grandpa!" Sy emerged from the shadows at the corner of the house. Andrew turned in his direction, but Sy was across the snowy yard in a flash, stopping short before Solomon, hand out for the horse's lead.

"Father."

"Thank you, Seymour," Solomon said with answering formality, then softened into the familiarity he so wanted. "Let's see to this together, all right? I'll be with you in a moment."

His son nodded once and clucked for the horse to follow him toward the barn.

Andrew released the dog to go with the boy. After the cutter passed between Solomon and Andrew, the two men were alone again.

"Solomon, I'll not have—"

"Nor will I." Solomon approached the porch and stood at the bottom step, drawing the glove off his right hand. "I'm beholden to you and Mother Watson—and to Calista—for your care of the children while I was . . . while I was ill. But I'm better now, and I wish to take my children into my care very soon. I'd like to speak to you of these things in the morning, if you're willing."

"I'm ready to hear you out," Andrew said, "but I won't have you stirring them up—nor frightening Callie—with whatever you have in mind."

"I don't want that, either. The children are first in my concerns—I can assure you of that." Solomon returned his hat to his head and put his right hand back in the glove he carried—a handshake could wait.

Solomon started toward the barn, and Andrew slipped into the warmth of the house where Solomon imagined the Watson women cooed to his little girls in safety and quiet cheer. He turned to follow his son.

SOLOMON SAW CALISTA give her father a sidelong look, and at his nod she swooped Callie into a festive welcome, easing her little charge into confidence at Solomon's reappearance. Then she scooped Nettie from Sally, who sat cradling her by the front-room fireplace, and deposited the infant into Solomon's arms—an example for Callie of what ought to be. Finally, the tableau complete, Calista stepped back and left him to make the best of it.

"See, Callie?" Sy said with a grin, "I told ya he'd be back—for Christmas, anyway." Sy took Solomon's violin case that he'd brought in from the barn and set it on the piano bench, then fetched the jars from the box by the door and held them up for Calista. "See? More from the German lady!" Then Sy took them into the kitchen.

"Callie?" Solomon coaxed, "would you undo the satchel there? Maybe Mama Calla can help you."

Callie stood a pace away from where he sat with the baby on his knees, her finger in Nettie's closed fist, the closest Callie would come to her father. Calista encouraged her with a hand fluttering toward the satchel, and Callie scrambled over and undid the strap by herself.

"Just inside there is a cloth wrapped around a dish. Careful, now. Draw it out."

Calista appeared at Callie's side to help and undid the knotted corners of cloth at the top, revealing Lillianne's teacakes.

"These are special sweets from the Franklin Hotel in Lowell," Solomon said, "made by a baker there, called a chef, for the hotel guests."

Callie's eyes were drawn to the delicate confections covered with sifted white sugar, and at Calista's nod she selected one. "And one for your brother," Calista said, holding out a teacake for Sy. "The rest we'll save." She knotted the cloth again and set the plate on a small table.

For the next quarter of an hour, the forms of polite inquiry for the sake of the children were borne by all, and then the welcome bedtime hour finally arrived, and the domestic details needed to be seen to. Solomon found himself spooning milk into the eager mouth of his baby daughter and chatting about town news with Father Watson—while Sy lingered and had to be called upstairs twice, finally roused by a gruff word from his grandfather.

Once the older children were abed, Calista came to fetch Nettie from Solomon, and Andrew helped his wife up the stairs, the yellow hound clicking up the stairs behind them. Solomon, alone in the front room, looked about for what he could do. He carried the plate of teacakes into the kitchen and closed them into the sideboard, safe from mice, then poked and banked the fire for the night. He was glad to have just finished when Andrew came down to do the job.

"Well, thanks for that." Andrew gestured toward the fireplace. "Calista is getting your bed ready for you. We let Sy take your old room, so you'll share with him."

"All right," Solomon answered, straightening up and dusting ash from his knees. He picked up his bowler from where it had fallen by the coat hooks and hung it carefully—*in my old place.* Then, as his father-in-law blew out the lamps downstairs, Solomon followed the light of the one on the wall upstairs and went up to his old room.

*　*　*

The next morning Calista was muttering and banging pots as she bustled around the kitchen, but she went quiet—her back to him, a spoon upraised in one hand—when Solomon pulled back a chair at the table.

"Good morning, Calista," he said brightly.

"G'mornin'," she mumbled. She set down the spoon but hovered her hand over it, as if she had forgotten what she was doing. Then, picking it up again, she scooped out some lard and plopped it onto the griddle, where it skittered over the surface and hissed. "Children stirring yet?"

"Not that I heard," he replied. "Sy snores more than I'd have thought seemly for such a small fellow, and he was still at it as I left the room. I peeped in at the girls, and they were more decorous, which is a comfort." He smiled at the scene he'd just enjoyed upstairs—all his children, safe and at peace.

"He's a flailer," Calista said, "so it was a mercy to Callie to give him the other room—suits us all."

"He slept pretty still last night—"

"They were all up far too late." She wiped her fingers on her apron and pried the top off a tin of cinnamon, which she sprinkled into the bowl in front of her.

"I want to thank you for sending my violin with Talbert. And the scarf. I had to buy a rough one in Lowell and was glad to see that one."

"Jennette would have wanted you to have it . . . and the violin, too," she said with a softer tone.

"It was good of you to think of it, especially with all the rest you have to do ..." While he looked around for something he could do to help, she dropped a spoonful of batter onto the griddle, then raised her head sharply, listening. Her dimple—just like Callie's—deepened with her frown of concentration. He joined her at the stove. "I'll flip those for you if you like." He held out a hand for the spatula; Calista hesitated, then gave it to him.

"I think I heard Nettie," she said, "and if I don't get there first, Callie will try to haul her out of the cradle." At once she was gone and he was alone. A little pot next to the griddle held dried apples bubbling away in maple syrup, and she'd already stacked plates and forks on the sideboard. Solomon flipped the pancakes, then quickly laid the places around the table and set out the pitcher of buttermilk and cups. A high-chair was pulled up next to Andrew's armed chair at the other end of the table. *Nettie is already big enough for that?*

Solomon heard his father-in-law stamping snow off his boots on the back porch and telling the dog, "You stay, Penelope," then Andrew came through the kitchen door and pulled off his gloves, jacket, and battered work hat and hung them on pegs. The two of them exchanged greetings as Solomon slid the first batch of pancakes onto a plate and spooned more batter onto the griddle—several small ones and one larger—*Callie will like the little ones,* he thought. *And Nettie.* Like her older brother and sister before her, Nettie would no doubt examine the tiny pancake held in her fingers, discovering her powers and the world around her—even if it was just the small world of her tray and her food—finding what she liked and disliked, taking her place in the family.

Before long, he heard Calista coming down the stairs with the children. Sy burst into the kitchen well ahead of her, and immediately began talking excitedly to Solomon. Callie was silent but attentive to her little sister, who set to banging her fists on her tray as soon as Calista had fastened her into the seat with a dishcloth tied around her middle and another tucked into her collar. Andrew had gone upstairs and returned with Sally, who was breathing heavily and shallowly at the same time, exhausted by the effort. Each one had his or her place. Solomon was there but not really of them, even with Sy chattering on to him about the rabbit he'd snared and skinned the week before.

"So," Andrew said, as Calista presented the plate of pancakes whose preparation she had smoothly taken over from Solomon a few moments before, "shall I ask a blessing?" Calista slid onto the bench by Solomon and set Callie at her other side, and all bent their heads, Callie and Seymour with their hands clasped before them.

"Father God, we thank thee for the bounties thou hast prepared for us by these hands in thy service, for the blessings of the land ... and for the presence of all the family here today. Be with us as we seek to serve thee in this day. Amen."

"Amen," Solomon murmured with the others, and then Andrew sent around the plate of pancakes. One adult tended to each child, leaving Solomon with nothing to do but take his own portion when the plate came by, then the apples in syrup, and then the pitcher of buttermilk.

Solomon's visit was an interruption to their routine. But in the natural course of things, he would have been taking his place as the householder. Andrew was plainly weary, and Sally needed the attentive care of a husband not so occupied with the main responsibility of a farm—or a maiden daughter not so occupied with her sister's children.

As if reading Solomon's thoughts, his father-in-law said, "Solomon, now that you're here, would you be willing to help me tomorrow with some repairs in the barn? I need another man's strength, and Daniel's been busy tending to his own place."

"Of course," Solomon said, "I'd be happy to do my part—"

Calista looked up sharply and Andrew gazed at him levelly as his words hung in the air. Solomon felt the cloud of doubt and blame descend over him.

Then Callie knocked over her buttermilk as she stood on her seat to reach toward her baby sister, and all was in a tiny uproar that spared Solomon further awkwardness.

* * *

When breakfast was finished, Solomon offered to drive some of them to worship in the cutter—not all would fit—but Andrew declined, saying he'd already chosen a sermon to read to them all. He opened the door to the kitchen porch and let in Penelope, who must have been waiting for the opportunity. They had a service in the front room while Nettie took her morning nap. Sy read the passage, sneaking a look at his father from time to time, and Callie came to life, belting out "O Come, O Come, Emmanuel" and losing the words but not the tune as Calista accompanied her on the piano. The rest of the Sabbath was spent in quiet reading and naps, the dog stretched out before the fire, as was the Watson practice, but the children's building excitement about Christmas hung in the air. Andrew confided in Solomon after dinner that he and Sy were outside when Bert Talbert had come by with the things Solomon sent and that Bert and Sy had hidden them in the barn for the holiday.

"Grandpa and I will cut down a tree tomorrow!" Sy announced when Calista handed him and Callie some pencils and paper to draw while she cleared the supper table.

"Or perhaps your father would like to do that," Andrew said, then took a long draw on his pipe. "Grandpa's bones are getting old for that sort of thing."

Solomon smiled at Andrew in gratitude, and Sy pointed out the east window and said, "Over there? Where we got it last year? Mama said it was the fluffiest she'd ever—"

He fears to speak of her, but only for my sake. Well, for Sy's sake, and for his own, no matter how it pained him, Solomon must set an example. *How else can we go on?*

"You remember that, son? Your mother was proud to see you grown and carrying the top of that tree out of the woods, holding it out of the snow. And Callie, I remember another time, when you were just a baby Nettie's size . . ." He spread his hands apart, and Callie lifted her big blue eyes to look at him, still gripping the pencil she'd been drawing with. "Just *this* big, with hair the color of corn silk like your mother's but in curls like Mama Calla's."

He went on to tell the story of the spindly pine he'd brought in that Christmas in Orange, insisting it would fit just so in a particular corner, its sparseness setting to great advantage the ornaments Jennette was preparing to hang on it. She had despaired of his aesthetic sense but borne with his provision. Every Christmas since then she'd commissioned a hunt for a full, round tree . . . *Was it really just a year ago?*

"So, what sort of tree should we cut down this year?" Solomon asked the children. "A fluffy one such as Mama liked best, or a spindly one that would make her laugh?"

"Fuffy!" Callie called out, and it was decided.

After breakfast on Christmas Eve, Sy took Solomon by the hand to the barn and to the horse stall.

"Papa, I visited her this morning and brought her treats, even before you were up!" Then he showed where he and Bert had tucked away the Christmas gifts. The rocking horse was wrapped in burlap and resting on the join of perpendicular rafters, and the other parcels were in the space Daniel had drawn the fishing gear out of so many years before.

"I didn't even look, Papa, I promise. Grandpa said it was our duty to keep the secret, and it would be less ten . . . ten . . . tation to me if I didn't know the secret to start with."

"I admire your forbearance, son. I don't know if I could have done it myself."

They took down the packages but left them in the barn for the time being. They had decided to walk into the woods with a hand-sled for a tree, saving a cutter ride for Christmas Day.

Solomon selected a hatchet and some rope from the barn, then pointed to the sled that he wanted Sy to drag over. "Do you remember when your Grandpa Ramsdell lived nearby, when we lived in Orange Township?"

"Yessir!" Sy answered. The sled was propped against the wall and he pulled it to the dirt floor of the barn and dragged it toward his father, leaving ruts on the way out to the snow.

Solomon secured the hatchet to the sled with the rope and added his own strength to drag the rig out of the barn. "He loved to come to our place back in Orange and give you rides on his horse—even when you were so little he had to hold you atop the beast."

"And I," Sy added breathlessly, "would mount from the big stone!"

"You remember that?" *You weren't more than three!* Together they got the sled into the snow, where it began to glide properly behind Sy on their way into the woods.

"Yessir. It was a roan, wasn't it?"

This one's entranced by horseflesh, it seems. So be it.

In a streak of yellow, Penelope overtook them and bounded out in an arc before them, planting herself square to face them with a single commanding bark.

"Do you like Penelope, son? She seems to have a lot more energy than old Puck did."

"Yessir. But I miss Puck."

"How did he die, son? Was he sick?"

"Not like Mama," Sy replied, shaking his head sorrowfully as he leaned into the hill they were climbing.

Solomon took the rope of the sled and finished the climb with it. "Go on, son."

"His back legs got weak, so Grandpa had to help him in and out of the house. Then one day nobody saw him all day and Grandpa and I went looking. I-I almost fell over him— he was curled up in the leaves under that maple tree by the front porch."

"So he died in his sleep," Solomon said. "Your mama did, too. That's a gentle way." He stopped at the top of the hill and motioned to Sy to stop while he rested a moment. The boy had his hands stuffed in his pockets and studied his shoes, Penelope sniffing around the two of them, looking up to see what was next.

"I helped Grandpa dig the grave by the lake path," Sy said.

"That was a manly thing to do—good for you." Solomon put out a hand to draw his son to himself, and the boy rested his head against his father's waist and then threw his arms around him, squeezing tight.

I must be a father to him.

Solomon held him several long moments, then dashed away his tears. He put his hands on either side of Sy's head and tipped up his tearful face up to look at him.

"The lake path was a good place for it," Solomon said, releasing Sy's head and resting one hand a moment on the boy's shoulder. "Puck loved that lake. I remember the first time I went there, he went for a swim and came out shaking lake water all over me—your mama and Mama Calla and Uncle Daniel had a good laugh over that."

Sy smiled and wiped his nose on the back of his mitten. "Yeah, he was a good shaker!"

They both laughed. Solomon rejoiced to have made this connection to his son, and he pressed for more as he gestured for them to continue. "Let's keep an eye out for that 'fuffy' tree we're after, all right?"

"All right!" the boy said, and ran a few steps ahead with the dog at his heels. When Solomon caught up again, he started a new line of conversation.

"Sy, you know Grandpa Ramsdell lives in town now. In Lowell, where I've been this fall. He has a shop for saddles, and I've been working in a shop for furniture. That's where I made the—oh!" He clapped a hand over his mouth and raised his eyebrows comically high to draw a giggle from the boy. "Never mind!"

"In any case," Solomon said, after they'd stopped laughing, "I've been considering doing business in town, leaving off the farming I used to do, like your Grandpa Watson still does, and Daniel. What would you think of moving into a big house in a town? Maybe Lowell . . . maybe elsewhere."

"Just us two?" Sy asked. "With the cutter?"

"No, your sisters, too. And this cutter is borrowed, like the horse, but we could have our own someday soon— maybe a two-horse cutter—and a stable with others' horses, as well . . ."

"And Mama Calla?" Sy looked at him with wide, clear eyes, and their gazes held a moment.

Solomon sighed. "No. Your Aunt Calista would stay here with Grandma and Grandpa Watson."

"I'm a big boy," Sy said. "I can sleep alone—or with you. But who will my sisters sleep with?"

* * *

Who will my sisters sleep with? Sy's question kept ringing in Solomon's head all morning as they made the pleasant work of searching the woods for just the right tree. They eventually found a full white pine, a little smaller than the last year's, and chopped it down. Sy made a few bites into the trunk with his axe and was surprised when the blade repeatedly stuck and threw him on his rump, and his trousers soon soaked through from the snow. When Sy's teeth began to chatter, Solomon finished the job in a few quick strokes, finding the effort a pleasant memory— though he had to wind his shoulder around a few times to work out the kinks.

Who *would* Sy's sisters sleep with?

Lillianne would certainly be kind and bring them up in refinement. But she stood her ground with her own plans for herself, requiring him to bend to those plans if he wanted her. That was clear. With a nanny, the children would lose something of the family life they had known.

In the Jacob Ramsdell home, invisible currents connected everyone, even if some were troubled. He remembered his mother's relative, a medium, doing some conjuring years before, calling up spirits of the dead. But in his own home—and in the Watsons'—flowed a more wholesome spirit. He could feel it running through him after being back in their midst for only a few brief days. Where did it come from?

There were other commonalities, too. Callie's hair was pale gold like Jennette's. Sy held his shoulders with a stoop forward as he walked, like Andrew Watson, but he had Jacob Ramsdell's—and Solomon's own—high brow and straight nose. Nettie bore the family likeness in the slender strength she used to brace her little legs and stand on the lap of whoever held her—baby Seymour had done the same.

His family was an admixture of himself and Jennette, and Jacob and Andrew and the two Sallys, and all the brothers and sisters of those generations. Sy's stoop perhaps owed more to habit and imitation than to anatomy, but what else was to be expected when his grandfather had been as a father to him for much of his young life?

What was Solomon proposing to do? Take his children to a young girl who had never met them? Who thought of them only in the abstract, however well-meaning she might be?

Absorbed in these thoughts, Solomon let Sy run around in the woods, wearing himself out. Solomon followed slowly with the tree, taking a more direct route to spare his hip.

Suddenly all was quiet around him, the sun near its peak but filtered through the bare branches to the south. Full, dark spruce loomed in those woods, and the seeming skeletons of the deciduous trees, paused for winter, their summer finery transformed and drifted to the ground, now covered by the blanket of snow. Directly above him the fingers of each high tree's branches reached for those of another, some not quite touching—establishing their individual realms—and some intertwined.

Solomon blinked out of his reverie, smiling at the vision of his son and the dog in the distance, romping through the snow.

Our lives are knit together. No doubt some of Sy's current exuberance was from having his father back—a young boy should have a young man as a father, a man who could bring him alongside as he made his own way into the future. Andrew was a loving grandfather, but he was tired and world-weary, ready to take his place on a porch or by a fire, as should be.

What had seemed just days before a real possibility— the children's removal to Lowell, to a new life in a town with servants and paneling and rich carpets—nearly made Solomon laugh aloud as he hauled the sled out of the woods, working against the rheumatism in his hip. Sy kept running ahead toward the farm and then back to Solomon, and when they finally got close enough, he ran to the door to call everyone out to see the tree.

Solomon beheld the house that had sheltered his family when he was unable to—ill in mind even more than in body—and knew it was time to return and take his place.

He hadn't yet begun courting Lillianne, so there was no shame there ... Solomon shook his head with the realization: that must have been why Arza King had loaned him the cutter, so he could clear his mind and truly see his prospects.

Right here is what I should have wanted all along.

After dinner, Andrew and Solomon went to the barn to see to the work Andrew had mentioned, while Sy stayed in to help decorate the tree. Calista had cleared a corner for it, and she'd found the ribbon-tied pinecones and paper chains they'd stored last January. Ginger cookies pierced for hanging were waiting in the kitchen—they would go on last.

"Father Watson," Solomon began, as he pulled down the lengths of wood Andrew pointed out in the rafters, "my time in Lowell has been instructive, to the point where I've been considering some promising lines of work. There's something pleasant about working with materials provided to you, rather than fretting over whether a crop will come in, or whether a hailstorm will carry it off."

Andrew chuckled. "Ever since Adam that's been the trouble. But even manufactured goods have vagaries of weather and such upstream."

"That's true," Solomon said. "And vagaries of men as well. Kopf—the man I'm working for—brought in two fine chairmakers from New England, and all was in a smooth hum of production and sales. But it was their high temper that set the business in a lull so I could come for Christmas. One got in a pet and took off for home, so the other—not be outdone—left too."

"And what's a businessman to do when his stock runs out?" Andrew said. "It's not much different, I guess, from when the foxes come for our chickens." He patted a spot next to him on the bench outside the cow stall, and after stacking the planks, Solomon joined him. The barn warmth would make it comfortable to sit for a little while. The work could wait.

"My father gave up farming for shopkeeping," Solomon said, "but being back on this land has reminded me how much farm work suits me. If I'm honest, I must admit my soul is fed just being among the trees, or taking measure of a field to find its best yield. There's a mystery of an elemental sort in the land."

"But what of your temperament, son? Are you able to be the children's father again? I ask plainly, for if you don't mean to take up your family again, it will be a shame upon you. Even worse, it won't do for you to be around the children, raising their hopes."

"It's a fair question for you to ask, sir," Solomon replied, "but I assure you—in these weeks away I have become sounder. Like you, I'm considering the needs of the children first, and I know I must carry on what their mother would have wanted for them."

"Your departure—and your behavior before that— didn't evidence such care."

"I know, and I ask your pardon for that. I left in great part because I feared the darkness within me. This time last year Jennette brought healing to me after my mother died. I was able at last to unburden myself of some things I had carried from the war, and my spirit was lightened."

"Yes, I saw that. You were a different man last spring— the one I remembered."

"Yes, just that!" Solomon said. "All seemed at last restored to me—"

"'The years that the locusts had eaten,'" quoted Andrew. He pulled his pipe from between his teeth and pointed with it toward the barn rafters.

"—But then," Solomon hunched over and clenched his fists between his knees. "I lost it all again." He relaxed his hands.

His father-in-law—a man whose life had been peaceful, who was losing his wife to sickness but over many months and after many years together, a man whose son had returned from war whole—remained quiet.

"I was undone," Solomon said just above a whisper. Only a low moan from the cow and the rustle of a hoof in the straw disturbed the silence. "What is that verse? 'I was foolish . . . like a beast . . .' Really, I feared what I might do."

His father-in-law turned a little sideways on the bench and studied him, waiting for what more he would say.

"I can never repay you, sir, for your care of my family when I couldn't care for them myself. It's a testament to all that you are . . . that I could in essence run away without thought of what would become of them, because I could rely on you."

Andrew shook his head and poked at the tobacco in his pipe. "If I didn't know you better, Solomon—remember better of you, know my daughter's love for you—I'd say you must've learned some pretty words from sharp-dealing shopkeepers . . . even lawyers!"

Both laughed then, and Andrew pulled off his cap and beat it once on his knee, scattering the dust.

"I'm ready to take care of my family," Solomon announced. "I have obligations at Kopf's for some weeks yet to come, but I'm hoping we can discuss how best to arrange things for the good of all." He held out a hand to his father-in-law as he stood. "Should we see to that broken cart, then, and mull things over?"

Andrew took the proffered hand and eased himself up to standing, bending first one knee and then the other to work out the stiffness, and they set about their work. Over the next hour, while Solomon helped Andrew repair the bed of his wagon, they discussed parcels of land and established farms that Andrew knew were for sale, and their prospects for the kind of farming that would best answer the call of the future. They agreed to take the cutter out on Christmas afternoon to have a look at the hills in their winter finery.

CROSSING
LATE DECEMBER 1866 – MARCH 1867

Proposal

THAT EVENING, at his father-in-law's direction, Solomon's family read the Nativity story from the Gospel of Luke in turns, Sy reading aloud the Magnificat with a purity that settled a golden spell over them all. They sang "Silent Night" together but would save the more boisterous music for the next day. Jennette would have loved to hear Sy read the passage and would have had difficulty restraining her excitement over the Dickens Christmas planned for the next day.

Once the children and their grandparents were in bed, Solomon crept out to the barn for the gifts and brought them in to place under and on the tree. The ribbon and the mane on the rocking horse were a bit worse for wear after the journey.

Calista came into the front room from the kitchen, bearing gifts wrapped in newspaper, and stopped short at the sight of him on his knees working on the rocking horse.

"I'm having a bit of trouble here," Solomon said, holding two lengths of leather that had been wrenched out of the mane. "Do you have an awl—or something like it—that I could use to press these back in?"

She let her parcels tumble gently onto a side table and returned to the kitchen, then came out with an ice pick and a knitting needle, holding them out on her open palm.

"Thank you," he said, trying the knitting needle first. She stood silent, the ice pick still on her outstretched palm.

"Is something amiss?" he asked. "You haven't said much this evening."

"It's a solemn time. Missing Jennette . . . contemplating the Gospel. I wonder how Mary was able to take in all that was happening about her, and in her . . ."

"Doesn't it say she pondered all those things in her heart?"

"Yes, but I mean, she was willing to carry the child despite what would be whispered about her. She saw the larger purpose, and she was willing." Calista closed her hand around the pick and slipped it into her apron pocket. Then she looked down again, untied the apron, and laid it across a chair.

"So"—she cleared her throat a little and continued in a strained tone—"so when do you mean to take the children to Lowell? Seymour said—"

Solomon looked up, eyes wide, as soon as he realized his blunder. How much his mind had changed since he'd uttered those words! *Why did I blabber that to the boy?*

"I mean," she continued, bracing herself with a hand on the back of the chair, as if she'd practiced the speech, "I could see Sy going now, but Callie will need help getting used to the idea. And Nettie . . . could . . . could you leave her with me for a while?" Her voice caught on the last word and a tear coursed down her cheek. She wiped it away.

Knit together they are, and Calista would be torn to lose them. Solomon could see that she would have hidden her emotions from him but for the desperation she felt to speak on the children's behalf, and his heart went out to her.

But before he had words to reply, she continued: "I could even"—she swallowed and her chin quivered a little—"come to town for a time to help them adjust."

"No! No, I could not have that!" he protested, climbing to his feet as Calista sank into the chair, her face drained of color. He had no idea where to begin, no idea how to fix the mess he'd made.

As he sought to find his way among the tangle of threads in his mind and heart, attempting to sort them like the leather strands of the rocking horse mane, he discovered a part of himself that was wounded by her wounding. Even though it had been a misunderstanding, his heart flooded with sorrow at her pain.

At last he found some words. "I'm not taking them," he said, his tone betraying his shame that he'd even considered such a thing. He remembered Arza King's suggestion that she be the children's nanny, and Solomon's heart leapt up to defend her. *She is so much more to the children—*

A log thumped down in the fireplace and threw a few sparks into the room, and it all came to him then, what he was too dull to see before: Calista had become a part of him when he'd become part of her family. Calista bore Jennette's life history, of which he'd shared less than a decade. They both loved Jennette, had been her confidantes, were the keepers of the memory of her shining joy. Even though Jennette was gone, Calista conveyed her love to the children—and loved them in her place.

But Calista wasn't just an echo of Jennette. Solomon looked down at her bowed head and smiled, his thoughts rushing over him in the silence that filled the room. Those bronze curls—he held himself back from touching one— that trim waist in a figure more generous than her sister's.

He remembered Jennette looking down at her own small bosom that long-ago June day she'd described her sister to him in the wagon on their way to visit the Watsons.

And Calista's music . . . she had all of the technique and expressiveness that Lillianne could offer.

To offer his hand to Lillianne, he'd have to cross into a new realm; he'd be entering into *her* world. But Calista already inhabited his world—no, she was the *keeper* of his world, of his beloved children. He had only to look more deeply into what was true to find her there.

"Calista," he said with a directness that lifted her head. "Calista Diantha, please forgive me. I've caused you distress." He was surprised by the deep tones in his voice—so long since he'd heard himself like that—only Jennette had drawn such emotion from him. But Calista didn't put out her hand to receive the apology, so he continued. "I have no intention of taking the children, but I won't abandon them, either. I'll be with them. I'm myself again, and I'm seeing things clearly now."

She waited, watching him without expression.

"You've carried all Jennette's intentions for the children, something I was unable to do when I lost her . . . when I went mad, to be plain about it. You've been their mother while waiting for their father to return to them. I should have seen it—"

"You were ill," she said, "and now you seem better."

"I am. I'm finally coming to myself, and I can see now how you reached out to me, to remind me of my family— the violin, the scarf . . ."

"Jennette's work."

"Yes, it was, and you knew what she would have told me with those articles, so you said it yourself. You have forborne with me, and I thank you for that."

"So will you look for a farm, then?" she asked, taking refuge in practical conversation.

"Yes, and . . ." It came to him all in a rush. "I'll want to plant this spring. If it can be managed."

"So soon?"

"So late, rather," he said with a small note of laughter. "Jennette would be pleased, don't you think?"

"Yes." She paused a moment, smiling to herself. Then she gave a small nod of decision. "I could keep the children here, nearby, so you might accustom them to the new life." She stood and draped the apron over her arm again, then picked up the parcels and began to put them beneath the tree.

All business, she is.

"But Calista," he said, catching her hand and pulling her up from where she knelt by the tree. "Might you be willing . . ."

She left her hand in his and looked at him directly, waiting.

He took a deep breath. "Would you be willing to let me court you, if your father approves?"

She flushed, her face in confusion. "I thought you—but I wouldn't want—"

"Nor would I. I know the children need a mother—and you've been as a mother to them—but that shouldn't be the foundation for a marriage. Some would say we're just doing what's expected, but I never took it for granted, marrying my wife's sister. Stupidly, I didn't think of it at all—I was too ill. You're far too substantial for anyone to assume such things of you. Unfortunately, I have been taking *you* for granted—and your parents as well—but only because I knew I could rely on you absolutely."

She smiled wryly. "That is not much of a proposal, Mr. Ramsdell."

Clever Calista. And with Callie's dimple.

"Jennette wouldn't expect you to accept such a slender proposal—and neither would I," he said, his voice bearing the deep tones of love that were welling up in him. "So I mean to court you properly. And prove to you that I want you for yourself—though I can tell you, as sure as I'm standing here, it's quite plain to me now. It should have been clear from the beginning, but I was unable to see it."

"I look forward to your proving it to me, then." She squeezed his hand, then let it drop.

Brusque and self-possessed once again, she nevertheless raised an unconscious hand to tuck a curl behind her ear, and he remembered the flowers she'd worn there the first day they'd met, when she came down that staircase with Jennette, into this very room.

Reconciliation

THE MORNING AFTER CHRISTMAS, Solomon stood in the cutter and waved exuberantly to the family gathered on the porch, then guided Arza King's bay up the lane and then onto the road back to Lowell. The snow had frozen hard and the northwest wind howled across it, forcing Solomon to tie his bowler on with his scarf to keep it from blowing clear to Ohio. But he whistled snatches of every tune he knew, the lines whisked off his lips by the scouring wind. He even laughed aloud a time or two at the lightness of his heart.

As promised, Solomon had taken everyone on rides through the sparkling white countryside on Christmas Day, first Calista and the children—even Nettie, bundled up like a parcel, wiggling and laughing at her siblings' excitement. Then he took Andrew and Sy to view the nearby farms that were for sale. Sy almost burst with pride at being included in the manly expedition. After Sally—minding her cough— had allowed herself a brief ride with Callie, Solomon tipped his bowler to Calista and helped her into the cutter for the final ride of the day, and the two of them carried a single basket to a poor family. Mother Barlow had passed in October. At the end of the day, full of Christmas warmth, they'd bundled up to bed, all but Solomon and Calista, who enjoyed a quiet hour together before the dying fire.

Now Solomon had other things to contemplate. When Lowell came into view, he began to consider how best to accomplish the business before him. He'd raised expectations with several in town and had left unresolved the quarrel with his father. Not three months before, he wouldn't have had these troubles, for he'd been in no state to attract partnerships nor answer for his behavior. But by the relentless power of love, by the slow work of others' faithfulness to provide for his children and wait for him, he had finally come to himself. He had blinked awake and looked around him, seen anew the consolations of this world.

My sweet Jennette, I can no longer live the dream we shared, but I can enter a different dream, one that still contains much of you.

Once he'd arrived, he happened upon Arza King in the stable after leaving payment for the attendant to take care of the horse and cutter.

"Well, Solomon, I hope you enjoyed your Christmas," King said, shaking Solomon's hand.

"I did indeed, Arza, and I'm in your debt for the loan of the cutter. Not only did it allow me to visit my family, but it gave us much pleasure in several jaunts yesterday."

"And how *is* your family?"

"The children are well, and though time is taking its toll on their grandparents, we had a pleasant visit." Solomon anxiously clutched the china plate he was planning to return, and then decided a plain declaration would be the best course.

"After considering all my options," he began, "and the needs of my family, I've decided to go back to farming, and likely in the Grattan area. Andrew Watson and I were able to see some properties yesterday—thanks to the cutter."

"I see. I expect you understand Miss Baker is not likely to take an interest in such a future," King said, and Solomon nodded once. "But it's best that you both know your own minds in the matter."

"May I return this plate to the kitchen?" Solomon asked.

"You may give it straight into the hands of Miss Baker. I believe you'll find her near the piano."

As Solomon crossed the lobby to where Lillianne was sitting at the piano with her hands in her lap, he took in the serene picture of what might have been. Contrasting images of the farm flashed before him—a chick in a basket, laundry falling into the mud from a weakened clothespin, corn stalks sodden and broken from a hailstorm.

Lillianne raised her head and her jeweled comb glittered.

Solomon envisioned a toddler cradling the chick; he saw a flushed young farm woman snatching the garment from the ground and pinning it again. Such a woman—a woman like Jennette, or like Calista—would know, from the depths of her being, how to console a man taken to the edge of despair by the hailstorm—or any of the other frustrations of Adam in the field.

When Solomon reached Lillianne's side with the china plate in hand, a sleekly dressed young man rose from the other side of the piano with a sheaf of sheet music from the low cabinet. Lillianne glanced from Solomon to the other young man and back, judging Solomon's reaction, and Solomon bowed deeply to her, extending the plate.

"Miss Baker, I believe I need to return this to your keeping, with the thanks of my family."

She took it with a smile and rose to step away from the piano, holding the plate against her bodice. "Did you enjoy your visit, then?" she asked quietly, coolly. The other young man had sunk down behind the piano and was looking through the music cabinet.

"Yes, it was a precious time and a good reminder of what I've missed."

"The children?"

"And the land, too, and parts of my history I had let slip away." His eyes went to the velvet chair in the lobby and he pictured Penelope curled up in it. He huffed a little laugh. "Our evenings here with the music reminded me of the part of my life I'd lost since the war—I am grateful to you for that . . ."

She gave a knowing nod and waited for him to continue.

"But time with my family reminded me of other things I've set aside in the difficulties of the last year, and what I want to get back to." He tipped his head to glance at the plaster ceiling and then back down. "I've decided to buy a farm there."

Sparing him further awkwardness, she replied, "Oh, how lovely—and what do you plan to grow?"

All is well, then. And perhaps that young fellow there will be glad to see me gone.

He went on to chat a little about the farms he'd seen and when he expected to leave Lowell. A few minutes later, he left Franklin House, whistling. His next stop, Kopf's, was similarly galvanizing to his cheer and his purpose—John Kopf took the news well, clapping him on the back and saying how pleased Mary would be to hear of his plans.

* * *

All Solomon's spirited resolve drained from him as he set his steps toward the saddlery. The last time he'd seen his father, the man had been sitting in stony silence at his dining table, sputtering lamplight shifting dark shadows across his face. Solomon, in his fury, had stormed off, taking the young man's way of escape.

My words were honest, no doubt. From my heart but untempered. Perhaps his father needed to hear those words . . . but what was the value of airing a truth if it didn't lead to better relations between people? Yes, an old idealist might need a lesson—but at what cost? To what end?

Men go to war that their sons might farm and do business, that their sons might make art and music . . . wasn't that what John Adams said? Well, Jacob Ramsdell was in that middle generation, and what did he have to show for it? His family's farms were scattered and sold up, and his wife— who'd labored with him toward these easy later years—was dead. Rosette was enduring a sorry marriage, and Ellen had been cast off by her own husband. Jerome was off to pursue a trade, and young Frank showed promise as scholar—so there was at least hope there.

But what, in Jacob's mind, had become of Solomon?

What would I want for Sy . . .? What does any father want for his son? What does he fear?

Solomon had been leaning into the wind on the icy road toward the saddlery, leaning into his task to set things right with his father and start life anew. But this last question stopped him short in front the shop. What *did* he fear? As Solomon took a deep breath and reached for the door handle, his dutiful stiffness was suffused with warm light, as a flame brings alive the cut glass of a fancy lamp. Bells jangled as he stepped in.

Jacob Ramsdell looked up over his spectacles from where he sat behind the counter, tooling a design into a leather strap. He didn't speak.

"Father," Solomon said and set down his satchel, threading his cane through the handles to support it. He lifted his bowler by the brim and unwound his blue scarf. He held the hat and scarf a moment, then turned to hang them on the hooks by the door. On a shelf above the hooks sat his father's top hat, presiding over the place.

Solomon turned back and cleared his throat. "A belated Happy Christmas to you, and best hopes for the New Year."

His father unhooked his spectacles and folded them into a leather pouch hung around his neck, letting the words lie between them as they both waited for his reply.

"Son," he said at last, "I hope the Lord will see fit to send us a better year than this one has been."

"Amen to that," Solomon answered. *A good beginning . . . we could just start from there.* But more needed be said. "Father . . . things were awry between us when last I saw you—"

"Awry within us, too, no doubt," Jacob said, placing his hand to his heart, then holding it out to take in the room. "And about us. Have you become more settled since then?"

"It's thanks to mercy that I have . . . I was in turmoil too long. When I was cross with you before, it was during a time when I wasn't equal to the demands on me."

"I asked only that you do your duty, son—"

"And *every* circumstance asked that of me. I did my best . . . But this time, I was not equal to the task, not all at once."

Jacob sighed. "You were right to remind me of your larger duty to the nation—a duty that you fulfilled at great peril and personal sacrifice." His voice cracked with emotion and he looked up and revealed tears glistening in his eyes. "How you have suffered . . . You were right to remind me." He looked down and picked at a shred of leather on the edge of the piece he'd been working.

"So we're in agreement then, Father, on these points?"

"'It is good for brothers to dwell in unity,'" quoted Jacob.

Solomon smiled and finished with the old family quip, "Oil running down the beard," while scratching through his chin whiskers.

"As your father, Solomon, I hope I have wisdom to lend you, as it was lent to me from my father and others. But I mustn't forget you're my elder in war, and that I have wisdom to learn from you."

His father's eyes bestowed honor upon him. Humbled, Solomon dropped his gaze.

After a moment, he looked up with a playful smile. "Do you think, Father, that I might one day wear a top hat like yours?" He nodded toward the shelf by the door.

"Well, it was a bit cocky to start wearing that in my thirties," Jacob answered, "but it helped me feel the dignity of my office in Kalamazoo. A judge can make good use of a symbol—a gavel at the bench, a top hat about town."

"I understand that young judge also remembered his youth . . . for instance, in the matter of an outsize rocking chair!"

Jacob laughed and came out from behind the counter to embrace Solomon, who clasped his father with arms newly muscled from carpentry, and with a strengthened heart, too. Gesturing to a bench beneath a window by the glowing stove, Jacob invited Solomon to sit.

"Now tell me about these new mercies, son. It will do me good to hear of them."

Family

A LATE-MARCH BLUSTER sent great shadows of gray-bottomed clouds across the low hills, and shafts of sun sliced through the stubble of past crops. Solomon guided the horse and wagon over the rutted field—its good drainage allowed for the wagon wheels. Calista held Nettie on her lap with her left arm and gripped the side of the wagon with her right as the rig bucked and tossed over the uneven ground, and behind them Sy and Callie braced themselves against the sides of the wagon bed.

At last they came to the rise with the log cabin, so Solomon called "Whoa!" to the gray mare and pulled up the brake. Nettie held out her little arms to him. "Get down?" he asked, lifting Nettie from Calista's lap before holding out a hand to his bride-to-be. The older children had already swarmed over the sides of the wagon and were running about, arms wide in the wind.

The wedding was to be the next day, at the Watsons', and they were bringing another load of household goods to the cabin that would be their first home here. The proper house would go up after planting. The cabin was spacious— twenty feet on a side—and its previous owner had taken as good care of it over the last decade as he had of the fields. The barn was as fine a structure as Solomon could have wanted; he was already thinking of sheep. The farm was only a few miles east of the Watsons, its 160 acres cultivated by a man who was lost in the war, but now Solomon's to make a new start with. Solomon had spent many hours over the winter reading agricultural pamphlets and journals and making the acquaintance of those new neighbors who had likely establishments. The possibilities dizzied him, but he'd learned in Lowell how to judge business prospects, and those principles and his father's counsel had decided him on fruit trees as a primary crop.

He'd longed to spend the late evening hours with Calista, dreaming over their plans for their household. But he'd had to content himself with more occasional visits under her parents' supervising gaze and had spent most of his nights at the new property, taking covered pails with a couple of days' worth of food to last him as he worked. But whenever they'd had the time, they'd put their heads together at the Watsons' kitchen table and plotted out their future. Calista had ordered a table from Kopf that would be enormous when all the leaves were in it, and she'd asked Solomon for a spacious room that could house a singing school and hold attendees for piano recitals.

"I mean to have many young people about me . . . beginning with these three, and then as many more as we might have together. And if not more of our own, then the neighboring children who might want to come. I want to draw out their gifts, not just in music but in declamation and dramatics as well . . ."

It had been a joy to discover all that Calista had cherished in her heart those months that she'd left off teaching to care for the children. And though Mama Calla was a true mother for Sy, Callie, and Nettie, she never went a day without recalling her beautiful sister for them. Her stories delighted Solomon, too, for he'd never known so much of Jennette's early life.

A decade older than when he'd built his first home for Jennette, and with farming experience and some capital, Solomon had an advantage in this new place, and he now viewed the Orange Township property as his test farm. He'd possessed it since his boyhood, really, and had tried out many ways of growing crops and harvesting sugar—certainly enough to know what else he might like to try. And this wide, rolling place would give him that chance.

Before he began to unload the wagon, Solomon whistled two distinctive notes to call Sy and Callie over to help him with a spade, some slender fence pickets, a ball of string, and a wad of fabric scraps. He handed the fabric and string to Callie, who held them solemnly, awaiting his bidding. Sy was entrusted with the fence pickets. Then Solomon leaned the shovel against the wagon and reached in to unwrap a tarp from two leafless saplings about Callie's height that he'd carefully laid on their sides in the wagon, their root balls contained in a bucket. He grabbed the bucket and the shovel and headed out to a knoll, where he stood and waited for the others to catch up.

Once Calista had arrived, Nettie in her arms, Solomon began his speech:

"Children, starting tomorrow, this will be our home—this farm. We'll begin in the cabin, in close quarters, but we'll work together to make a new home here, right where we stand." He pointed to the road not far from them. "There, to the north, the road runs east and west, and our front door will face it." He then took the bundle of pickets from Sy and handed back one of them. "Son, drive this stake in right here. The ground should be soft enough."

The boy straddled the picket and pushed down mightily with two fists around the top of it.

"That's right. That marks our front door, in the middle of the house," Solomon said. "Now Callie, give me your string." He took the ball and wound a length around the top of the picket, after first making a notch with his knife to secure it. He then showed Callie how to let the string unwind from the ball as she walked, and she followed him as he strode west with a picket, counting paces as he went, stopping six paces away. He drove in the picket and then met Sy ten paces south from that spot.

"Calista!" he called once he got there. "Will this be your music room, then, this corner?"

"Yes!" she called from where she stood by the front door. "Southern sunlight all winter, and the sunset to boot. Callie, come help me with the flags—leave the men to finish with the stakes." She waved the little wad of fabric scraps and Callie ran stumbling back to her. Together they tied streamers to the first stake, then the second, leaving them fluttering to the northeast in the southwesterly gusts.

When all four corners of the house plan had been staked and strung, Calista showed the children how the kitchen would be in the southeast corner, a window on the eastern wall to let in the rising sun for breakfast. Solomon stomped up imaginary stairs leading straight up from the front door and then showed the children where their rooms would be. "Callie, if you look very hard to the west here, you might be able to see Grandma and Grandpa Watson's place from your very own window!"

"What about the sticks in the bucket, Papa?" Sy asked.

"I was just coming to that." Solomon held out a gallant hand to Calista.

"Miss Calista Diantha Watson—soon to be Ramsdell like the rest of us—follow me, please." He took Nettie on his own hip and placed his foot on the string so Calista might climb over more easily. He then led her a dozen paces south of the house.

"Sy, bring me that shovel." While Solomon waited, he eyed the front door stake to make sure that he was standing directly opposite and squared off with the string along the back of the house, then lowered Nettie to stand at his feet, letting her grasp his fingers as he stooped. She pulled against his fingers and tested her booted little feet against the dirt and grass, pumping up and down with glee.

When Sy returned, Solomon instructed him to pace ten yards to the south with fifteen big steps—about right for a boy—and set a stake, then head west five more paces and set another, lined up square with the house.

"Then run back to the middle stake, son, and head in the other direction, five more paces, and set a stake."

While Sy followed these directions, Calista squatted down a few feet from Solomon, eye-level with Nettie. She held out her hands and Nettie gurgled and stomped a tiny foot, pulling against Solomon's hold on her, and he shuffled forward as Nettie staggered a few steps toward Calista. Callie ran to Calista's side and squatted, too—and then Sy.

"Come to Mama, Nettie!" Calista called softly, and as Nettie tried her steps, Solomon gently pulled one finger out of her grip—she wobbled, then steadied herself—and then another. Solomon could see Sy holding his breath with the others. Nettie took one more step, stumbled, and Solomon swept her up, twirled her around, and set her into Calista's waiting arms while they all cheered her first steps.

"My turn! My turn!" cried Callie, running up to Solomon, arms outstretched. An ache bloomed in his chest at her eagerness, and Solomon drew his daughter into an embrace and then grasped her hands and spun her, her skirts and black-booted feet flying outward as she shrieked with joy. When he set her down, she staggered like Nettie, giddy.

Solomon gathered his family around him, and he and Sy took turns digging where the two stakes were, about seven yards apart, then lowered each sapling into its hole, root ball first, gently guiding the tap root deep so that it might re-establish there.

"So Sy, Callie, my dear Calista—and of course Nettie—do you know what these sticks are? It's hard to tell now, but they're shagbark hickories, and in the course of time they'll grow as tall as a two-story house and taller, and though they seem very far apart just now, as they grow taller they'll grow wider. Their branches will spread out all around, and one day, years from now, they'll meet in the middle and intermingle." He threaded the fingers of his two hands together and Sy and Callie did the same.

"When I married your mother—Jennette—I planted one of these trees in front of our house, next to the big rock Sy remembers climbing on when he was smaller than you, Callie." He reached down to lift her from under her arms to straddle his hip. "Just like children, trees grow and seem to take a long time to do it, but one day these trees will give us a crop of good hickory nuts. Do you know when that will be?" He set her down and knelt, motioning for her to pat the soil around one tree and then they walked over to do the same with the other. Calista cradled Nettie over her shoulder and followed. "Do you know, Calista?"

"Not for a number of years, I believe."

"That's right," Solomon said, pressing into the soil. "Sy, you'll be nearly a grown man before the first nuts come, and there likely won't be a good crop until you're a grandfather!"

"Grandfather?" Sy said, clearly taken aback.

Solomon chuckled—*It does seem impossible that boys can become grandfathers!*

Solomon dusted off his hands and handed Sy the spade and Callie the string and rag bundle. "Now run on back to the wagon, you two, and we'll take the other things into the cabin. You can give Silver one of those apples we brought."

The children lit off, and Solomon held out his hand for Calista's and led her further south, to another gentle rise.

The two of them stood there—Nettie asleep against Calista's shoulder—and looked back at the collection of saplings and stakes and string they'd planted.

"In the days to come, dear one," Solomon said, giving Calista's hand a gentle squeeze, "our home will grow here just as those trees will—and these children. Over seasons and decades . . . and even centuries. I don't know if the house we build will last that long, but the trees should—they're supposed to live three hundred years."

"I cannot even imagine it," she said. "Our ancestors haven't been in this continent for that long."

"One day we can teach the children more of what these trees represent—the longevity we hope for our marriage, our legacy."

"It's a good lesson." She turned to gaze up at him. "A lesson in patience, and in hope."

"But there's more to it," Solomon said, putting his lips to her ear as he curved his arm around her shoulders and drew her to him. "One day when Bert Talbert was in the shop in town, at Kopf's . . . we were just warming ourselves before he started back home . . . he told me a kind of story."

"I've observed that wood stoves are good for drawing a story out of a man," Calista said. "Shelling peas or working on a quilt frame does the same for women."

"I suppose it does. Well, he told me the folklore of husband-and-wife trees. Have you heard of the idea?"

"No, but I'm thinking that's what you've just planted." She nodded toward the saplings. "I heard what you said about the branches growing together, intermingling . . ." She threaded her fingers through his where he grasped her shoulder, and he squeezed them.

"Yes. But there's something else. These little trees won't know the advantage for years, so they'll be vulnerable until then—but if they make it, each will send its own taproot into the earth for the water deep down, and when they're more of a pair in years to come, each one will shelter and support the other, depending on which direction the wind or hail comes from."

"And when mature, they'll cast shade for the house," she added.

"I planted them far enough from the house so the nuts shouldn't damage the roof, by the way. But besides the taproot, they'll each have wide-spreading roots that will intermingle with the other, securing the soil around them and further buttressing one another."

"I can see even more." Calista took her hand back and shifted Nettie. "They'll draw up the water and goodness they need from deep in the soil—hidden from view. That's their real strength."

"And the source of their beauty," he murmured. He withdrew his arm to take her chin in his outstretched fingers, and he kissed her.

She returned his kiss, then put her hand up to caress his face, his beard already neatly trimmed for the wedding. "Thank you for this gift, Solomon. The trees will every day remind me of what you've said here today."

"And what I'll say in our vows tomorrow." He held out his hands for the baby. "May we grow together in such a way that we strengthen one another and those around us— just as the trees shelter birds and other creatures and provide food for many."

"I have no doubt that this blessing would have Jennette's approval," Calista said, placing baby Nettie into his arms. Then she lifted her skirts and began to walk back to the children.

For Jennette was ever only what she seemed to be, Solomon thought, and then followed his bride across the stubble-covered field.

AFTERWORD
"PIONEER PROFILE: THE RAMSDELLS"

In *The Rockford Squire*, August 9, 2001
By Susie Fair

The Ramsdells left their indelible mark on our community, our state, and our country and their story is one that spans many years. We begin with Joseph Ramsdell, born about 1620 and a native [of] Elland in the West Riding of Yorkshire, England. There, they were known by the name of Ramsden, lords of nearby Huddersfield. Joseph was the first to arrive to Plymouth Colony, the first English settlement in New England, founded by the pilgrims in December that same year. In 1645 or 46, Joseph married the first of two wives, Rachel Eaton, whose father [Francis Eaton] was a signer of the Mayflower Compact.

Their son, Daniel Ramsdell, served in King Philip's War and was given a land grant in "Narragansett Number Four" (present-day Greenwich, Mass.), which his son Thomas claimed when he came of age. Thomas and his wife Sarah had twelve children, the fourth of which was Gideon, born Sept. 13, 1712. Gideon had three wives, the last being Ruth Palmer, who bore him a daughter, Deborah, and a son, Noah.

On June 30, 1790 at the age of 20, Noah married Mehitable Whitmarsh. Together, they had nine children. Seventh in line was Jacob Ramsdell, born Sept. 8, 1806 at Abington, Mass. (about 20 miles southeast of Boston). Jacob was a man of high esteem and intellect, that carried on to succeeding generations. He taught school in New York state and in Wayne County, Michigan before settling in what would become Kalamazoo. Being a fine mathematician and experienced surveyor, Jacob was called upon to lay out Kalamazoo's early thoroughfares, and also served two terms as county judge. In 1845, he moved to Ionia County, having purchased a 160-acre tract in Orange Township where he erected a log cabin. He soon afterward sold this property and relocated to Lowell, where for years he was engaged as a saddler and harness maker.

Jacob Ramsdell and his wife Sally (nee Richardson) had five children, four of whom were still alive in 1900: Solomon, Jerome, Frank, and Rosette. Jerome was a tinner in Grand Rapids. Frank was a prominent lawyer in Deerfield, Wisconsin. Rosette was a teacher in both Kalamazoo and Ionia counties, and wound up in Fargo, North Dakota. This left Solomon, the eldest, to establish roots in our neck of the woods.

Solomon was born near Detroit on May 23, 1833. He remained with his parents until he reached the age of 26, when he married Jeanette S. Watson. They would remain inseparable until Dec. 31, 1863 when Solomon enlisted at Lyons with the Sixth Michigan Cavalry. While serving in the Civil War, he was captured and held prisoner by rebel forces. He discharged June 4, 1865—free to return to Michigan to start anew.

Unlike his siblings, Solomon was tiller of the soil, with a fine farm of 160 acres. That farm included the northwest quarter of section 17, Grattan Township, evenly split by what is now Belding Road. The farmhouse stood on the south side of the road, across from the present roadside

Afterword

park. By his marriage to Jeanette, Solomon fathered three children: Seymour, Nettie and Callie. Following her death July 9, 1866, he married her sister, Calista. To this union March 23, 1867 was born: Gregg, Floy, Gertrude, Bert, Frank, Orpha and Gladys. Nettie, Seymour and Floy were all school teachers. Callie was an accomplished musician and music instructor. Gertrude was an elocutionist and Frank, an orator and dramatic actor in his own right.

Frank Ramsdell's marriage to Gertrude Barker assured a life filled with excitement. Together, they shared 21 years on the stage, each in their separate roles. They made their debut in Chicago in 1901, but by 1911, had struck out for New York City. Gertrude starred in the leads and Frank portrayed characters in several plays, including "The Winning of Barbara Worth." They were also billed in many road shows touring the United States and Canada, rounding-out their careers in vaudeville, before retiring in 1921.

In 1917, the Ramsdells built a pavilion on the south shore of Bostwick Lake with a sandy beach, bath house and boats for rent which they operated as "The Pines" until 1944. That is what most people remember as their claim to fame.

Sources: History of Grand Rapids and Kent County, pub. 1900 by A. W. Bowen & Co; the Ramsdell Genealogical Archive (website) created by Ross D. Andrews, 1999; Rockford Register articles and various other newspaper clippings; writings by Richard Deyo Brooks, great-grandson of Solomon Ramsdell.

Used by permission and transcribed from an image of the story

ACKNOWLEDGEMENTS

THIS BOOK WOULD NOT have come to be without *Rosette: A Novel of Pioneer Michigan*, so all the acknowledgements given in that book apply here as well. As I researched and wrote that novel and sketched in Solomon's life there, I and my readers found him a compelling character, and I wanted to explore his story more fully.

For this book I would especially like to honor the contributions of those who came alongside me to read and respond to *Rosette*, the related short story "Blizzard," and/or this novel while they were in development. These professionals and friends include Grace Barber, Kristen Chavez, Janie Cheaney, Cheryl Dean, Mike and Carolyn Durak, Amy Edwards, M.L. Gardner, George Grant, Joshua Grasso, Monica Haynes, Patti Hobbs, Jen Hoos, Liz Horst, the Literary Fusion writing group, Lisa Lombardo, Kim Aulerich Mahone, Ben and Betsy Marsch, Glenn Marsch, Joy O'Toole, Will Rinaman, Cindy Rollins, Matthew Ross, Katey Schultz, and others I may have missed.

Finally, but foremost, I thank all my readers, especially Rosette's and Solomon's warm-hearted fans—you encourage me to continue this amazing adventure.

FOR MORE

If you are captivated by Solomon, as I am, you may want to learn more about him and about his sister Rosette, the subject of my first novel. Please visit RosetteBook.com to read entries from her journal and notes from my research. Join the Readers List at the site to receive news and special offers on additional publications.

These novels, the short story "Blizzard," and a forthcoming transcript of Rosette's journal constitute the *Ramsdell Family* series. Print versions of both novels are available, and *Rosette: A Novel of Pioneer Michigan* is illustrated with charcoal drawings throughout. Visit RosetteBook.com or MorainesEdgeBooks.com for more information.

Authors depend on the good words of their readers. Please review *Solomon Ramsdell* on Amazon.com (US and other markets) and Goodreads, and send me a note if you're curious about any details of the Ramsdell family.

Thank you!

Cindy Rinaman Marsch
Moraine's Edge Books

www.morainesedgebooks.com
www.rosettebook.com